LUCKY NUMBER

NINA KAYE

A CIP catalogue record for this book is available from the British Library.

Cover art by Jane Dunnet.

To Mum and Dad, thank you for everything.

Chapter One

I hold my breath as I wait for Robert to speak. Everything is riding on this. My whole career, my entire future. I drink in the vast modern office space with its tastefully decorated walls, plush carpet and luscious green plants that add a distinct feeling of health and vibrancy to the environment. My brain conjures up an image of me perched on one of the high stools in the 'creativity hub' brainstorming innovative growth strategies with like-minded colleagues. Yes, this is where I belong. I cross my fingers.

'OK, Emma...' Robert leans forward in his seat. 'Thanks for taking the time to meet with me again. I know it was an intense selection process.'

'It's been a pleasure, Robert.' I ensure I sound as confident and professional as possible. 'A really... insightful experience.'

'Glad to hear it. Now, as you know, it's company policy to deliver all candidate outcomes face to face. We are true believers in giving everyone – even those who are unsuccessful in securing a position – useful feedback they can take away and work with.'

Jeez, that doesn't give much away. He's really making me wait for this.

'So, I've come to a decision. It took a lot of consideration and the competition was stiff. In fact, this might be one of the toughest hiring decisions I've made in some time...'

Just spit it out.

'Emma...' He's looking at me intently, tapping his index fingers together as if he's still not fully through that decision, and I almost can't bear it. I want to jump over the desk, grab him by his impeccably stylish silk tie and beg him to put me out of my misery. 'It is my absolute pleasure to say... welcome on board.' Robert stands up and extends his hand.

In my shock, it takes me a moment to catch up. He's not offering me the door. *I've got the job.* I shake his hand vigorously, trying to think of something clever to say, but all words have escaped me.

'Are you pleased?' He eyes me with a curious expression.

My arm is going numb from the repetitive motion, so I quickly let go. 'I'm... delighted. Really delighted. And so grateful for this opportunity.'

'Well, that's a relief. Although, there is one thing I must mention.'

'Of course. I'm always open to constructive feedback.'

He seems hesitant. 'Well, this is a tad awkward, but before you start, you'll need to do something about that smell. It will really put people off their work.'

'I'm sorry... what smell?' My smile freezes as a rich putrid stench engulfs my nasal passages...

I wake with a start, my head jolting up like a gazelle braced for danger. *Oh my god, I fell asleep.* I only meant to rest my head for a moment, but I actually properly nodded off at my desk and now I'm even more behind schedule than I was.

Clutching my face anxiously, I'm perplexed to discover

that the right side feels bumpy, which can only mean one thing: I have a visible keyboard impression on my cheek. *Shit.* Clear evidence of my indiscretion, which must also look ridiculous.

While trying to get myself together and back to being productive, I suddenly remember the smell from my dream and take a tentative sniff at my underarms, but they're fine. At least that wasn't real. Though neither was the amazing job offer, sadly. The only thing I can smell is my boss, Karla. Or rather, her perfume. Overpowering, musky, suffocating – just like Karla herself, and a tell-tale sign that she's nearby.

I grab my makeup compact to check my face but there's no time. A rustling to my far right is followed by the click-clacking of Karla's skyscraper stiletto heels, and she appears at her pristine, photograph-laden desk – most of them of her and her friends, pets, Z-list celebrities she's met – just feet away from mine. With a tense jaw, I keep my eyes on my computer screen, hoping she doesn't look across and clock my new temporary facial feature. Thankfully, she stalks off in the other direction.

After a quick rub at my cheek to encourage the blood flow, I start typing furiously, aware that I'm seriously running out of time. A few minutes later, Karla materialises at my left shoulder.

'Have you not finished that yet? You're leaving this *ridiculously* tight, Emma.'

'Sorry...' I type even faster. 'Nearly...'

'I'll be back in half an hour,' she barks. 'Get it done pronto, or we'll be having a conversation about your performance. Fifteen copies of the report plus appendices, and make sure they're in colour. Nobody gets a medal for saving a few measly pence.'

I do a mock salute, quickly changed to a scratch of my

head, as she turns and stares at me briefly, before flicking her sleek dark hair over her shoulders and stalking off again.

'You know, Emma...' she calls over her shoulder. 'You're going to have to be much more proactive if you want to get anywhere in this business.'

As Karla disappears from sight, my phone lights up on my desk, signalling a new message, but I don't dare look in case she comes back. I know who it's from anyway.

Sighing resignedly, I look round the dull, dingy office, surveying the yellowing walls and the ancient grey carpet tiling, taking its colour from the years of dirt and dust ground into it. My despondent gaze sweeps across the sea of untidy desks, crammed into the less than generous office space. There's nothing here that resembles an inspiring work environment. Such a stark contrast to my dream.

I reluctantly drag my focus back to the Board paper and resume work on the final changes, then thirty minutes later, having done the printing and binding at lightning speed, I hand over the finished reports.

'Down to the last second, *once again*,' Karla spits.

I say nothing.

'Don't forget you have another deadline for close of business on Tuesday.' She can't resist one last parting shot before she leaves for the meeting. 'You might want to consider dragging yourself away from your precious social life this weekend if you're as behind schedule with this next paper.'

This time she really hits a nerve. My fatigued eyes prick with tears as the injustice of the situation wrenches through my body. I can't let her see me cry. I can't let her know that the excessive workload she's piling upon me, as well as the complete lack of any kind of mutually respectful working relationship, has me nearly at breaking point.

She takes off in the direction of the boardroom, leaving me dabbing at my eyes with my sleeve, and as I'm packing away my things, my phone lights up again, this time with an incoming call.

'*Finally!*' the voice at the other end hollers as soon as I answer, and so loudly that I have to hold the phone away to preserve my ear drum.

'Hello to you too,' I reply.

'*Where the hell are you?*'

'I'm on my way, don't worry.' I laugh, feeling my misery start to lift. This kind of greeting is not alien to me by any means.

'Well, move your arse, will you?'

'I'll be there in five.'

Instead of confirming this is as an acceptable arrangement, the caller simply hangs up.

Relieved to be finally out of the office, I wander across Festival Square, where I pause briefly to call my newest FaceTime contact.

'*Aunt Lottie!*' I break into a delighted smile when an elderly face appears on the screen. 'You managed to get set up. See, I told you it was easy.'

'It was easy to follow your highly detailed instructions, Emma, yes.' She returns my warmth.

I try not to wince on noticing that the background lighting, coupled with the close-up perspective of the video call makes Auntie Lottie's increasing age and frailness ever more evident. Though she looks happy enough, her face is wan, etched with the strain of several decades of a life that wasn't kind to her, her grey hair limp and lacking vitality.

'Great. That's us sorted then. We can see each other anytime, not just when I visit.'

'Indeed, we can. Thank you for this, dear girl. You really are an angel. Is that you finished for the week?'

'Yup. And I'm about to meet the others.'

'Well, you run along then,' she chastises me. 'You've got better things to be doing than talking to an old woman.'

'*Aww, no way.*' I vigorously shake my head. 'You're top of my list. But you're probably right that I should go. Amber's been digitally harassing me for the last two hours. I'll speak to you sometime in the next few days, and... I'm really sorry again that I can't visit this weekend.'

'My love, please stop fussing.' Aunt Lottie purses her thin lips and frowns at me. 'I'm just fine. I have George for company. And plenty of films and programmes to watch on the not TV thingymajig—'

'You mean *Now* TV.' I giggle.

'That's what I said, isn't it?' She's oblivious to her error. 'Go and enjoy yourself, and don't give me a second thought.'

'You're the boss.' I grin. 'Over and out.'

Aunt Lottie's chuckling face freezes on the screen as I end the call.

Putting my phone away, I tune into my surroundings: the excitable buzz of the Edinburgh after-work crowd and the growl of the traffic on Lothian Road. It's a beautiful evening too. The spring air is fresh and warm, with the longer days making it feel earlier than it is. I take a deep breath and stand for a moment, allowing the stress of the last few hours to drain away. After what feels like an unbearably long week, I'm finally free. And I'm actually feeling slightly refreshed from my impromptu nap. *Ah yes*, this is going to be a brilliant weekend – and it starts now.

Chapter Two

'*Freedom!*' my long-time friend, Amber, whoops when I join her and my bestie, Cat, in Blue Bar on Bread Street – a stylish wine bar and favourite after-work watering hole of the local office workers.

They've clearly been here for a while.

'Yes, and thank god. This week couldn't end soon enough.' I hug Cat while Amber ducks away from me, not one for shows of affection.

It's actually Thursday. We're having a long weekend to celebrate my birthday – a bit of a tradition I have with my three closest friends, one of whom will be even later than me.

'Cheers.' I clink their glasses once Cat has poured me a glass of Merlot from the open bottle on the table. 'What time did you two get started?'

'About five-thirty.' Amber's tipsy grin and burgundy-stained upper lip are proof of this. 'We messaged you.'

'You mean *you* messaged her,' says Cat.

With a wry smile, I pull out my phone and scroll through the dozen or so unread messages, all from Amber. They start with a simple 'what time will you be here?' and progress to borderline verbal abuse as drinks evidently flowed and my continued absence was noted. Amber, being pint-sized, with freckles and long wavy auburn hair, may look cute and innocent, but she's got one hell of a mouth on her and the self-assurance to match.

'Emma, you need to sort out that bitch boss of yours,' she says. 'Keeping you in the office 'til seven p.m. on your birthday weekend is *bang* out of order.'

'I know.' My shoulders slump. 'She has no idea it's my birthday though – despite regularly pulling my employee file to see if there's anything she can use against me.'

'What an evil cow.' Amber scowls.

'Tell me about it. She knows nothing about my life. Not even that I'm good friends with the CEO's PA, more fool her. I'm never going to get any credit for anything I do while I'm working for Karla.'

'Oh, Emma.' Cat gives my shoulder a sympathetic rub. 'It hasn't gotten any better then?'

'*Nope*. She shamelessly sits in front of the Board taking full credit for every piece of work I produce. A lot of it work that she's meant to do herself. Sara tells me every time and it drives me insane. I can't decide whether having a friend on the inside is a good thing. I mean, at least I know what's happening, but I'm worried that I'll eventually lose my shit and get fired for bawling her out.'

'*Ha*, that I'd like to see.' Amber scoffs. 'You're a total wuss, Emma. There's no way you'd do that.'

Knowing Amber's right, I'm momentarily transported back to the hopelessness I felt in the office.

Cat puts an arm round my shoulder and pulls me in for a much-needed hug. 'Hey, chin up honey. Don't let her ruin tonight as well.'

'You're right.' I let my head rest on her shoulder and attempt to ward off the impending tears. 'It's just not that easy when I'm made to feel useless and incompetent every single day.'

'So, quit,' says Amber.

'I can't. I have bills to pay.'

'Oh yeah, that's right. Tell me again why you're paying rent to your rich boyfriend who owns his Quartermile apartment outright?'

'It's not rent as such, it's... complicated. I don't want to be a freeloader.' I look away as Amber eyeballs me.

'*Anyway...*' Cat saves me from an uncomfortable exchange. 'The important thing is that, until you can escape Karla, you need to find a way to get on with things without snapping. *Everyone* has their breaking point.' She throws Amber a look, but Amber just snorts and turns to me.

'If there's one thing she won't do, it's fire you. Then who would do the work? You both went for the same job and she won, but it was close, so she's keeping you down. You're her biggest threat.'

'I suppose you could be right.' I shrug, not entirely convinced. 'But even if she won't fire me, she'll make me suffer big time. It's so frustrating. That job should have been mine.' I grab my glass and take a large medicinal swig.

'Do you know when Sara's joining us?' Cat says, in a clear attempt to move the conversation on.

'Oh... *Sara*. What am I like? Here I am complaining when poor Sara's still *in* work – at the Board meeting – and that goes on 'til eight-thirty.'

'That's different. Sara loves her job. She also gets treated well and paid for the extra hours – you don't.

'Maybe she gets treated *too* well.' Amber winks.

'*Amber*,' I scold her. 'You have no proof Sara's seeing her boss – it seems to be nothing more than a figment of your overactive imagination – and there are people from my work in here, so watch what you're saying.'

'*Come on,*' Amber protests. 'Those extravagant pieces of jewellery? She might love expensive gear, but there's no way she could afford all that on her salary. And she's always *working late.*' She air quotes those last two words for effect. 'He's her CEO sugar daddy. No doubt about it.'

With neither me nor Cat biting, there's a lull in the conversation, so Amber engages in her favourite pastime of scrolling through Instagram reels with the volume turned up – all for the purpose of irritating other punters she considers too 'up themselves'.

So, our celebratory weekend starts in the same way they always do. Too much wine, and only remembering to eat when a passing member of staff takes exception to Amber's boisterous nature and politely suggests we move on.

We get that much-needed fuel at a cosy pizzeria on Lothian Road, and I notice while we're eating that Cat seems a bit distant.

'You OK?' I ask her, when Amber takes her second trip to the ladies.

'Eh... yeah, I'm fine.' She swallows the mouthful of pizza she's eating, straightens herself in her seat and gives me a bright smile.

'It's not Amber, is it? I know she can be hard going, but she doesn't mean any harm.'

'No... um... it's... I know she doesn't. In some ways, I'm actually a bit envious of her. Like, she has an amazing husband and she doesn't care what anyone thinks. Don't you sometimes wish you had her level of self-assurance?'

'Totally.' I nod. 'It would help solve my problems at work.'

'And maybe I'd have something resembling a successful relationship instead of a string of failed romantic liaisons.'

'Aww, Cat. That most recent one lasted for, what – four dates? That's not so bad.'

'It's not good either, though, is it?' She chews her lip with an apprehensive expression.

'You need to believe in yourself.' I give her a meaningful look. 'We're not in high school anymore. I know those scars still run deep for both of us, but look at you, you're a grown woman with a successful career. There are no braces or nasty nicknames...'

'For being an "immigrant hiding behind a British name"? It's OK, you can say it. It's how it was.'

'They were cruel little shits, Cat. Firstly, they were wrong, and your British-Asian heritage is something to be proud of.'

'I know that, and I appear to "fit the mould" enough these days to avoid the hate, but you're right, those scars do run deep.'

'Well, I think you're gorgeous. Inside as well as out.'

'Thanks.' Cat gives a weak smile and I clutch her hand affectionately.

'Your perfect man will turn up and he'll see what a catch you are, I just know it. Hang in there.'

'Don't worry, *I* will. But I'm not sure how long my self-esteem will hold out.'

We laugh and then fall silent. Cat stares off into the distance, her dark-brown, poker-straight hair framing her hazel eyes and cute button nose. It's something that I really can't understand – why someone as amazing as Cat can't find love. I cross my fingers that she'll meet the right man soon.

'So, you're all right?' I ask again.

'Yes... fine. Just tired today.'

'OK. But you know I'm always here if you want to talk.' I let the matter drop. Not because I believe her, but because I know she'll tell me when she's ready. 'So, I've got Lottie using FaceTime now.'

'Honey, that's great.' Cat perks up on hearing this. 'I meant to ask how she's doing. That will be so much better than chatting on the phone.'

'Yup.' I take a sip of water. 'I worry about her spending so much time alone. A cat is not a replacement for real people and relationships. And she's really getting old now. It actually scares me a little.'

'I know what you mean. I felt the same about my nan. She was the matriarch in our family, and then suddenly she was so small and frail. She barely recognised us anymore. It was horrible.'

'Of course. You know exactly what I'm talking about.'

'What are you losers wallowing over now?' Amber surveys us woefully on returning to our table.

Cat and I exhale heavily, then start laughing. Amber's indelicate observation is exactly what we need to snap out of it.

~

After eating, we head to another lively bar near the Grassmarket. We're finally joined by Sara, who's been part of our friendship group since she moved to Edinburgh a few years ago and I met her at work.

Strutting up to our table as if on a catwalk, causing all (straight) male eyes in the room to follow her, she greets us in turn with her signature European-style air kisses. She then collapses into the seat beside me, sighing dramatically while piling her long, thick, glossy blonde hair on top of her head.

This reveals the discreet tattoo on her slender neck, further raising the testosterone levels in the room. She's the personified goddess every woman longs to be.

'So, girlfriends...' Her green eyes twinkle in the half light. 'What have I missed?'

Despite having worked a fourteen-hour day, Sara is pristine, her glamorous makeup perfect. She's also later than expected, further fuelling Amber's suspicions.

'Late finish for the Board, Sara?' She asks with a devilish grin.

'No, actually...' Sara seems wise to Amber's game 'I had some... essential tasks to see to.'

Now well inebriated, Amber misses the cues in Sara's reply. She turns to Cat and me, wide-eyed, and we shake our heads despairingly.

'Good night so far?' Sara asks again.

'Eventful.' I nod my head in the direction of Amber. 'Sorry you've missed most of it.'

'Comes with the territory of being an Exec PA.' She shrugs, inspecting her perfectly manicured nails. 'Anyway, what I'm looking forward to is our chill time at the spa tomorrow.'

'Oh, me too.' Cat adopts a dreamy expression.

As the night passes, I can't help feeling slightly envious as I watch how Sara has to fend off one guy after the next. There's almost a production line of them, each leaving like forlorn puppies when their advances fail. I suppose it could become irritating after a while, but to be that desirable – what a confidence booster.

A bit later on, the conversation turns to matters of the heart. That is, matters of *my* heart.

'So, what's the royal Dave up to tonight?' asks Amber.

'Please don't,' I reply automatically.

'*What?*' She feigns innocence. 'I was asking a simple question.'

'You *so* weren't.' Sara raises a perfectly arched eyebrow at her.

Amber tries to protest, but she's not sober enough to cover it up. 'Fine. The dickhead deserves it. Has he apologised for leaving you stranded in the pouring rain last week?'

'That was a mistake.' My eyes flit to hers and away again. 'He lost track of time, and he did buy me flowers. That's as good as an apology.'

'*Bullshit.*' Amber scoffs. 'That's as good as a guilty conscience. He's got you whipped, but you're so obsessed you can't see it. He's one hundred per cent selfish.'

I shift uncomfortably in my seat.

'Amber, quit having a go at Emma.' Sara comes to my defence. 'You may not like Dave, but that's *your* opinion.'

I shoot Sara a grateful look, but she's already become distracted by a new male admirer who has 'accidentally' bumped her chair when passing our table. Her supportive words give me a boost, nonetheless.

'He's a good guy, Amber.' I fiddle with the stem of my glass. 'You just don't know him well enough. The other week he surprised me with a pair of designer jeans—'

'Buying your affection once again.' Amber folds her arms and scoffs.

'He's also taking me to France for a long weekend for our four-year anniversary.'

'Touché,' she says. 'And he's probably using your rent money to pay for it.'

'*No, don't say that.*' I'm desperate for Amber's approval of Dave, but equally uncomfortable with this exchange. 'He's put a lot of thought into it. We're going to this seaside town

I've always wanted to visit, and he's booked an amazing restaurant. We're even doing a vineyard tour. The whole trip is organised around things *I* like. That's not buying my affection.'

'Ignore her.' Cat, who's been distinctly absence from this exchange, tries to soothe me. 'Amber's had too much to drink.'

Amber starts to correct Cat on that point, but a waiter's approach miraculously silences here – to everyone's relief.

We put in our drink orders while I search my friends' faces, insecurity oozing out of me. Sara glances over and gives me a little wink, Cat seems to have drifted off again, and Amber changes the subject, so I decide to label that a success and move on with the conversation.

Chapter Three

Our night out comes to an end earlier than expected. Instead of the usual birthday ritual of hitting the cheesiest club we can find and dancing 'til our feet can't take anymore, we make the conscious decision to avoid spending our spa day like the walking dead. That is, all of us except Amber.

'*Come on, you lightweights!* You're nearly thirty, not drawing your pensions.'

I roll my eyes at the others. 'You may not get hangovers the size of Ben Nevis, but I'm afraid the rest of us do. If we're old and boring for wanting to enjoy our spa day headache-free, then fine.'

'Bunch of losers, the lot of you,' she mutters.

After quickly agreeing our meet up plan for the next day – my birthday eve – we each get our revenge by treating Amber like a small child with a quick goodbye kiss on the top of her head.

While meandering home to the Quartermile apartment I share with Dave, my mind wanders to the rest of the weekend, and what he might be planning for my birthday.

I'm not expecting anything elaborate, but there's a tiny part of me that's hopeful of a different surprise...

I allow myself to lapse into my well-rehearsed Hollywood-esque fantasy. Dave taking me to one of Edinburgh's best restaurants, ordering champagne, and then instead of saying cheers, getting down on one knee in front of all the other diners. I, of course, feign complete surprise, squeal my assent and jump into his arms, even though I've been waiting for this moment for ages. We kiss passionately while the diners around us clap and cheer, the women wiping tears from their eyes. It would be *so* perfect.

I mustn't get ahead of myself, though. We have our France trip coming up, and that would be an even better setting for the ultimate romantic proposal.

Emerging from my daydream, the gap in my mind is instantly filled by Amber's tirade about Dave. I try to chase it away, but it buzzes round my brain like a tiny relentless fly. OK, so our relationship isn't perfect, but I don't expect it to be – I'm not deluded. Why does she have to be so hard on him?

On reaching our exclusive apartment building on Simpson Loan, I take the lift to the third floor, let myself in and wander along the art-bedecked hallway, towards the spacious modern kitchen living room. I'm expecting to find Dave glued to his laptop, but the room is empty and the only thing suggesting his presence is that the lamp next to his spot on the sofa is on. Wondering if he's in bed already, I go through to our bedroom, but he's not there either. That's strange. He had no plans this evening. Surely, he would have let me know if he was going out.

'*Dave?*' I call out. '*Dave, are you here?*'

There's no reply.

I initially settle myself with the thought that he's nipped

out to a late-night shop, but after twenty minutes that no longer seems viable. My mind starts to tick. Where is he? And why is the lamp still on? An uneasy feeling creeps over me. What if something's wrong?

Grabbing my phone from my handbag, I try to call him but he doesn't answer. Then I try him again. This time, he answers on the fourth ring.

'Dave, is everything ok?'

'Yeah, babe, I was grabbing a beer from the fridge.'

I look at the fridge. 'Sorry... what?'

'I was grabbing a beer, that's why I missed your first call. How's your night out? I hope Amber's behaving herself.'

'What fridge?' I'm still stuck on his first statement.

'What are you talking about? *Our* fridge. You know, the big silver thing with the water dispenser in the—'

'Yeah, I know it. I'm looking at it. And unless I'm in some kind of parallel universe, you're not here.'

There's silence at the end of the phone.

'Dave, where are you?' I start to feel anxious. *Why is he lying to me?*

The silence continues.

'Dave?'

'OK, don't get all paranoid...' There's an air of irritation to his voice. 'I'm at Melissa's. Her dad's been rushed to hospital and she needed some support. What are you doing back so early anyway?'

Alarm bells clang in my head. He's with *Melissa*? His stunningly beautiful, ex-university sweetheart. And he's mopping up her tears? *Really?* Don't panic, Emma. You have to stay calm.

'Emma?' Dave has clearly picked up on my insecurity. 'I said, *don't* get paranoid.'

'I'm not... I'm... really sorry to hear Melissa's dad's not

well. It's just that I'm wondering... would she not be better with her mum and sister, or at the hospital?'

This is a dangerous move but I can't help myself. The insecure teenager from years ago has taken over. I can hear her desperation-fuelled voice, and I hate it, but I'm no longer in control.

'I'm not saying you shouldn't be there for her,' I rush to add. 'But isn't it a bit... *convenient* that she called on you for support?'

It's out before I can stop myself. I brace myself for the inevitable.

'*Excuse me?*' Dave's voice is incredulous. 'What the hell does it matter who Melissa called? She's in bits and all you can think about is yourself.'

'No, it's not like that... I'm not—'

'And you wonder why I didn't tell you where I was.' The acidic tone of Dave's voice makes me squirm. 'You've always had issues with Melissa. It's pathetic, Emma. You need to get a grip.'

'I'm not thinking about myself, I promise.' I feel hot with embarrassment. 'I'm just... I don't know... I've had a few drinks. It's late. If you'd let me know where you were going—'

'So, I have to tell you my every move now, do I? You want to know every time I take a piss too?'

This is turning really sour. I'm desperate to avoid an argument but it's gone too far.

'Of course not. But maybe in certain circumstances it would be helpful to know where you are. Like maybe this one?' My voice tails off almost to a whisper.

'Let me get this straight,' says Dave. 'You want me to read your mind, work out what you might and might not be comfortable with, and then pander to your paranoia? Sure, I'll do that – and you carry on as you are.'

I so badly want to quell this unbearable confrontation, but the insecure teenager in me needs reassurance.

'I know I'm not perfect, Dave.' My voice is trembling. 'But she's... your ex-girlfriend. And... well, you did lie about where you were.'

'*For god's sake, Emma*, Melissa's a friend. I don't need to explain myself, and I'm not going to ditch her because you can't deal with it.' He cuts the call, leaving me staring at my handset in shock.

This is bad. I've never vocalised my mistrust of Melissa, although it's been fairly evident. But Dave's never lied about being with her either – not that I know of anyway. Tears of hurt and disbelief start trickling down my cheeks.

I spend the best part of the next hour crying and checking my phone to see if Dave's been back in touch. Unsurprisingly, he hasn't.

Then suddenly, I hear his key in the door.

Half full of dread, half hoping he's ready to make up, I wait for him to enter the living room. He walks in and stares at me, his normally alluring blue eyes cold as ice, and I recoil into the large plush sofa, my immediate instinct to avoid another confrontation at all costs.

'What was that all about before?' he says.

I avoid eye contact while frantically trying to think of a response that will ease the tension. 'I'm really sorry... I just panicked. You said you were at home when you weren't... and honestly? I don't trust Melissa. I see how she looks at you. I mean... you *proposed* to her.'

'You just had to bring that up, didn't you?' He towers over me menacingly, though he doesn't lose his temper. '*Yes,* she was important to me, *yes* I proposed... and she said no. It was five years ago.'

'I know. But surely you understand why I feel uncomfortable about your friendship with her. Like, if you really think about it from my perspective.'

Dave takes off his jacket and appears to soften slightly. 'I suppose I can kind of understand it. But you're imagining all this, you know. There's nothing going on between us.'

'Promise?'

'I shouldn't have to promise, Emma. You may not trust Melissa, but don't you trust me?'

'I do,' I say automatically, without giving his question any real thought.

'There you go. So, you don't need to worry about me hanging out with Melissa – and that means I won't need to hide it from you.'

I frown at this. 'You're saying you only hid it from me because you knew I'd get upset?'

'Yes.'

'So, it's my fault that you did it?'

'That's not what I meant.' Dave becomes visibly irritated again, sweeping a frustrated hand through his chestnut brown hair. His patience is wearing thin – I can see this – but I'm still not comfortable with his explanation, despite having told him moments before that I trust him.

'You have no feelings for Melissa whatsoever?'

'None.'

'You're *fully* committed to me?'

'*Yes.*' This response comes through gritted teeth.

'If that's the case, why does Melissa still have to be such a big feature in your life?' I ask. 'I'd never keep an ex that close out of respect for you. Especially not one I'd previously wanted to marry.'

Something unrecognisable flashes across Dave's face. Is it guilt? Acceptance of what I'm saying? He exhales heavily, then emits an emotionless laugh.

'You know what? This is *never* going to be OK. You'll never accept that I'm friends with Melissa, and I'm never going to end our friendship because you want me to.'

'But that's how relationships work, Dave. We have to consider each other. I've made plenty of compromises on my side.' I'm more or less begging him to see my point of view.

He scoffs and shakes his head. 'Yeah, well, maybe I don't want to compromise. I'm sick of being tied down. I'm barely thirty and I feel like I'm in a stale marriage already.'

'*Dave*... that's not... what are you saying?'

'I'm saying it's over, Emma.'

I'm completely winded. 'You don't mean that. You can't mean that. I'm sorry. I can find a way to be OK with you and Melissa being friends. This is just a rough patch. We're probably due one – you know what they say about the four-year itch—'

'I thought it was the eighteen-month itch.'

'Does it matter? It's the principle.' I'm aware that I've lost every last thread of dignity, but I'm desperate not to lose him like this. 'Couples have difficult times, but they work through them together. We can do that and come out even stronger than—'

'*Enough.*' Dave silences me with a look so ferocious that I cower away from him. 'You're doing my head in. I don't want to work through things. I want you to move the fuck out.'

I take in his contemptuous expression, tears tracking down my cheeks. He means every word he's said. A million panicky thoughts tear through my mind. What will I do without him? Where will I go? I have no place of my own. This is meant to be my home – with Dave.

Without knowing what else to do, I snatch up my jacket and handbag, and rush out of the room, my heels clattering along the echoey hallway. On nearing the front door, my eyes land on Dave's wine cupboard, and for no other reason than being in survival mode, I yank open the cupboard door, grab the first bottle I see and stuff it in my handbag.

Dave appears at the living room door, unaware that I've taken it.

'I'll pack up your stuff and you can collect it next week when I'm away for work,' he calls to me. 'Post the keys through the letterbox when you're done.'

I stare back at him, heartbroken and unable to believe how ruthless and unfeeling he's become.

'OK, Dave,' I choke, through endless salty tears. 'Whatever you want. I just don't get where this has come from. I mean, if you've been this unhappy, why all the nice gestures? Like the trip to France?'

I'm not actually looking for an answer, but Dave's sterile response, just before I close the door behind me, is the knockout punch.

'There *was* no trip to France.'

Chapter Four

Fifteen minutes later, I'm sitting on a park bench at the edge of the Meadows, sobbing over my heartbreak and cursing myself for not lifting a corkscrew. I pull myself together, trudge back up the path to a late-night shop on Forrest Road and quickly locate one. However, on taking it to the till, I find to my dismay that my purse is not in my bag. It must have fallen out in Dave's apartment.

'Sorry,' I mumble to the shopkeeper, while rummaging through the pockets of my coat and handbag in a desperate attempt to raise the funds I need.

I'm about to give up when my fingers graze some coins buried at the very bottom of my bag. Hastily scooping them out, my lack of care sends them scattering all over the floor, causing me to make chase in a very undignified way.

Once I've picked them all up, I count them out in front of the shopkeeper. '...one fifty... one seventy... two twenty... two twenty-five... two thirty-five... two-eighty-five... two-eighty-seven.'

I check the price tag on the corkscrew and my face falls. It's not enough.

Despite a valiant attempt to sweet talk the shopkeeper into a substantial discount, he's unwilling to budge. Not even when I switch tactics and recount my sob story, between real sobs. The miserable sod – he's obviously never had his heart broken.

'OK, I give up. This really isn't my day.' My shoulders slump and I head for the door. Then, to my surprise, the-man-previously-made-of-stone finally takes pity on me.

'All right, all right. You can *use* the bottle opener, but make sure it's clean for the next customer. And put it back where you found it.'

I don't have to be offered twice.

While I'm twisting the corkscrew into the top of the bottle, the shop door tinkles, but I'm so engrossed in my task, I barely notice the new customer. It's only when I shamelessly haul out the cork that I become aware of someone watching me – a man around my age, with dark hair and eyes and an air of confidence about him. He's dressed in casual office attire, his top shirt buttons undone, no doubt part of the corporate rat-race too.

'Oh, sorry.' I realise I'm blocking the till. 'I'll get out of your way.'

'No problem.' He smiles at me, then glances at my wine bottle and does a double take. 'That looks expensive... and possibly vintage.' He squints at the label.

Bewildered, I check the bottle. 'Erm... is it?'

He angles his phone towards the label and lets out a low whistle. 'It's vintage all right.'

'Says who?'

'Says Google – I did an image search. I hope you're sharing it with some very good friends for a *very* special occasion.'

I could lie, but I'm past caring what anyone thinks.

'Nope. I'm heading to a park bench in the Meadows to drink it – by myself.' I take a long swig as if to prove it.

'*OK...*' The man looks perplexed. 'You do realise it's worth about two grand?'

I choke mid-sip, spraying tiny scarlet droplets onto the row of crisp packets in front of me. Thankfully, the shopkeeper doesn't see this.

'Erm... no, I didn't.'

The man eyes me with a look that I can't quite decipher. Though he obviously thinks I'm nuts. Uncomfortable, I look away.

'OK... well, you have a good time,' he says.

'I will.' I focus my attention on reattaching the corkscrew to its packaging.

'You do that.'

'I... said, I will.'

There's a short silence, during which my skin prickles from the weight of his appraising stare. Feeling distinctly awkward, I decide I should elaborate.

'Look, if you must know, this bottle is to get me through the evening... after being treated like shit.'

'I never asked.' I catch him raising an eyebrow at the shopkeeper.

'Don't make out that I'm crazy.' I also don't care if I make a fool of myself. I'm never going to see this man again anyway. 'It's called self-preservation.'

'I never said you were.' He completes his transaction and turns towards me.

Shifting with unease, I'm suddenly aware that I must look a sight – all red, puffy eyes and tear-stained face. And who knows how far my eye makeup has travelled.

'Don't suppose you want some company?' he asks. 'I'm... intrigued by the wine – you could give me a taste.'

Thrown by his question, I falter. *Who is this guy?* I'm not heading off into in the dark with a total stranger.

'Um... no, I don't, but... thanks for offering.'

To avoid any further awkwardness, I walk to the back of the shop to return the corkscrew, hoping he'll be gone by the time I return. But he's still there, talking in a low voice to the shopkeeper. He spots me and calls over.

'Listen, I know this is none of my business, but... maybe you could consider sitting somewhere better lit, where people pass more regularly – like a bus stop?'

Still oversensitive from my fight with Dave, I feel utterly patronised. *I'm not a child.* Indignation flares within me, causing me to finally reach my breaking point.

'*Will you sod off and leave me alone.* I'm perfectly capable of looking after myself. You men are all the bloody same.'

The man scrutinises me once more. I want to stand my ground and stare him out but I'm spent, so I turn away and pretend that I'm interested in the magazine rack.

'Change of plan.' I hear him say to the shopkeeper. 'Thanks anyway, mate.'

Then the door closes, and when I turn back around, he's gone.

'Sorry,' I grumble to the shopkeeper. 'I didn't really mean that. I'm sure you're very nice. As I said, it's not my day.'

'If you're having that bad a day, you must be due some luck,' he replies. 'There's a UK Lottery draw tomorrow with a huge jackpot. You could return the favour for the corkscrew and buy a ticket?'

'I don't play the lottery. And I never win anything, so there's no point.'

'Someone's got to win.' He shrugs. 'But, fair enough.'

I decide I can't argue with his logic. I have absolutely nothing to lose, and things can't get much worse. What use is a couple of quid anyway? It's as good as having no cash on me at all, as I've discovered.

'Why not.' I sigh.

Appearing pleased by the result of his mini sales pitch, the shopkeeper asks me to choose my numbers.

'Oh, I don't know...' I'm struggling to think straight. 'Maybe just let the machine decide?'

'Where's the fun in that?' He smiles at me.

'No offence, but do I look like I want to have fun right now?'

'What about using memorable numbers, then? Maybe special dates? Some people look for signs in their environment. Or do you have a lucky number?'

'I definitely don't have a lucky number.' I give him a hopeless look while willing him to take pity on me, but he seems to be enjoying this too much. It must have been a slow night.

At a loss, I resort to looking around the shop in search of inspiration and spot a crumpled scrap of paper on the floor near the counter. Picking it up, I can see it that has what looks like a partial reference number on it. *Bingo*. I break it down into smaller numbers and relay the information to the shopkeeper, then hand him the piece of paper so that he can put it in the bin. He makes the necessary transaction and passes me my ticket.

On leaving the shop, I return to the Meadows, where, out of spite, I find a bench in the darkest, most isolated spot I can find, before sinking nearly a quarter of the bottle of wine without coming up for air. Then I cry like I've never cried before. A lost, broken howling that, had I been in public, I would never have allowed out my mouth.

As the wine reaches all the parts I need it to, I gain some

composure and realise that I'm angry with Dave. What has gotten into him? He's never behaved so cruelly before. I admit that I could have handled that situation better, but I certainly didn't deserve to be ripped into like that. I think about what Amber said. Could she see something that I couldn't? Is it possible that I don't really know Dave at all – just the version of him that I wanted to see? Maybe he really is a selfish wanker and that means I've had a lucky escape.

But I love him, a little voice creeps into my head, and I start to sob again, my heroic indignation prematurely brought to a close.

'Excuse me, are you OK?' A voice suddenly breaks through my weeping.

I look up and find myself face to face with a girl of around sixteen years old. There's also a small group not far away, obviously waiting for her.

'Erm... oh yes... fine.' I scramble to sit up straight, but misjudge things and over-balance, nearly falling on my face. 'I'm... just having a night cap.'

'Funny place for a night cap.' She gives me an odd look. 'You seem upset. And drunk. Would you like me to call someone?'

Since when have teenagers become the sensible upstanding citizens? When I was young, we were the ones up to no good. Though it's not this girl's fault that I feel completely patronised for the second time this evening.

'What? Don't be silly, I'm fine.' I aim for a light-hearted chuckle, but it comes out as more of a high-pitched squawk. 'I'm about to head home actually, and you lot should be doing the same. It's late.' I'm quite proud of my attempt to regain the moral high ground.

'If you're sure.' She's clearly not convinced by my act. 'We only came over because we thought a cat was in trouble. I've never heard anyone make a noise like that before. I hope you'll be all right.'

She turns and rejoins her group of friends, and I hear them whispering in an animated way as they walk off.

Great. Pity from a group of teenagers who thought I was a dying pet. And I thought things couldn't get any worse.

I sit for a while, swigging my wine. The Meadows is so dark and peaceful, it does have something of a therapeutic effect. Eventually, I dig my phone out of my handbag and indulge myself for a moment, imagining I have a boatload of messages and voicemails from Dave, begging me to come home. And on illuminating the screen, my heart flutters. I do have a number of notifications. Only, on closer inspection, I see that they're not from Dave. They're all from Cat.

My heart sinks. She knows what's happened. Which means Dave's spoken to her. Which means this is real.

I consider not calling her back, but the tiny part of my brain not marinated in red wine realises that, if I don't, she'll panic and call the police. Or worse, my parents. Taking a deep breath, I put my phone to my ear.

Cat picks up on the first ring, which even in my drunken state, makes me feel slightly guilty.

'*Emma, thank goodness,*' she breathes. 'Where are you, honey? I'm so sorry to hear about you and Dave.'

'I'm at the Meadows, behind the playpark. I'm drunk and cold... *and I'm homeless.*' I dissolve into tears once more.

'Oh honey, don't worry, I'm coming to get you. You can stay at mine for as long as you need, OK?'

'*Okaaay...*' I snivel between sobs.

'Stay exactly where you are. I'll be there in fifteen minutes.'

She hangs up and I'm left once again to my feline yowling, not caring a bit if the animal protection unit turns up.

Chapter Five

In the immediate period after my breakup with Dave, I camp out in Cat's guest room in a seemingly endless cycle of self-imposed misery, which includes 'forensically' trawling through his social media to try to figure out what went wrong. That is, until he heartlessly blocks me four days after our breakup.

My mind is in overdrive and my anxiety levels are through the roof, leaving me terminally exhausted. Because as much as I hate Dave for what he's done, I still love him, and I really miss him. It's like my heart and my head are in a never-ending war, which on top of my already challenging work situation, is just too much for my mind to cope with. So much so that I'm beginning to understand where the mindset associated with self-harm comes from. My self-critical inner voice, which seems to have hijacked all logical thinking, constantly berates and chides me to the point that I feel imprisoned in my own mind and desperate for some kind of release.

I go over and over things in my head, wondering if I'd done things differently, been a bit more independent, or not caused Dave to feel like he was always having to compromise, would things have been different? And what about the France trip – was it true that it never existed? Why would he make that up?

After a week off work on sick leave, I have a telephone appointment with my GP, who points me in the direction of some online self-help advice to ease my anxiety and signs me off for another week. I know I'm not capable of dealing with anything remotely challenging or pressured, never mind the boss from hell. Karla would rip what's left of me to shreds in minutes.

Of course, she's furious when I tell her I've been signed off with stress and anxiety.

'You wouldn't know the *meaning* of the word "stress". I'll be speaking to Lisa in HR about this. This is not going to look good, Emma.'

Luckily, when Lisa in HR receives my medical certificate, she confirms that my absence is genuine, so Karla has had no choice but to accept this predicament, leave me in peace and do some work herself for once.

~

Close to a fortnight on from what is now referred to as 'D-day', I venture out of hibernation in search of some company. Whether it's due to boredom or an improvement with my anxiety symptoms, I decide I can't lock myself away any longer, without seriously compromising my mental health. It may also have something to do with the return of my appetite.

Cat is in the kitchen, cooking a big pot of soup over the stove. She must sense me hovering in the doorway, because she turns and smiles.

'Well, well, Emma. You're out of your room. To what do I owe this honour?'

'I... erm...' I trace the pattern on the floor tiles with my toe. 'I thought – now I'm familiar with every square inch of wallpaper in your spare room – that maybe I could have dinner in here tonight.'

She laughs softly at my coyness. 'Of course, honey. I'd love to have your company. It's just soup and sandwiches tonight.'

'Sounds delicious.' I hop up onto a bar stool and watch Cat beavering away.

'So, does this mean you're feeling a wee bit better?' I can tell that she's treading carefully to avoid sending me scarpering back to my duvet.

'Yeah, I think so. I mean... it still really hurts and I still feel panicky at the thought of leaving the apartment, never mind going back to work, but I think I'm past the sobbing-at-every-nostalgic-thought stage.'

I smile weakly, suddenly ashamed. It's obviously not my fault that the combination of my relationship breakdown and my work situation have tipped me over the edge mentally and emotionally, but I feel guilty nonetheless. Especially when Cat's been running around after me, and there's clearly something going on with her. I've caught her with that same troubled look from our night out a few times since, but any time I've tried to bring it up she's said it was nothing.

'Can I tell you a secret?' Cat leans in conspiratorially and I nod. 'I'm really glad you're feeling better. You see... Amber's been very patient over the last few weeks, but that's only because Sara and I threatened to disown her if she wasn't.'

'You know, I was totally wondering about that.' My

mouth twitches with amusement. 'Her behaviour has been out of character – in a good way.'

'It took some effort, believe me. And there's no way it was going to last. The other day she said, and I quote, "if she doesn't get her sorry arse out of that bedroom soon, I'm going to come over and give her a lesson in just-freakin'-get-over-it".'

Cat giggles, but when I don't immediately respond, she pulls back and searches my face. 'Oh honey, I'm sorry. I thought you'd find it funny, but it's still too soon, isn't it?'

I'm a bit stunned for a second, but then a little snort escapes. Then another. And before I know it, I've dissolved into fits of laughter – which, it turns out, is a refreshing alternative to tears.

'Sorry.' I clamp my hand over my mouth. 'I don't know what's gotten into me. It's not even that funny, but I *was* baffled by this new improved Amber. It makes sense that it was an illusion.'

'We couldn't have let her loose on you,' says Cat. 'You were way too fragile.'

'Well, thank you for that.' I reach for her hand and give it a grateful squeeze. 'The wrath of our Amber is not for the faint-hearted.'

I start laughing again. I'm not really sure why but it feels good. I'm not at all put out by Amber's threat – and Cat and Sara sitting on her like that to protect me: that was so touching.

'You know what?' I rub my jaw thoughtfully. 'You guys are *amazing*. I mean... Amber, demonstrating some self-restraint for once. Sara, although she works ridiculous hours, still managing to pop in. And you, where do I start? You're the most incredible best friend anyone could ask for.'

Cat colours and starts to bustle around the kitchen again.

'Seriously.' I try to catch her eye. 'I can't believe you're still single. You're the most loyal, caring, selfless—'

'Oh, enough.' Cat cuts me off, clearly embarrassed.

'*No*, not enough. I know you're uncomfortable with this kind of chat, but tough. You've rallied around me, picked up my stuff from Dave's, made me food – although I have a confession, I've been flushing a lot of it down the loo.'

'I guessed that. But I figured if you were even eating a few mouthfuls then that was better than nothing at all.'

'*You see?* That's exactly what I mean.' I slap the worktop triumphantly 'You've worked from home, even taken a day's holiday – all for me. But you've also given me space to work through things myself. My parents would have suffocated the life out of me. I want you to know how much I appreciate it, and that I *will* repay the favour one day, I promise.'

'OK, thank you for your kind words,' Cat blusters. 'Now are you done?'

'I'm done.'

I sit back in my seat, satisfied that I've shown my best friend enough gratitude – for now.

'Speaking of your parents...' she says. 'Sorry again for letting it slip. I didn't realise you hadn't told them about D-day. How did you get away with that?'

'It's fine. They had to find out eventually.' I wave a non-plussed hand. 'As we only speak on weekends – you know, because I tell them that I'm too busy on workdays – I knew I'd be safe once the mandatory birthday phone call was out of the way. They were so busy singing *Happy Birthday* and reminiscing about my early years, they didn't even notice that I barely said a word.'

'Oh honey, it's such a shame that you missed out on your birthday celebrations.' Cat has a slightly distracted look on her face. 'Dave's timing really was appalling.'

I raise my eyes to the ceiling to keep any rogue tears at bay.

'But anyway...' She realises her error and swiftly changes the subject. 'Since I let things slip to your parents, it's been a different story, as you know. Your mum called. *Again.* I tried to reassure her that you're OK, but I'm not sure how much longer I can stave her off. She's going to turn up here eventually. You must realise that.'

'OK, I'll call her.' I'm irritated by my mum's persistence.

'Promise?' Cat waggles her finger at me.

'Promise.' I cross my fingers behind my back. '*Jeez,* I don't need to call my parents. I've got a ready-made mum right here.'

I duck as Cat playfully lobs a piece of carrot in my direction. 'You're definitely feeling better, you cheeky monkey. And what about Lottie? Have you been in touch with her? She'll be worried if she's not heard from you all this time.'

'Don't worry, I've been messaging her. I told her I was unwell and wasn't up to calling her, which is the truth. I didn't want her to see the state of me. I'm the one who should be looking after her now, not the other way around. She's done more than enough for me over the years.'

'She has.' Cat nods. 'But that doesn't mean you need to be made of steel. I'm sure Lottie would want to offer you some support at a time like this.'

'I suppose.' Now I'm thinking more rationally, I realise that Cat's right. 'I'll FaceTime her in a bit and tell her what's happened.'

'Good plan. So...' Cat ventures once again into the unknown of my emotions. 'Now that you're feeling a bit brighter, if you don't mind me asking, how did you come to be hammered in the Meadows at 2.30 a.m. on D-day night? I only realised earlier today that you weren't that drunk when you left us.'

I cringe at the memory. 'It's a bit ridiculous really. I was rushing out of Dave's apartment and I guess my survival instincts kicked in. I made off with one of his bottles of red to numb the pain – turns out it was vintage and worth a couple of grand.'

'*You didn't*. Goodness, he'll be livid. Did it taste amazing?'

'No idea.' I wince. 'I was hardly in the right frame of mind for savouring it. I wonder if he's noticed yet.'

'Maybe not,' says Cat. 'And when he does, he might not even realise what's happened. I wouldn't usually say this, but he did kind of deserve it. And it's not like you took it as revenge.'

'No, I didn't. I'd never have taken it if I knew how much it was worth, and I did get a shock when I found out, but it was already open by then.'

'And how *did* you find out?' Cat asks. 'Tell me the whole story.'

I flush with embarrassment while filling her in on what happened in the shop that night, including my frustrating encounter the bloke who clocked that the wine was vintage and how the shopkeeper conned me into buying a lottery ticket with my last couple of quid.

'Gosh, you had a right ordeal that night – and the last thing you needed was some wise guy making you feel small,' says Cat, once I'm done. 'Although... I don't think it was so bad that he was concerned for your safety.'

'He wasn't concerned for my safety.' I scoff. 'He was showing off. Trying to be the big hero rescuing the damsel in distress. He thought I was a right flake.'

'Well, that's not nice. I can't believe that the shopkeeper

persuaded you to part with the only money you had left too. I take it you didn't win anything on the ticket?'

I make a face. 'Obviously not. I mean, I never checked it, but the odds of winning more than a few quid are like a billion to one.'

'So? He might have been a wheeler dealer, but he was right that someone's got to win. Why don't you check the ticket, just in case? Even a twenty-pound win, wouldn't that feel a little like karma?'

'I suppose it would, but I'm not even sure what I did with it. My memory of that night is so hazy. I'll have a look.'

I go through to Cat's guest room and rummage through my jacket pockets, where I find nothing but used bus tickets and receipts. I then empty my handbag onto the bed and rifle through the contents, but there's no sign of the ticket.

Returning to the kitchen, I re-locate myself on the bar stool. 'No ticket, I'm afraid. I must have dropped it in the Meadows.'

'Oh well, as you say, the odds of winning are very slim.' Cat looks mildly disappointed on my behalf.

'Exactly.'

'You feel up to a glass?' She opens a fresh bottle of red. 'Or even half a glass?'

Having not touched a drop of alcohol since D-day, my stomach's first reaction to the suggestion of wine is an uncomfortable nauseated flip.

Despite this, I hear myself say, 'Sure, why not.'

Cat pours us a glass each, then tentatively proposes a toast. 'To new beginnings?'

'To new beginnings.' I clink her glass with mine. And I realise that I actually mean it.

Chapter Six

After dinner, I curl up on the double bed in Cat's spare room with my phone and dial Lottie through FaceTime. As the video call connects, I feel an unpleasant churning in my stomach at the thought of having to say the words out loud.

'Emma, how lovely to see you.' Lottie's kind but timeworn face appears on the screen. 'Are you feeling better? Golly, you're looking quite pale.'

'I'm fine, Aunt Lottie.' I force as natural a smile as I can. 'I have something to tell you. It's the reason I've been unwell.'

'Oh?'

'I'm sorry, I should have said before but I didn't want to burden you with my problems.'

'Why, Emma? Because I'm old?' Lottie appraises me over her spectacles, making her look like an old schoolmistress.

'No...' I cringe.

'Young lady, I might be getting on a bit and unable to do a lot of the things I used to, but I also like to think that I'm wise. Wise enough not to shoulder other peoples' issues at the expense of my own wellbeing. And wise enough, perhaps, to offer some helpful guidance and support to the younger generation. If you take that away from me, you may as well starting digging—'

'Don't say that. Of course, you are. I'm sorry, I guess... I wanted to protect you.'

'I can understand that, even if I don't agree with it. Now tell me, what's happened?'

'Dave broke up with me.' My eyes sting with emotion and I swallow thickly to keep my composure.

'Oh, darling girl.' Lottie's gentle voice becomes heavy with concern. 'I'm so very sorry to hear that. You invested a lot in that relationship.'

'I did.' I sniff, losing my battle as an army of tears advances down my cheeks. 'I really did, Aunt Lottie. I thought we were going to get married.'

'I know you did. And I don't think it was unreasonable to have that hope, particularly with David's extravagant and very public displays of affection.'

'Me neither.' I nod miserably. 'Although... having had time to think about it, there weren't many of those over the last year or so. He spent money on me, but he was emotionally distant, and I failed to notice. I've been really stupid and naïve.'

'No, you haven't. You've been in love,' Aunt Lottie consoles me.

'Amber always hated him. Like *really* hated him. Did she see something I didn't?'

'My love, I'm not sure it will do you any good to analyse it. You won't come up with any definitive answers, and it will only extend your suffering.'

'But I need to know, Aunt Lottie. It's been driving me up the wall. *Please.* As you quite rightly pointed out, you're wise, and I really need some of that wisdom right now. Even if it means you end up slagging Dave off.'

'All right,' she says. 'Although I'm not sure being wise is about "slagging people off". David is... very showy, Emma. He likes nice things, so having a pretty young woman like you on his arm would have suited him. However, I never got any real sense of depth from him.'

'What do you mean?' I wipe my nose and give it a soft blow.

'Every time I saw him – which was not often, bear in mind – he had a new and expensive item that he would draw attention to. Like a car or a watch or piece of designer clothing. David's view of the world, and his ability to discard and replace his possessions so easily, well... it may have crept into his personal life.'

'You mean he just saw me as another "possession" that could be thrown away?' I frown in response to my own question.

'I wouldn't go as far as that, but he perhaps doesn't possess the emotional depth to create a lasting bond with you.'

'You know, you're right.' I rub my forehead in realisation. 'I remember he once said that his parents told him the most important thing in life was to make money, because wealth meant power and a nice life with nice things.'

'Well, there you are. There might be some truth in what I say. Although it's just an educated guess, Emma. Don't take that as fact. One can never know exactly what's going on for other people.'

'Of course. It's just been so hard to accept, you know? And things at work have been really tough too.'

'I understand, my love. And I really wish I could take the pain away. What I can say, is that, although it will take time, you *will* get over this. And sooner than you think. Believe me, all wounds, no matter how deep, are capable of healing – to some extent at least.'

As she says this, I'm flooded with guilt. Here I am, thinking my partner ending our relationship (which it appears everyone but me knew was doomed anyway) is a near apocalyptic disaster, when Aunt Lottie has had to endure far greater pain in her life. This realisation is enough to kick me back into the gear I reached earlier with Cat.

'You're so right. I need to suck this up and move on.'

'Just don't push yourself too hard,' Aunt Lottie warns me. 'If you do, you'll only knock yourself back.'

'I won't. Thanks, Aunt Lottie. You're the best. Oh, I forgot to ask how you're doing. Is everything OK? Do you need me to do anything for you?'

'I'm fine, my love. For now, put your focus on getting back on your feet.'

'OK, but I'll be round to visit really soon, I promise.'

'I know you will.' She smiles warmly.

'Bye.' I blow kisses at her until the screen freezes and she disappears, then I wander through to the living room, where Cat is lazing on her corner sofa watching the latest reality dating show on Netflix. I settle down next to her, but I struggle to pay much attention to the TV because I'm stuck in my own head.

'I think I need to reassess my life,' I philosophise.

'What makes you say that?' asks Cat.

'Well, my relationship's gone down the drain, I have nowhere to live, my boss is a bully, who constantly threatens and belittles me. And I'm desperately trying to build a career for myself that – at this rate – I'm never going to achieve.'

'Well, when you put it like that...' She throws me a sympathetic look and mutes the TV. 'OK, let's talk about it.

The best way to solve a problem is to break it down, so we'll start with the easy bit. You do have a home. Right here with me. You can stay as long as you want.'

She may be my best friend, but I'm still bowled over by this gesture. 'Gosh, thanks, Cat. Are you sure? You have no idea how much that means to me.'

'Totally sure.' She grins. 'What could better than flat sharing with my bestie? Now, onto the next... your breakup with Dave. It has been painful and a huge shock, but you're over the worst of it. In fact, I'm willing to bet that in around six months' time you'll barely think about him anymore.'

'Probably true. You're good.'

'Maybe for others. But not for my own issues.' She rolls her eyes in a self-deprecating way.

'We all have our areas of challenge. Keep going.'

'So, that leaves us with your boss and your career. I think Amber's right, Karla will probably never fire you. That would leave her exposed. She needs you but she also knows you're a threat, so she's keeping you down.'

'But it's unbearable, Cat. If Karla will never actually fire me, at what expense do I stay there?'

'Hold on, this is a process. What was the feedback you got from your interview again? Why is it that Karla got the job over you?'

I sigh. 'Because apparently, I lack the "coat of armour" that she's got... whatever that means.'

'Well, what do you think it means?' asks Cat.

'Does it matter?'

'Of course it matters. If you don't understand your weaknesses, then how do you ever expect to overcome them?' She gives me an affectionate nudge with her foot.

'I hate to admit it, but you have a point.' I suddenly feel a bit sheepish for not trying harder to solve this one myself.

'OK... well, I *think* it's to do with avoiding conflict. I'm reasonably confident day to day and I'm damn good at my job. But when it comes to difficult or aggressive people, those who think that their opinion matters more than mine, even if I know I'm right, I just seem to buckle and step aside. And I let them get to me.'

'There you go. That wasn't so hard, was it?'

'I guess not, but it doesn't really help me. Maybe Amber's right. I am a wuss.'

Cat ponders my words. 'No, I don't think so, honey. But if you really want that career move, you'll need to work on that area. Do you think Karla would treat you the way she does if you made it clear it's not acceptable?'

I shrug. 'Maybe not.'

'And do you think Dave would have spoken to you the way he did if you'd held you own that night – or even throughout your relationship? It did seem like he was a bit self-centred at times, making sure he got what he wanted. If you never stood up to him, you made it easy for him to do that.'

'You never said anything.'

She hesitates and seems to choose her words carefully. 'It wasn't necessarily a deal-breaker in itself. And you seemed happy. All couples have issues of some kind – so I'm told.' She looks pained for a second. 'Anyway... the point is—'

'I could transform more than just my career if I can turn this weakness into a strength? Or maybe just get better at it.'

'Yes.' Cat grins at me. 'Exactly that. You see, sometimes we just need a little steer to find a way forward ourselves.'

'Cat, you're a *total genius*.' I launch myself on her with a huge hug. 'I mean, I've no idea how I'm going to do it, but at least I know where my opportunity for a happier life lies. No wonder you do so well in your career. Maybe we should apply the same logic to your love life?'

'Whoa, no thanks.' She holds up her hands as if to ward off my idea. 'That one is best left alone. It'll happen when it happens.'

'Seriously, though.' I hug her again. 'Thank you so much – for everything. I'm going to come back from the gutter, and I really will return the favour one day.'

'There's no need.' She sighs. 'You've bailed me out of more than enough dating blunders over the years.'

Settling back on the sofa, I feel lighter, and not just because I've had some wine. I know that something's changed. I've accepted things and I can now start the process of moving on.

∼

A few hours later, while I'm getting ready for bed, it dawns on me that I've turned Cat's spare room into a dumping ground. I start picking things up and putting them away, and as I see the progress I'm making, it becomes almost compulsive. The tidier the room becomes, the further my mood lightens and my sense of new beginnings grows, and in not much time at all the room looks inviting again. Pleased with my work, I'm about to jump into bed and snuggle under the duvet, when I notice something sticking out from under the divan frame. Reaching down to pick it up, I discover it's the missing lottery ticket.

'Hey, Cat, I've found that lottery ticket,' I call to her.

'Oh, fab.' She appears in the doorway. 'Are you going to check it then?'

'May as well, eh?'

I fire up my laptop and find the right web page.

'It wants me to select the date of the draw and enter the numbers on my ticket,' I inform her unnecessarily.

She comes into the room and sits on the end of my bed, while I add the numbers and click the 'submit' button. To my surprise, the refreshed web page informs me that I've won a prize.

'Ooh, I'm a winner. Maybe I'll get that twenty quid after all.'

'Well, good,' says Cat. 'You deserve a break. Whatever you win, you have to treat yourself, OK?'

'Defo. I'll buy us a round in the pub, or a meal if it comes up good. To celebrate my new beginning.' I click through to view my prize. 'So, it seems...' I study the information in front of me. '*What the*...? That can't be right.'

'What? What is it?'

I blink at the screen, checking and rechecking the numbers I've entered.

'*Tell me!*' Cat loses her usual self-restraint.

'It says I've won...' I shake my head in disbelief. 'Seven-hundred and eighty-four thousand, five hundred and sixty-three pounds and forty-seven pence.'

'Very funny.' She makes a face and sticks her tongue out at me. 'What have you really won?'

'I'm serious, Cat. That's what it says here.'

'Let me see.' She clambers across the bed to get a look at the screen. 'Oh... my... goodness. *Oh my goodness!* Emma, that's the second top prize. One more number match and you'd be a multi-millionaire.'

'Aww... what a way to burst my bubble,' I joke, but I'm tingling all over. I turn to her in disbelief. 'Cat, I've just won three-quarters of a million pounds.'

Chapter Seven

Lost in a daze, I check the information on how to claim my prize, and discover I need to call a dedicated telephone number. Unsurprisingly, it's closed for the day and I have no choice but to wait until the morning – however, my night doesn't end there. I mean, how can it? This is the equivalent of having three cans of Red Bull for a night cap and expecting to drift peacefully off to sleep.

Cat and I are so wired from the shock and excitement that our bedtime plans are hastily abandoned in favour of hot chocolate and fantastical chit-chat, and by the time we finally part company for bed, we've mentally spent my winnings several times over.

I carefully place the ticket in my bedside drawer and try to go to sleep, but it inevitably becomes a frustrating night of tossing, turning, and continuously checking it's still there. It's ludicrous because I have absolutely no reason to be so paranoid – and *obviously* I'd trust Cat with my life – but things like this *never* happen to me.

At some point I must finally doze off, because I'm woken

just after eight a.m. by the sound of Cat crashing around the flat in a very un-Cat-like way.

'*Morning,*' I call to her, after checking the ticket is still nestled safely in my bedside drawer. 'Everything OK?'

I hear something fall to the floor, followed by a brief yelp of pain.

'*Morning,*' she calls back from the kitchen. 'Sorry, everything's fine, but I'm super late. I slept through my alarm.'

'Eek, I'm sorry. You're only late because of me.'

'No, don't worry at all. I should still make the start of the weekly management meeting.' She appears in the doorway briefly with a toothy smile and a thumbs up, then disappears again.

'How about I buy you dinner later to make up for it?' I decide on a whim, then jump out of bed and join her in the hallway. 'Or, even better, I'll buy you all dinner as thank you for your support these past couple of weeks.'

'There's no need for that.' Cat hops around on one foot trying to do up her ankle boots. 'Are you even feeling up to going out?'

'I'm sure I'll be OK if I'm with the three of you. And I know there's no need. But I want to show you girls how grateful I am for your post D-day support. Yours especially, of course.'

'OK, sounds great.' She heads for the door. 'But make it somewhere cheap and cheerful.'

'Uh-huh.' I only semi-agree to this, because I already have a place in mind. 'Oh, and I want to surprise Amber and Sara, so don't say anything to them.'

'My lips are sealed. Good luck with your call.'

Once I'm alone, I look around the silent apartment,

suddenly apprehensive about making the call to the lottery people. I've checked the details over and over, but what if I've made a mistake? In my heightened state, I consider calling Aunt Lottie first – a habit well-ingrained in my daily life – but then think better of it. I'd hate to get her excited, and then find out I'd got it wrong.

Just make the bloody call, Emma.

Grabbing my mobile, I take the ticket out of the drawer and dial the number on the lottery website.

'Good afternoon, you're through to the UK Lottery claims line. My name is Sumaira. Can I take your name please?'

I freeze. 'Oh... hi. I think... I've won a shedload of money,' I trumpet down the phone, then curse myself for not being more cool and collected. Or starting with my name, as requested.

'No problem, madam. Let's see if I can help you. Please can you give me your name?'

Sumaira has clearly dealt with my breed of idiot before.

'My name is Emma... Emma Blake.'

'Thanks, Emma. Now, please can you give me the draw date and the numbers on your ticket?'

I keep tripping up and talking over her as I relay the information. It takes three attempts to get it right, and she has to read it all back to me, to make sure.

'OK, thanks for that, Emma,' says Sumaira. 'Give me a moment to check this, please.'

She's so calm and professional, it makes me feel like a hummingbird on amphetamines. Hold music plays in my ear for what feels like an eternity, and I realise that I'm holding my breath. Exhaling, I try to breathe normally, but it's like I've forgotten how to do it. This causes me to panic and while I'm getting myself in this little flap,

Sumaira comes back on the line, shocking me back to normality.

'Sorry to keep you. Could you give me a note of your address and telephone number, and I'll arrange for one of our lottery advisers to call you back, hopefully in about an hour.'

'Sure.' I give her my details. 'Wait, does that mean I've won? Or have I got it wrong? Oh no, I knew this would happen. I'm so mortified. Please don't tell anyone I called.'

In my renewed panic, I've missed that Sumaira's trying to get my attention.

'Emma? Emma, can you listen to me for a moment? Please just stay calm. Perhaps take some long deep breaths.'

'OK... OK... really sorry about this,' I say, between huffing and puffing.

While I fight to get my breathing under control, I can't help wondering if people ever die of shock when they find out that they've won. Or worse, that they haven't, like me.

'Emma? Are you OK now?' Sumaira asks.

'Yes, yes, I'm fine.' I'm consumed by embarrassment.

'Glad to hear it. Let me explain the process to you. I can't confirm anything over the phone. Your lottery adviser will do that once they've met with you and verified your ticket. They have to do those checks because we do receive claims that are not genuine.'

'What, you mean my ticket might be fake?' I'm horrified at the thought. 'But I bought it from a shop with a lottery machine. It wasn't some dodgy back-alley deal.'

'It's just a precaution, Emma. Most are genuine, but unfortunately, there are people out there who try to make money in dishonest ways. Mistakes can also happen too. All I ask is that you stay calm and open-minded until the relevant checks have been done.'

'OK, sure, I can do that,' I say, knowing fine well that I can't.

On hanging up from my call with Sumaira, I sit and wait, watching the second hand go round and round the clock on the wall. Never in my life do I remember time moving so slowly. After about fifty minutes of that, along with pacing and scolding myself (in case I've gotten this worked up over nothing), my phone buzzes beside me, causing me to yelp with fright.

'*Hello?*' I squeak down the phone.

'Good morning, is that Ms Emma Blake?'

'Yes. Yes, it is.'

'May I call you Emma?' the voice asks.

'Of course.' I'm now so high pitched, I'm surprised the crystal in Cat's apartment is still intact.

'Thank you, Emma. My name is Vivienne Caldwell and I'm a lottery adviser. I've been speaking with Sumaira, who has told me you may have had a substantial win.'

'Yes... that's right. But I might have got it wrong, so I'm keeping an open mind. It's really... open.' I wince in embarrassment. *What has happened to me?* I'm an intelligent, capable woman, but this situation is turning me into a blithering idiot.

'That's good, Emma. Now, shall we get a few formalities out of the way before we talk about next steps? Is that all right with you?'

I nod enthusiastically, then on realising she can't see me, I confirm that I'm happy with this plan.

Vivienne spends the next ten minutes or so checking that I'm OK (something that's clearly needed, judging by my behaviour), chatting me through her role in looking after me as a potential winner and explaining the prize claim process, including the required verification of my win. She also asks me to confirm my ticket details again.

'Well, Emma,' she says eventually. 'Provided everything we have discussed is accurate, the ticket is genuine and you're able to produce it for inspection when I visit, your win will be confirmed.'

I gulp. *It's real.* This is actually happening. It seemed a bit ridiculous when I thought about it myself, but now that Vivienne is confirming it, it sounds utterly absurd.

'Are you *absolutely* sure?' I ask. 'Because I'm not sure I'd come back from this if it were a mistake.'

I can almost hear Vivienne smiling down the phone. 'I am absolutely sure – pending what I've said. I've done this job long enough to pick up on potential issues at this stage. I also tracked the ticket sale before we spoke. We do it all electronically. Just you keep that ticket in a safe place.'

'Oh, I will. I'll guard it with my life.'

'Good. Now before we do the necessary admin, tell me, do you have anything planned over the next few days? We generally recommend that you don't make any substantial purchases before everything is confirmed. I would also recommend seeking some financial advice and/or taking a few days away to help you think through what you want to do with the money. Also, be wary of making snap decisions that you might regret.'

'That seems like sound advice. Well, tonight I'm hoping to take my three best friends out for dinner,' I tell her. 'To a restaurant we often eat at. Does that sound OK?'

'I'm sure that won't break the bank,' she says. 'And I'm sure your friends will appreciate the gesture – just bear in mind that everything is not yet signed and sealed. Have you told your friends yet?'

I'm starting to get excited now.

'My best friend was with me when I checked the ticket. But no one else knows. I'm going to surprise the others. I've had a difficult time recently and I owe them a huge thank you for their support.'

'I'm sorry to hear that you've had a difficult time, Emma. That sounds like a lovely way to show your appreciation. Now, a few other important things... Please do not make any promises to anyone, and be extra vigilant when it comes to people who might appear out of nowhere if they hear about your win. I recommend asking your friends to keep it a secret while you figure out how public you want to be about it.'

'Thanks, that's great advice.' I'm so appreciative of Vivienne's rational mind at this particular moment, especially as I seem to have lost mine.

While we go through the more administrative based part of the process, I can't help focusing on one thing – what she said about people appearing out of nowhere. Would Dave do something like that? Surely not. He made it clear that things were over. A sudden U-turn would be pretty suspect. *Although, at least I'd have him back* – that little voice creeps in again. Annoyed with myself for allowing this thought to form, I push it away and make a mental note not to get sucked by any 'declaration of regret' if he does turn up again.

∾

By lunchtime, the excitement of my call with Vivienne has worn off. In fact, it feels like a bit of anti-climax, because her visit isn't for two days, and I don't know what to do with myself to pass the time until then. Remembering my conversation with Cat about my career and life success in general, I look up some online articles on assertiveness, but I can't concentrate. I then consider going for a walk, however, the thought of that conjures up a big ball of nerves in my stomach.

I'm absolutely terrified at the idea of leaving the ticket alone in the apartment. *What if we got burgled?* And I'd feel equally worried taking it out with me in case I lost it. Then, there's the fact that my incredible stroke of luck hasn't magically cured the anxiety triggered by my breakup. In fact, the surrealness of this experience and the limbo I'm facing while I wait for confirmation of my win seems to have temporarily worsened it.

Eventually, I decide I can't sit on something this huge any longer. I have to at least tell Aunt Lottie.

I dial her on FaceTime and wait for her to answer. It takes a while, but eventually her face appears on my screen.

'Emma, lovely to see you. How are you coping?' She peers at me with a concerned face.

'I'm doing OK, actually.' I'm physically twitching at the thought of telling her my news. 'How are you?'

'You don't have to pretend with me.'

'I'm not pretending. I'm honestly a lot better. Something's happened, and it's kind of... massive.'

'Oh?' Her thinning eyebrows lift.

'Aunt Lottie...' I pause for effect. 'I've won the lottery.'

'You've won some pottery?'

I giggle. 'Not pottery. *Lottery.* I've won the lottery. Not the top prize but a big one.'

She still seems a bit confused, which isn't all that surprising – I'm struggling to get my own head around it – so I fill her in on the events of the last few days to help her understand.

'That's just lovely, Emma,' she says once I've told her how it all happened. 'You were in need of a little boost.'

'Don't you want to know how much I've won?' I ask with a grin.

'That's not really my business. Though I'm hoping it's enough for you to treat yourself to something nice after the upset you've had.'

'Oh, it is. I've won... *wait for it*... just over three-quarters of a million pounds.'

Aunt Lottie studies me over the video feed. 'Good grief, Emma. You're not kidding.'

'No, I'm not.' I shake my head, eyes wide from my residual disbelief. 'I feel like I'm in a dream and I'm about to wake up. But it's actually real.'

'Well... I'm a bit lost for words.' Aunt Lottie looks quite overwhelmed. 'This is... *wonderful* news. I'm ever so pleased for you.'

We chat excitedly for nearly an hour, and I arrange to visit her on Friday, then I message Amber and Sara about dinner – they don't know I'm planning to pay, of course – but my idea to spontaneously surprise them doesn't work. Unlike me, they both have lives and already have plans for the evening. Instead, we agree to meet on Thursday, which actually works better, because by that time my win should be confirmed. It will also give me a chance to get out and about and work up to being in a crowded restaurant. How I'll keep myself from telling anyone else for two more days, though, I really don't know.

I even consider calling my mum as 'fake promised', but she's incapable of keeping a secret. Feeling slightly guilty that she's worrying about me, and that I'm not sharing the most exciting moment of my life with her and my dad, I send her a text to say that I'm fine and I'll pop up to see them on Saturday. A visit trumps a call, so that should help me win back some brownie points.

So, with that ticked off and a noticeably absent attention span, I lock all lurking thoughts of Dave firmly out my mind and indulge myself in a spot of daydreaming about what I'll do with my big win.

Chapter Eight

By the time Thursday morning arrives, I'm just about climbing the walls. However, as the clock in the living room hits 8.55 a.m. – five minutes before Vivienne is due to arrive – my impatience is replaced by a jangling nervy feeling. Not so much because I'm worried that she'll tell me it's all a big mistake, or that the ticket will spontaneously combust (it's sitting on the table in front of me pinned down by an empty vase), but because this is the moment when it becomes real. It feels a bit like the adrenaline-fuelled final minutes before an important presentation, or an interview for the perfect job. Only this time the outcome is almost guaranteed to be a good one.

I walk slowly round Cat's living room, taking slow, deep breaths as per the self-help advice the doctor pointed me to, all while contemplating how my life is about to change. After this meeting, I shouldn't have to worry about money ever again (provided I don't lose my head and blow it all in a matter of months). It's not enough to live the life of a socialite and I'd never want that anyway. I still want a high-flying career. But it's definitely a game changer. I smile at the thought.

The apartment buzzer sounds and I go to the video entry system, where I see woman with cropped dark-brown hair waiting patiently. I buzz her in and stand at the open door until she emerges from the lift.

'Emma, it's a pleasure to meet you in person,' says Vivienne, as I let her into the apartment. She's middle-aged, probably in her fifties, with a kind face that matches her phone manner.

'Would you like a cup of tea or coffee?' I ask, after inviting her to have a seat in the living room.

'Tea with a spot of milk would be lovely, thank you.'

I make our drinks and return to the living room, where I place the tea laden tray down on the coffee table and invite Vivienne to help herself the assortment of chocolate biscuits I assembled after raiding Cat's cupboards. I've also brought out Cat's best porcelain cups and saucers for this grand affair. It feels a bit like having a visit from royalty.

Vivienne takes a sip from her cup, and lets out a little gasp of satisfaction. 'That is good tea, thank you, Emma. Nice and refreshing after a long drive. So, first things first, do you have the winning ticket to show me?'

She's obviously being polite because the ticket is in plain view next to the tray on the coffee table, still held captive by the empty vase.

'Ah, yes. My ticket.' I launch myself at it rather over-enthusiastically, knocking Vivienne's elbow in the process, and to my horror, her tea slops over the saucer and onto her pristine outfit.

'*Oh god, I'm so sorry.*' I quickly take the crockery from her. 'I'll get you a fresh cup and saucer. And I'll pay to have your outfit dry-cleaned. You didn't get scalded, did you?'

Vivienne puts a hand on my arm. 'Emma, dear. It's fine, really.'

'It's not, though, is it? That might stain.' I'm now trying to dab at her outfit with a wad of clean tissues. 'Think I'm a bit overwhelmed by all this.'

'Come on, leave that.' She gently takes the tissues from me and guides me back to my seat. 'My outfit is fine. It will wash out. Now, allow me to make us another cup of tea while you settle back and relax. Do you have decaf, per chance? Or a nice camomile?'

'All the teas and infusions are on the counter.' I murmur, my face puce with embarrassment.

I'm left sitting awkwardly, while Vivienne bustles round the kitchen. When she re-enters the room, she's carrying two sturdy looking mugs of tea, one of which (mine) is an infusion blend that goes by the name of 'Calm'. I sip at it gingerly while nibbling at a chocolate biscuit and it does seem to bring me back down to earth.

'All right, Emma.' Vivienne's tone is gentle and soothing. 'Shall I take a look at that ticket?'

I hand it to her, and she checks it against her paperwork.

'Well...' She looks up at me and smiles. 'I am very pleased to tell you that all is as it should be. Congratulations. You're about to become the proud recipient of seven-hundred and eighty-four thousand, five hundred and sixty-three pounds and forty-seven pence.' She reads the amount off the sheet in front of her.

Although this is exactly why Vivienne came here today, I'm completely thrown on hearing her say it.

'How do you feel?' she asks, and this has the effect of kicking my brain into gear.

My eyes widen, my mind playing back what she said. She's confirmed it. This is really happening. *I'm rich*. Heart pounding with adrenaline, my calmer demeanour is snuffed out in an instant.

'I feel... AMAZING!!'

To Vivienne's amusement, I jump up and shamelessly dance around the living room.

~

After Vivienne leaves – with multiple reminders that I must contact her if I have any questions or concerns – I spend the rest of the morning logging in and out of the banking app on my phone. She said the money could take several hours to come through, but I just can't help myself.

For what feels like an age, my rather unimpressive current account balance stares back at me defiantly, as if too stubborn to give in. Then, *boom*. Just as I've sat down in front of the TV with my lunch, it's there. The six-figure sum is so alluring, it's almost as if it's dancing in front of my eyes – or maybe the shock of seeing it there is giving me double vision. Even though I knew it was coming, it's a total head wrecker to see that enormous figure in my bank account.

A whirlwind of excited thoughts rush through my mind: how this will change my life; the financial security I now have; all the things I can now do that I couldn't before. But one thought in particular returns over and over. Aunt Lottie. What I want more than anything is to return the kindness and support she's offered me all these years. And I know just how I want to do that.

Dragging myself back to reality – and I'm not sure if it's my residual anxiety at play again – I suddenly feel an enormous responsibility to keep my money safe. Seeing it there on the screen is incredible, but it also instils a fear in me that someone will hack my bank account and I'll watch it disappear in front of my eyes. I've read about that actually happening. I decide that I'll take Vivienne's advice and head to my bank after my lunch to see if I can get some financial advice and some help to keep my money more secure. I need to get out and about anyway, and the thought of speaking to a faceless person on the phone or through a chat window about a figure this size gives me the heebie-jeebies.

Although I took a couple of short walks yesterday and the day before, I didn't venture into the bustle of the city centre, and it's a bit of a shock to the system at first. Thankfully, by focusing on my breathing and the excitement of my big win, I make it to George Street without feeling the urge to dash home and hide under the duvet. That's what I call progress.

On entering the bank, there aren't any available staff members for me to approach, so I join the small queue for the cashier. While waiting patiently, I take in the hum of the lights and the self-service machines, the murmur of hushed voices and the bustling activity around me, and find myself noticing – probably for the first time – how stressful everyday life is. The man at the front of the queue taps his foot impatiently, eyes boring a hole through the head of the woman in front, willing her to finish her unnecessary nattering with the cashier. A woman with a crying baby and a toddler having a tantrum struggles to use the self-pay-in machine. She looks so stressed that I feel a rush of sympathy for her. An elderly man with mobility issues struggles his way across the foyer, an immense effort just to enter the building and join the queue. Watching them, I realise that I'm in a situation that few people ever have the fortune to experience – which means I need to make the most of it.

The impatient man gets called by the cashier, and as I shuffle forward, a voice comes from close behind me.

'How was the park bench?'

'*Excuse me?*' I turn around, perplexed. 'I think you've got me mixed up with... *oh.*'

I find myself looking, not at a local pervert, but at the man from the shop on D-day night. The one I told to sod off for patronising me.

'Hello again.' He grins at me. He's dressed in the same office wear, only this time he's sporting a stylish blue tie. His dark eyes lock on mine.

'Hi.' I shift self-consciously, averting his gaze, then I turn back around, hoping that he'll take the hint.

He doesn't.

'Was the wine good?'

I ignore him.

'Come on...' he persists. 'I've always wondered what a bottle worth that much would taste like.'

'It tasted like wine,' I throw over my shoulder.

'You must have noticed some difference from the plonk most restaurants and bars sell.' He sidles up to me and nudges my shoulder playfully with his own, causing me to flush with embarrassment.

'Nope, not a thing.' I grit my teeth and remain front-facing so as not to encourage him. 'I... basically downed it.'

'I see. *Respect.*' There's almost a mischievous tone to his voice. 'You said it was to help you through the night. Are you OK now?'

'Fine, thank you.'

'That's good... I was concerned about you. Thought about giving you my number, just in case.'

This comment strikes a nerve. 'As I said in the shop that night, I can look after myself. I'm not a child.' I may be overreacting, but I don't care.

'Hey, sorry, didn't mean to offend you.' He flashes his

palms in a clear gesture of surrender. 'What happened, if you don't mind me asking?'

'Actually... I kind of *do* mind.'

'Right. I'm James.' He doesn't take the hint. 'And you are?'

'What... erm... Emma. And I'd rather... Look, I just want to forget about that night.'

'Got it. Sure. Sorry.'

Even though I can't see his face, I feel like he's enjoying this. Glancing around self-consciously, my cheeks flaming, I see to my discontent that we're being watched with interest by the other customers in the queue.

'It's nice to meet you, Emma,' says James. 'Properly this time.'

'It's not, though, is it,' I bat back.

'Not what?'

'Not properly. It's hardly meeting *properly* if I have to introduce myself, under duress, in a bank queue.'

He sucks his teeth. 'I guess you're right. Perhaps we should start again. Over coffee or something? You know, to make things more... formal.'

'Or perhaps not,' I mutter.

'Huh.' He's undeterred by my comment. 'So how does a person get past introductions with you, then? Like, if they want to ask you out on a date? Do they have to apply in writing?'

I hear a snigger from further back in the queue, and as a knee jerk reaction, I glare at James, just in time to catch his self-gratified smile – no doubt his response to discovering he has an entertained audience. 'What... I... *no*. Of course not.'

'All right. Good to know.'

My face is now like a furnace, my heart starting to pound. *Who is this joker?* I really can't deal with another walking ego who thinks he can charm the pants off every woman in sight. Like sodding Dave.

'Excuse me, madam?'

I realise I'm at the front of the queue, and the cashier is calling me forward, not for the first time, it seems. Relieved at being rescued from this unbearable interaction, I rush forward.

'Great to see you again, Emma,' James calls out from behind.

'Hi.' I ignore him and focus on the cashier, while trying to calm myself.

'Good afternoon, madam.' She smiles at me, likely unaware of the ridiculous exchange that has just taken place. 'How can I help you today?'

I look at her, then at the room around me, suddenly aware that I'm surrounded by several pairs of ears. I hadn't considered the lack of privacy.

'Madam, are you OK? Can I help you?'

'Erm... yes, thanks. I'm fine.' I try to sound bright and carefree, then I lower my voice to almost a whisper. 'Is there someone I can talk to for some financial advice on a large sum of money?'

'I'm sorry, I didn't catch that. Could you say it again, please?'

I repeat my request, not raising my voice at all.

'Forgive me, I still can't hear you.' The cashier leans forward in her seat. 'Can you speak up?'

'No, I can't.'

'Madam, is everything all right?'

In her agitation at not being able to hear me, the cashier's voice has been rising and has attracted quite a bit of attention. Exactly what I didn't want. I start to get flustered.

'I can't speak any louder.' My frustration causes my voice to rise too. 'This is a *personal* matter.'

Wrapping my arms around myself protectively, I scan the vicinity and my eyes meeting those of James, who's now with the cashier two along from mine. He does that same raised eyebrow gesture from the shop on 'D-day' night, which gets me even more worked up. My stomach gives an uncomfortable flip, and I look away quickly.

Just when I'm about to tell the cashier to forget it, another staff member materialises at my side. She flashes him a grateful look.

'Madam, I'm the Assistant Manager. Would you like to go somewhere more private?'

'*Yes.*' I exhale with relief at his presence. 'Yes, that would be great. Thank you.'

Chapter Nine

An hour later, as I'm leaving the bank, I'm pleased to note that Mr Cocky himself, James, is nowhere to be seen. And as I'm in town, I decide to pick up a few things I need before returning to Cat's place.

'How was your meeting?' She pounces on me the moment I walk through the door. 'Tell me everything.' It's clear from the fact that she's still in her work gear that she's only arrived home minutes before me.

'It went great. Or as great as it can when you've soiled the lottery adviser's outfit within minutes of her arriving.' I wince at the memory.

'You what?'

'Never mind. That's not important. As I said, it went great. The money's in my account, and thanks to a very helpful Assistant Bank Manager, I've even just had a meeting with a financial adviser.'

'Check you.' Cat looks impressed. 'That was sensible doing it so quickly.'

'It was more out of feeling vulnerable having that amount

of cash sitting in my current account if I'm honest. But Vivienne recommended I do it, and I realised on the way home that it should help to keep my parents at bay as well, so it was doubly beneficial.'

We each have a quick shower and then I go through to Cat's room so I can fill her in on my day while getting ready to go out for dinner.

'That's so exciting,' she says, when I've given her a chunky summary of Vivienne's visit and my meeting with the Financial Adviser. 'Everything is really turning around for you, isn't it?'

'It certainly seems that way.' I flash her a guilty grin, as if somehow, I don't deserve it. 'Though there was one thing that didn't go so well. Do you remember how I told you about the annoying guy in the shop on D-day night?'

'The one who wanted to be your babysitter in the park?'

'Yeah, him. Well, I only went and bumped into him again today, didn't I?' I roll my eyes at the injustice of this. 'In the bloody bank queue, where I had no chance of escape – not without losing my place in the queue anyway.'

'*Yikes*. What happened?' Cat pauses mid-way through applying her lipstick to give me her full attention.

'He got my back up *again*. Was all smarmy and superior. Made out he was just a concerned citizen and even pretended to flirt with me, all for the purpose of entertaining himself and making me look stupid.'

'Hmm... that's not so good. But... are you sure he wasn't actually flirting with you?'

'I really don't think so, but who knows?' I wave my eyeliner like it's the tail of an irritated cat. 'If it *was* an attempt at flirting then he can get lost. He gives off major Dave vibes so he's best given a very wide berth.'

'Got it.' Cat nods and turns back to the mirror. 'Here's hoping you won't cross paths again.'

'Absolutely. Though, in a city this size, what are the chances of that happening?'

~

At seven p.m., Cat and I walk through the door of *Chez Nicolas* – a stylish French bistro in the West End – and see that Amber and Sara have already arrived.

Cat joins them at the table, while I catch a passing waiter, and discreetly ask him to ignore the drinks order from our table and prepare a couple of bottles of champagne – the first to be served on my signal once we've ordered.

'So, what's the occasion?' Amber demands, before my backside has even hit the seat.

'What do you mean? And hi to you too.' I do my best to look innocent, which under the circumstances is very difficult.

'I mean, why are we in our favourite restaurant on a random Thursday? And while you're still signed off sick?'

'Thanks for the reminder.' I purse my lips, while self-consciously glancing around the restaurant at the other diners. 'I'm already feeling super guilty and paranoid about that. This seemed like a great idea until I thought about being spotted out by someone from my work.'

'Hey, honey... we talked about this on the way here.' Cat reaches across the table, giving my hand a reassuring squeeze. 'You're just getting yourself out doing things like this again. Anxiety is something you have to address with small steps forward in a safe environment. We're that safe environment, so you have *nothing* to feel guilty about.'

'*Anyway*...' Amber's impatience takes over. 'It's clear there's something going on. I can smell it. You're not pregnant, are you? Or, wait a minute... you're not back together with that selfish prick? That would be no cause for celebration whatsoever.'

She's clearly back to her normal self again.

'No, I'm not pregnant. And I'm not back with Dave either – I haven't even heard from him. But thanks for the care and concern.' I feel suddenly deflated. 'I may be doing better, but I'm still far from over him. And everything that happened. That's going to take a while.'

I'm aware of Amber getting a gentle kick under the table from Cat, which makes me smile. My bestie has become a proper minder.

'Anyway.' I gather myself together. 'I just thought it would be nice to catch up, so please can we relax and have a laugh tonight?'

I hope my attempt at evasion works. I only need about fifteen minutes.

'Whatever works for you, girlfriend.' Sara slings a comforting arm around my shoulder while pulling her compact mirror from her purse to check her pristine makeup, no doubt for the hundredth time today. 'It's fabulous to have you back.'

'It really is.' Cat raises her water glass, and as we're clinking, the waiter appears.

After we order, a fizz of nerves erupts in my stomach and the moment that I've been so looking forward to becomes a bit daunting. What if Amber and Sara aren't as happy for me as I think they'll be? After all, it's me that's won, not them. Do people actually like hearing about the good fortune of others?

I glance at Cat. She's clearly trying to send me a telepathic message. She grabs her phone and starts typing, then a few seconds later my phone buzzes. I read her message.

What are you waiting for? You're going to miss your moment. And the girls are expecting drinks that aren't going to arrive!

She's right, but before I can reply, another message comes in.

And stop worrying! They won't think you're boasting or selfish. They'll be nothing but happy for you.

Cat's mind-reading powers are clearly on point. Though, to be fair, she probably knows me better than I know myself.

Giving her another fleeting (and grateful) look, I catch the waiter's attention and signal to him to bring the champagne in five minutes' time. He salutes back with a little wink.

When I tune back into the conversation, Sara and Amber are chatting away about some A-lister's latest affair.

'Awww, sweetie, you're so naive.' Sara pushes her long blonde hair behind her shoulders. 'Celebrities go into the world of fame knowing that they'll be cheated on and that their relationships won't last. That's the trade-off for being in the limelight and earning a packet. Also, we live in the twenty-first century. Marriage isn't the sacred and eternal act it used to be.'

'Huh-uh, that's bullshit.' Amber scoffs. 'Cheating is so low and especially the way he's done it. Women should be given the right to inflict castration as a punishment. *That* would be the perfect deterrent for slippery schmucks like Leo Perrera.'

I feel lighter as I allow myself to be entertained by the familiar pattern of their conversation – two super confident women with very different views on life. Taking a deep breath, I clear my throat.

'Erm, ladies. Can I interrupt for a second?'

They both stop and look at me.

'I actually do have something I'd like to share with you. Some good news.'

'*I knew it.* You're bloody pregnant, aren't you?' Amber unhelpfully broadcasts, causing the other diners nearby to turn and stare at us curiously.

'No, I'm not pregnant, you idiot.' My heart hammers in response to the unwanted attention. 'But thanks for telling the whole restaurant I am.'

'So, what is it, Emma? What's the big news?' Sara asks.

'It's... well...' I've rehearsed this in my head, but now that the moment's here, my memory has completely failed me.

'Gonna just spit it out,' says Amber. 'The way you're behaving you'd think you'd won the freakin' lottery or something.'

'Erm... well...' I splutter, unable to believe that inadvertently she's guessed it.

Cat giggles and I decide I have to ditch the speech.

'Well, actually, that's kind of it.'

'Um... what's kind of it?' Sara looks flummoxed.

'What Amber said.' I shrug. 'On D-day night, I bought a UK Lottery ticket with my last couple of quid because a shopkeeper said I was due some luck. And... it came good. I won over three-quarters of a million pounds.'

For a moment, no one says anything. Amber and Sara survey me with sceptical expressions.

'It wasn't the jackpot,' I rush to add, feeling flustered by their appraising eyes. 'But it *was* the second biggest prize.'

There's another lengthy pause while the two of them take in what I've said.

'*Yeah, right.*' Amber opts for dismissing my claim.

'Ha, good one,' Sara gives a tinkling laugh. 'You nearly had us there. So, what's the real news?'

This is certainly not the reaction I expected, though I guess I can understand it.

'It's not a joke.' I lean forward, elbows on the table. 'I'm deadly serious. Ask Cat.'

Their faces blanch as they look from me to Cat and she nods.

'It's true,' she confirms. 'I was there. Emma's a near millionaire.'

The stunned silence lasts another few seconds, before it's broken.

'*You lucky cow!*' Amber cries, this time earning herself dirty looks from other diners.

'*Wow!* Nice one, sweetie.' Sara looks seriously impressed. 'I'm well jel.'

'Thanks, I still can't quite believe it myself.' I can't help grinning from ear to ear.

'So, what's the deal?' Amber asks.

'The deal?'

'Exactly how much have you won? And more importantly, are you sure you've won? You'll look like a right dumbass if you've got it wrong.'

'Oh, I've been through all that already, believe me.' I

cringe, thinking back to my idiotic behaviour on the phone with Sumaira from the UK Lottery helpline. 'I checked and re-checked about two-hundred times. The lottery adviser visited me today and the money cleared in my bank account not long before I got here.'

I quickly fill them in on the rest of the story, during which Amber's jaw drops further and further towards the floor. Sara takes it more in her stride, giving me recommendations for upcoming designer sales and her favourite premium makeup products. She also teases Amber for acting like a star-struck teenager, while Amber retaliates with her usual choice language.

'So, anyway...' I round things off. 'I obviously wanted to tell you my good news. But I also wanted to thank you from the bottom of my heart for your support over the last few weeks.' I try to ignore Amber sticking her fingers down her throat.

'It's no big deal.' Sara shrugs, while simultaneously applying her lip gloss and tutting at Amber. 'That's what friends do.'

'I know. But I honestly don't think I'd have got through it without your visits and messages of support. At least, not nearly as quickly as I did. So, to show my gratitude, dinner is on me. And...' I signal to our waiter, who canters across enthusiastically. 'So is the champagne.'

'Ooh, I love champagne,' Sara coos. 'You're really spoiling us, Emma.'

'Honey, I thought you were going to follow the lottery adviser's advice and buy something affordable, like prosecco.' Cat is anxiously leafing through the wine menu. 'That's... *one hundred and twenty-five pounds a bottle.*'

'Hey, Cat,' says Amber. 'How about... *shut the hell up.* This is awesome. Bring on the champagne!'

'It's fine,' I reassure Cat. 'I've got the money now and it's hardly going to make a dent in my winnings. I want this to be a proper celebration.'

The waiter discreetly pops the cork, pours us each a glass, then places the bottle in a free-standing ice bucket and disappears. For a moment, I'm hypnotised by the effervescence of the bubbles and what they represent.

'*Speech!*' Amber shocks me back to reality.

'What? No, definitely not. I don't do speeches.'

'Come on, girlfriend,' Sara urges me. 'This is a huge moment for you. At least make a toast.'

'OK, I can do that, I suppose.' I smile and my three friends beam back at me. 'To... an incredible change of luck?' I hold up my glass.

'*To an incredible change of luck.*' Their chorus is punctuated by the clinking of our flutes.

I take a sip and savour it. The champagne is fruity, dry and beautifully chilled. And right now – probably more because of what it represents than anything – I'd say that it's the most heavenly drink I've ever tasted.

'Hey, Emma.' Amber elbows me in the ribs, interrupting my zen. 'I want to make a toast too.'

'Erm... OK. But please keep it reasonably clean.'

'*Obviously.*' She rolls her eyes.

She makes a show of composing herself. 'To Emma's brand-new start. I couldn't have wished this to happen to a better person...'

'Aww, thank you, Amber.' I'm genuinely touched by her sincere gesture.

'Wait, I'm not done.' She holds up her hand to keep us silent, then resumes her speech-making posture. 'Especially as Dave the wank stain is out of the picture and won't be getting a penny of it.'

I choke on my champagne. Cat and Sara both eyeball Amber with disapproving looks, and then turn quickly to me to check I'm OK.

'Oh, why not,' I concede. 'Nothing's going to get to me today.'

We clink glasses again, doing our best to chant a repeat of Amber's rather longwinded and totally un-PC toast.

What follows is lots of cheering and whooping, random toasts – which become more obscure the merrier we get – and some really good chat.

After much coaxing, we manage to get out of Cat that there's a new bloke on the scene. I can't believe I'm living with her and I didn't even know that. Apparently, they're two dates in and it seems to be going well. She doesn't give us any real juice, though, despite some rather disconcerting interrogation tactics from Amber. Sara shares the gossip from the office, none of which includes any evidence (or even hints) of her alleged affair. I chat a bit about how I'm feeling after my break-up, but that conversation is short-lived due to a lack of tolerance from Amber. Finally, Amber rounds things off with her regular husband assassination slot, which is more about the comedic delivery than any real issues within her marriage.

There's also another obvious subject that keeps coming up – my new-found wealth. But I try to steer the conversation in other directions so that it's not all about me.

I'm so happy that my friends are pleased for me, and that they're accepting my token of gratitude. Broken heart aside, it's one of the best moments I can remember (as well as a well-timed distraction). And I get to celebrate again tomorrow with Aunt Lottie.

Before we leave the restaurant, I take a quick trip to the

ladies, and I'm drying my hands, when a voice comes out of nowhere.

'Well, what do we have here? Little miss I'm-too-heartbroken-over-my-split-from-my-boyfriend-to-turn-up-for-work.'

It seems my luck has run out. I turn and find myself face to face – with my boss.

Chapter Ten

I'm rigid with fear, unable to look at her, the shock having rendered me mute. This was not how tonight was meant to go.

Karla takes my silence as a welcome opportunity to reprimand me.

'What does it say on your medical certificate again?' She's clearly enjoying watching me squirm. 'Ah yes, stress and anxiety. You don't look particularly *anxious* to me.' She sni s the air. 'Is that alcohol I smell?'

This is not good. I may be signed o from work for genuine reasons, but bumping into her here definitely does not work in my favour. And especially not when I've been on the champagne. Why did this have to happen tonight, of all nights?

With my stress response in overdrive, I'm late catching onto the reality of the situation. First, that Karla's standing too far away to smell anything. Second, she looks like she's had a few more than me. However, as comforting as these revelations are, they do little to get me out of this unbearable confrontation.

Obviously well aware that she has the upper hand, Karla continues to make the most of her fortuitous find.

'*Tut tut*, Emma. HR will not be tolerant of this. Probably amounts to gross misconduct, in fact, faking an illness.' There's a slight slur detectable in her voice.

She walks towards me, only coming to a stop when I've been treated to a mouthful of her sickly, musky perfume. I can also smell alcohol on *her* breath. Repulsed, I take a step back.

'What's the matter? Finally realised you're expendable? *Took you long enough,*' she sneers, wobbling slightly.

A huge swell of anxiety rises within me. This is too much for my already challenged brain and body to cope with. Especially with her threatening my job and career while she bullies me into submission. My friends have their suspicions that she's bluffing over firing me, and I've so wanted to believe them. But that nagging voice of worry in my head always overrules any rational thought. After all, if she sees me as a threat, would it not be better to get rid of me? She could always find someone else to dump her workload on.

I'm at the point where I think I'm going to pass out, aware that my body can only endure so much stress, when my 'flight' instinct suddenly kicks in. I dodge out of her way and make a beeline for the door, Karla's gleeful laugh taunting me as I go.

Once I'm outside the toilets and in relative safety, the familiar feeling of regret kicks in. Why couldn't I have stood up to her – for once? Why does she always get the better of me? I stop and steady myself on the wall, gulping down deep breaths in a bid to calm my racing heart and the shaky feeling in my legs.

Then something strange happens. I stop trembling, the heat in my face subsides and I find myself regaining some control. I'm still terrified of her but I suddenly feel a primal urge to defend my position. *She's* the one in the wrong here. She's always been catty and nasty, but this is *too* far. I've been through hell over the last two weeks, and the moment I'm starting to get back on my feet, she does this. Bullying me in the office is one thing. Threatening me outside of work is quite another.

I'm in a strange moment where time seems to have stopped, and it's like I'm watching myself from a few steps away. My brain is battling with itself: one part telling me to run back to my friends, while another is building momentum, saying enough is enough. As Cat has quite rightly pointed out, I haven't actually done anything wrong. This *is* all about control, about keeping me down, and continuing to steal the credit. She's *nothing* without me.

I take one more deep calming breath, then I turn around and walk straight back into the toilets, where Karla's topping up her lipstick in the mirror. She seems surprised to see me return, but at the same time delighted at the opportunity to have another pop at me. She looks almost feral, eyes narrowed, a nasty superior expression on her face.

'Come back to grovel, Emma?'

'No. I've actually been thinking about what you said, Karla...' I'm not yet sure where I'm going with this, but my survival instincts seem to have well and truly kicked in.

'And?' She folds her arms and leans against one of the sinks with a gloating smile.

'I suppose you're right. I mean, here I am, signed off with stress and anxiety, and I have the audacity to be out enjoying myself.'

The smug look remains, but it's fixed, as if she's detected that this isn't quite moving in the direction she expected.

'Of course. Getting out and living would actually... how do I put it... oh, yes... *help* me with my recovery.'

I'm barely able to fathom the words coming out of my mouth, and I can see Karla's trying to think of a smart response to regain the upper hand, but I've caught her off guard. She expected my usual submissive response.

'I see what you're doing,' she says. 'You may be able to hide behind those ridiculous HR policies – for now. But you'll slip up again, Emma, and next time you'd better watch out.'

'Watch out for what exactly?' I'm still full of disbelief that I, Emma Blake, am taking her on. 'That you drunkenly confronted and threatened me while I was on sick leave? I'm sure the "ridiculous" HR department would be pleased to hear about that.'

I pause for effect. This time I've really shocked her into silence. *How am I doing this?* Thankfully she can't mind read, because that would definitely lose me this one.

'And just to top it off,' I continue. 'I can add in you stealing credit for my work – of which I have *a lot* of evidence.'

'*You wouldn't dare.* You don't have the guts.'

I can tell I've really riled her now. She's clearly not used to people standing up to her and she's getting desperate. This tells me that her bark and her bullying must be a cover for the fact that, deep down, she's no better with true confrontation than I am.

'Oh, I would, Karla. Things have changed for me more than you know.'

I see her shift uncomfortably. She doesn't know what's at the root of this unexpected transformation, but I can tell she's convinced by it.

'Lucky for you...' I'm now on full autopilot. 'I have other

options. You can consider this my verbal notice of resignation. My formal letter will be in the post tomorrow.'

'You what? You can't just resign like that.'

'I can. And I just did.'

What the hell am I doing? Alarm bells clang in my head, but my autopilot ignores them.

'You know what's even better than outing you through a formal process?' I go in for one final swipe. 'It's knowing that you'll crash and burn all by yourself without someone in the background doing your work for you.'

With that, I turn on my heel and sweep out of the ladies toilets, leaving my speechless, soon-to-be ex-boss behind.

Chapter Eleven

I'm buzzing with adrenaline as I take in what's just happened. *Where did that come from?* I just accused my boss of being a liar and a manipulator – and quit my job – something I would never have dared to do in a million years. *Who even am I?*

'What took you so long? You got the runs or something?' Amber's arms are folded with impatience when I collapse into my seat at the table.

'Honey, are you OK?' Cat has picked up that something's not right.

'I'm... yes... no... I think so. I just bumped into Karla in the toilets.'

'*Oh no,*' she gasps. 'Are you OK? Lottery win or not, that was the last thing you needed.'

'Tell me about it.'

'What did she say? I can't believe she's here. This is going to make things even worse for you at work.'

'Actually...' I smile guiltily, my heart rate returning to normal. 'I just stood up to her for the first time ever. And... um... I quit my job.'

'*What?*' Cat and Amber just about keel over in shock.

'Nice one, Emma!' Sara slaps me a high five. 'Never had you down as so spontaneous... or brave. So proud of you. Now you can chill for a bit and—'

'*Hold on.*' Amber cuts her off. 'You – Emma the wuss – kicked some bitch-boss arse in the toilets? No way. You're making it up.'

'I'm not.' I shake my head, eyes wide as saucers. 'I really can't believe it myself. I don't know what I was thinking, or if I was thinking at all, but I did it.'

I play back the scene from the toilets in a low voice while my friends listen intently. Once I'm done, there are vastly contrasting reactions to my heroic moment of liberation.

'Point her out,' Amber demands. 'I'll tell her exactly where being a nasty manipulative cow's going to get her.'

'Thanks, Amber, but I'll politely decline your kind offer of support,' I reply, relieved to note that Karla is nowhere to be seen.

Cat seems the most concerned about me having quit my job. 'Emma, I know this all happened in the moment and it's a bit of a rush, but have you really thought this through? What about your career aspirations? Surely, they're not off the table all of a sudden. You said yourself you haven't won enough to live the life of a socialite. And what about your work references? Karla could really mess—'

'*Chill,* Cat.' Sara plants a calming hand on Cat's shoulder to power her down. 'Emma needs this. She's been miserable for ages and I know exactly what Karla's like. Now's the perfect chance for Emma to get out of there and find her dream job.'

'That's right.' I flash Sara a grateful look, because it's not just Cat that needs convincing, I do too. 'I know it was a snap decision in a heated moment, and I have no idea what

I'll do next. But I'm kind of excited too. I already feel freer. Cat, we talked before about me having a brand-new start. Now I've got the opportunity to do it properly. I can find myself a new pad – mortgage free – and take some time to work out the right career path for me.'

'I guess you're right. So, I suppose that means you're moving out.' Cat's tone is laced with disappointment.

Ah, shit. I was so pleased to get the approval I needed from Sara that I've missed the impact on Cat. She's loving us being roomies. And she made such a kind offer of a time-limitless place to stay. I can't just dismiss that.

'*Oh, Cat.* No, not yet.' I grab her hand and squeeze it tight. 'The new place can wait. I should probably go slow on the big decisions anyway, and with that one I can *really* take my time.' I give her a little wink and she perks up. 'But as I'll be staying on with you for a bit, I want to pay my way – rent, bills and everything, all right?'

'OK, sure.' She smiles. 'There's no need for the rent part, but if it makes you feel more comfortable, then that's fine.'

We leave the restaurant and say our goodbyes, and as Cat and I wander along Fountainbridge to her apartment on West Bryson Road with a cool gusty wind whipping round us, I'm still buzzing with excitement and incredulity. Like one of those wind-up toys that keeps going and going.

'I have no idea what happened to me,' I say to her. 'I was in control like I've never been before – something just took over me. It was like I was her equal or even that I had power over her, and I can't put it down to anything other than having some extra cash in the bank.'

Cat shrugs. 'You have had an adrenaline-boosting few days. The alcohol probably played a role as well – giving you extra courage.'

'Yeah, maybe. But you know... it really is amazing the

feeling of security that comes with money. It makes my worries seem less huge – like all the fear I had was rooted in my financial vulnerability, and now that I'm better off, I'm not scared anymore. I've never felt so liberated in my life. I know people say money can't buy happiness, but at this particular moment, I *really* can't agree.'

'Hmm... I suppose. Quitting your job like that was a bold move and you do seem like you're in a better place. Just don't let the money go to your head, though, eh? Don't want you turning into a right diva on me.'

'Promise.' I laugh, linking arms with her.

'So, will you work your notice?'

'Yeah, I will. You were right about my references. I want to keep them clean. I could contact the doctor and try to get signed off again, but I'd have to fake it and that's not me.'

'Sorry, honey.' Cat grimaces. 'I don't envy you having to face Karla after what's just happened.'

'I know.' I mirror her expression. 'I can't say I'm relishing the thought. However, things have shifted between us. She doesn't have the upper hand anymore, so I'm hoping she'll leave me alone.'

'Fingers crossed. And what about your mum and dad? When will you tell them? You can't leave it much longer.'

'I know. I'm visiting Aunt Lottie tomorrow, so I've said I'll go and see them on Saturday. Will you come for moral support?'

'Sure.' She grins. 'No way I'm missing that entertainment.'

'Thank you. So, what about you then? Who's this mystery guy you've met?' I give her a playful nudge.

'He's... just a guy.'

'Well, come on. Spill.'

'I... don't want to.' Cat looks at the ground. 'It's early days and I really like him. I don't want to jinx it.'

'Oh, Cat.' I feel a rush of sympathy for her. 'You won't jinx it. If it's meant to work out, it will.'

'I know. It's just that I always get my hopes up about the new guy on the scene, and then a couple of weeks later I have to admit it's over. It's humiliating, Emma. I've decided that from now on, I'm not sharing any details until I find myself in a proper relationship.'

'Well, good for you. Play it cool and let him do the chasing. Looking back, I should have been more that way with Dave, though it probably wouldn't have made any difference.' A lump of emotion forms in my throat and my voice cracks. 'You know, even with how horrible he's been, I still miss him. Pathetic, huh?'

'It's not pathetic at all...' Cat's suddenly wearing that same troubled look I've seen on her recently, and I realise that what I'm saying probably has her pondering her own situation. That must be what's bothering her. She's worried that this new guy isn't who she hopes he is, which means she must *really* like him.

Chapter Twelve

On Friday morning, I see to some admin essentials before leaving to visit Aunt Lottie. This includes writing my letter of resignation from my job, which turns out to be one of the most therapeutic things I've ever done. It takes multiple versions and a lot of censoring, but the final piece is clean and professional. Then, spurred on by the combination of having my boss's balls in a vice grip (metaphorically speaking, of course) and a deep reluctance to set foot in that office ever again, I decide to chance my luck and follow up with a call to Lisa in HR.

I explain that my resignation letter is on its way, and that there are personal circumstances (I don't elaborate) that make it impossible for me to work my notice. I also ask her to speak to Karla on my behalf and let me know if there's a problem. Lisa's a bit taken aback, but fortunately agrees. I know I could be sued for breach of contract, however, I've hedged my bets on Karla not wanting anyone looking into what particular 'personal circumstances' have led to my sudden and mysterious departure.

It pays off. An hour later Lisa calls me back to say that

Karla is dreadfully sorry to hear that things have become so difficult for me, she certainly doesn't want to make an already challenging situation worse, and she wishes me all the very best in my future endeavours.

Yeah, right.

Before I say my final goodbye to Lisa, I can't help asking if they'll be replacing me straight away.

'It seems so,' says Lisa. 'Karla's requested that I get straight on the phone to the agencies to find some exceptional candidates who are immediately available.'

Just as I'm thinking there's no such thing as karma after all, Lisa restores my faith.

'I might have to bump that request to the bottom of my "to do" list for a week or two,' she says, with the slightest air of conspiracy. 'I'm busy with other priorities right now. Good luck with whatever you move onto, Emma. It's a shame we had to lose someone as good as you.'

～

Shortly after midday, I arrive at Aunt Lottie's cottage in Ratho and crunch my way up the gravel path, an explosion of beautiful spring flowers either side. Before I can ring the bell, the sage-green door opens and her slight frame comes into view.

'*Hi.*' I sweep her into a comforting and extended embrace. 'Oh, it's so good to see you.'

'And it's lovely to see you smiling.' She pats me on the back.

Leaning on her walking stick, Aunt Lottie leads me through the hallway into her pristine but dated living room. She bends awkwardly while settling into her embroidered armchair, a clear sign that her arthritis is playing up, but she waves me away when I rush forward to help her.

'I'm fine. Just stiff. But if I don't use it, I'll lose it, as they say.'

Reluctantly accepting this, I retreat to the matching sofa, kick off my shoes and make myself comfortable.

'Your flowers in the garden are beautiful,' I say. 'Gorgeous colours.'

'Thank you, my love. I planted them a few weeks ago. Thankfully, there's been no late frost and they've been able to bloom nicely. Tell me, what's been happening with you? That must be more exciting than talking about an old woman's flowerbeds.'

'Not at all.' I vehemently shake my head. 'Your flowers are high on my list of favourite things. After you, obviously.'

'How very *Sound of Music*.' Aunt Lottie chuckles. 'So, are you going to tell me if this big win of yours has been confirmed, or do we have to critique the vegetable patch first?'

I giggle. 'How about I make us a cuppa, and I'll tell you all about it?'

'Now that I won't say no to.' She smiles gratefully, while I head for the kitchen to put the kettle on.

Once we're settled again, with tea in hand and a plateful of pre-lunch biscuits my mother would never approve of, I bring Aunt Lottie up to date with the events of the last few days. This includes the news that I've quit my job, though I give her the PG adaptation rather than the post-watershed version.

'So, that's it,' I finish recounting my tale. 'The money is in my bank account, and I've got a chance at a brand-new start.'

'Dear girl, this is just *wonderful* news.' She looks quite

emotional. 'I couldn't be happier for you, especially when you've been having such a difficult time with that supervisor of yours. It's a relief to know that you can now get out of that situation and find a better job. And well done for standing up for yourself. I know you've found that difficult in the past. This really is a whole new beginning for you.'

'I know. Isn't it amazing?'

'It is,' she says. 'Just one thing bothers me, though. You know I'd never tell you what to do, and I wouldn't be best placed to advise you, but I feel that such a great sum of money will need careful handling. Have you thought about how you'll manage it?'

'Don't worry,' I reassure her. 'I've already had an initial meeting with a financial adviser who's given me some advice and options to think about.'

'That's good. You're a sensible girl. Golly, I feel like we should be drinking champagne, not tea.'

'We can still have a celebratory toast.' I hop off the sofa and gently clink her gold rimmed china teacup with my own, before returning to my seat. 'So, there's something related to my win that I want to share with you.'

'What's that, dear?'

'Well, I really want to do something for you, you know, to thank you for the friendship and support you've offered me over the years.'

'Oh, Emma, that's simply not necessary. You've given as much in return.' Her eyes mist over, leaving me in no doubt of the still-painful memories that have been invoked within her.

I'm not immediately concerned by this, but I trot across and sit on the floor by her armchair nonetheless. Aunt Lottie has spoken openly to me about her loss and has always been adamant that it's an important part of keeping the fond memories alive. The bad ones being nothing more than an unfortunate by-product.

'I know that.' I squeeze her hand. 'But it's something I really want to do.'

'Let's hear it then.'

'OK, you know how we've talked about Caroline and Sophie many times over the years?'

'Yes?' Her elderly face is a mix of nostalgic grief and curiosity.

'Well... it makes me feel like I almost know them. If that makes any sense at all?'

'It does.' She nods slowly.

'So, anyway, what I was thinking, is that I'd like to make some charitable donations in their memory. Twenty-thousand pounds to be split between two charities of your choice.'

Aunt Lottie sits quietly for a few moments, staring ahead, while I wait patiently. This is something she needs to digest. Eventually, she turns in her seat and looks down at me.

'Emma, I think that is one of the kindest and most thoughtful gestures anyone could make. And though my instincts are telling me you should keep your money, I appreciate that you feel the need to do this.'

'I do. I *really* do.' I shift onto my knees. 'I want to do some good with my win and I know you'd never take any money from me—'

'You're certainly right there.' The schoolmistress look comes again. 'I have everything I need. Even a *cat*...' She eyes me with pretend disapproval.

'You love George.'

'Yes, I believe I do. Six months ago, I'd have been chasing unwelcome feline visitors from my flowerbeds. Now,

I have a walking, furry hot water bottle as my second-best friend.'

'You're welcome.' I give her a toothy grin.

'Being serious for a moment.' Aunt Lottie's face clears. 'I can't think of anything that would mean more to me. And I know Caroline and Sophie would feel the same.'

'Good. That's sorted then.' I get up and give her a hug. 'You OK?'

'Of course, my love.' She smiles, and I can see just how touched – and slightly overwhelmed – she is. 'Now, let's get the lunch on.'

A short time later, we're sitting in Aunt Lottie's dining room, surrounded by display cabinets crammed with photographs and ornaments, enjoying her homemade lentil soup and making our way through a pile of triangular sandwiches. Outside in the back garden, the birds are tweeting their merry spring tune.

'Emma, I've been thinking about your win and your kind gesture,' she says. 'And I'd like to ask something of you.'

'I'm not reducing the amount.'

'That wasn't what I was about to say. I know better than to ask that.'

'Sorry, carry on.' I sit back in my seat.

She puts down her spoon and clasps her hands. 'I have few regrets in life, but there's one thing that does bother me.'

'What's that?'

'I spent a lot of my younger years worrying and not getting as much from life as I should have. And when Sophie and Caroline died, I believed that I didn't deserve any enjoyment at all.' She pauses briefly and I allow her this space. 'I'd lost my daughter and my granddaughter in a short space of time. Then, through my grief, I drove my husband away and distanced myself from the people who cared about me. It felt like a life sentence – until you came along, with your unrelenting determination that I was to be your friend. I'll never forget the day I found you sitting in the shed at the bottom of my garden reading your book. You were so like Sophie. You spooked me at first.'

'I can imagine I did,' I say. 'Eight-year-old me, using your garden to hide from my overbearing parents, with no clue as to what you'd endured in your life. I used that hole in the hedge like I was part of *The Great Escape*.'

'You've always had such an imagination.' Aunt Lottie smiles at me affectionately. 'You were the catalyst to me living some sort of life again, and now that I'm the age I am, I've realised that I shouldn't have shut myself away. That neither Caroline nor Sophie would have wanted that.'

'So, what do you want me to do?' I'm unclear where this is going. 'Anything, just ask.'

'My ask of you is simple. Use some of your win to enjoy yourself. Life is precious, Emma, and it's short. Believe me. You young people spend so much time with your noses in your phones, I worry that you'll find yourself at my age wishing you'd looked up and made more of your time on this earth. I also know that you take the weight of the world on your shoulders, Emma. I want you to have memories of carefree fun and laughter to look back on. I'm not suggesting you fritter your money away – far from it – but a touch of self-focus is no sin. Will you do that for me?'

'Erm... sure.' I shrug my shoulders. 'If that's what you want. It would be even better if you would join me.'

'Dear girl, no.' Aunt Lottie lifts her hands in protest. 'I'll only hold you back. I'm too old and slow, and my stamina's nothing like it used to be. But you can tell me all about it.

Bring your stories back to me and we can laugh and have fun together.'

'OK...' I say, not totally convinced by her reasoning for not joining in. 'One condition, though. I want to know what you would have done if it were you.'

'Oh, I don't know. Give me a second to think.' She rubs her forehead, while I bring up the notepad app on my phone, ready to start to tapping away. 'There's nothing concrete that springs to mind, but maybe I'd do something relaxing. Something fun. Perhaps something indulgent. Even something practical if it gave me an experience I could look back on and laugh. Or smile. And definitely something outlandish.'

I scan the words in front of me. 'Think I can manage that. I'll come up with a plan this evening. Gives me something to do.'

'That's settled then.' Aunt Lottie nods, a rare satisfied look on her face. 'Actually, I do have one more request...'

'Name it.'

'Perhaps you could just call me Lottie. You're a grown woman now, and as much as I've enjoyed being your adopted aunt, I think we can address each other as friends do.'

'Not a problem,' I say.

'Good. Now eat your soup.'

Chapter Thirteen

The next morning, Cat and I set off for my mum and dad's place in Perth. Despite all the excitement and positivity around my big win, I'm not looking forward to this visit, because I'm all too aware of the lengthy lecture I'm about to receive for my lack of contact with them after my breakup with Dave.

Oh, well. I can't stop the inevitable, but I can put it out of my mind until I get there.

'Any more plans to see your mystery man?' I ask Cat, as we zoom across the Queensferry Crossing in her car.

She purses her lips and I realise my error, having momentarily forgotten what she said before about not being ready to share.

'Sorry... I'm not fishing for details. I'm just checking that things are still on between you.'

Keeping her eyes on the road, she seems to relax and her face spreads into a coy smile. 'They are going well. He's away with friends this weekend, and he's having a mega busy time at work, so we've arranged to go for dinner and drinks next Saturday night. I did wonder if the work thing was an excuse and whether was cooling on me, but he's already sent me two messages today – while he's with his friends. That must be a good sign, surely?'

'Definitely a good sign.' I gaze across the Firth of Forth, the water glistening in the spring sunshine. It's a view I always enjoy taking in when I come this way, especially how North Queensferry looks like a perfect little toytown from this high up.

'For once, it seems like he's as keen on me as I am on him.' She gives me a little side glance.

'Awesome. Keep it up, and you'll have him hooked.' I'm pleased that she's felt confident enough to share this tiny but significant titbit, and that she seems more at ease with her new bloke. I haven't noticed any more of those troubled looks she had before, which must also be a good sign. 'So, are you ready to face the wrath of my parents?'

'Are *you* ready to face the wrath of your parents?' she hurls back.

'No, never.' I chew my lip in apprehension. 'But needs must. I'm dreading it a little less after seeing that financial adviser the other day.'

'Oh, yeah. Surely your parents will be pleased you've done that.'

'We'll see. I wish they were more like Aunt Lottie. She's so chilled compared to them, and she actually has faith that I can look after myself.'

'You'll be fine,' says Cat. 'Your parents are overprotective because they want the best for you.'

I give a sarcastic laugh. 'Correction: they want what *they* think is best for me. Don't get me wrong, I love them to bits, but they're incapable of seeing me as a grown woman who can look after myself. There's no question that this is going to be a painful experience, so buckle up and get ready for the ride.'

～

Less than an hour later, we pull up outside my mum and dad's three-bedroom semi-detached house. The door is flung open and my mum gallops down the path, swallowing me in a suffocating hug the second I get out of the car.

'*Emma, how are you?* I've been so worried.' She holds me out at arm's length appraisingly, before yanking me back in. 'Have you been eating properly? You look like you've lost weight. Why you wouldn't let your dad and I look after you through that awful time, I'll never know. There was no need to go through that alone'

I wriggle out of my mum's grip, which is remarkably strong. 'I'm fine, Mum, honestly. I wasn't *alone*. Cat was with me the whole time, and I have to learn to deal with these things myself. You and Dad won't be around forever.'

She hates it when I say things like that.

'Yes, well... while we *are* around, we're here to help. That's what parents are for. I wish you would let us do our job.' She turns to Cat. 'Hello, Cat. It's nice to see you again. Thank you ever so much for looking after our Emma. That goes way beyond what's expected of you as her friend.' She throws a look in my direction.

'It was no problem at all, June,' says Cat. 'I've really enjoyed the company, and Emma's been there for me more times than I can count.'

My mum ignores this statement as it doesn't support her cause. 'In you go, girls, before you get cold. Your dad's dying to see you.'

Cat and I are ushered into the kitchen-slash-dining room

where my dad is setting the table and my mum has the cooking underway.

'Ooh, this smells delicious. Hi, Dad,' I greet my father and brace myself for another ticking off but I'm in luck. He's not great with matters of the heart, so I don't get the lecture I might have if I'd announced I was off on a year-long pilgrimage to Machu Picchu.

'Hi, pumpkin. It's good to see you.' He gives me great big bear hug and Cat a kiss on the cheek before returning to his task.

We sit down to a tasty brunch and I decide, so that we can at least enjoy our meal, that I'll wait until we've finished eating before telling them my news.

To begin with, the conversation is light, mostly filled by my mum updating me on her involvement in one community project or another. But that doesn't last long.

'Oh, Emma, did you hear about the Roystons along the road?' My mum's grey blue eyes come to life as they always do when she's got some juicy gossip to share.

'No, who are they?' I roll my eyes at Cat.

'They're the family that moved in the year you went to high school. Their oldest was a couple of years younger than you. Susie? Or was it Sally?'

'No idea. Don't remember anyone by that name.'

'Well, anyway, they're getting a divorce, it seems. The parents. It's a bit sad because they're a nice couple, but apparently, he had an affair.'

'Well, these things happen.' I put on a bored voice but she doesn't take the hint.

'And then there's Mr Collingsworth on the corner. He's been behaving very strangely. I was chatting with Marjory from number forty-seven the other day, and she was saying that he won't answer his door to anyone anymore. Just shouts at people to go away. She thinks it might be dementia.'

'Or he's sensible and knows that this place is full of nosey parkers,' I mutter.

I'm becoming irritated by my mum's behaviour.

'Marjory also mentioned that he has no family, and it reminded me of that ghastly woman who lived in the house next door,' my mum unashamedly continues her gossiping, in between mouthfuls. 'Remember, the one who wouldn't give anyone the time of day. Then suddenly turned up on our doorstep one day, telling me how I should be bringing you up. *What a cheek.* What was her name again? Maybury was the surname. Ah, yes, Charlotte Maybury. Vile woman.'

'She wasn't *vile.*' My irritation has turned into annoyance. 'She was – and probably still is – a nice quiet lady who unfortunately experienced a lot of sadness and heartache in her life. Something you wouldn't know anything about.'

'*Emma*, don't speak to your mother like that,' My dad's bushy salt and pepper eyebrows knit together as he scolds me and I mumble a half-hearted apology.

My mum looks shocked for a moment, but quickly recovers. 'What would you know about her life, Emma? And why would you even care? You didn't know her.'

'I don't... care. But I do know that her granddaughter died because of a rare genetic disorder at seven-years-old, and then her daughter, the mother of the child, died by suicide because she couldn't get over it. It was a total tragedy. No wonder her marriage broke down and she ended up living the way she did. That would break anyone.'

My mum is temporarily silenced.

'Right, well, that is tragic,' she says eventually. 'How do you know all this?'

'Must have got it from someone at school.' I shift my

focus to drinking my tea. 'I'm just saying that you shouldn't judge without knowing the facts. I'm sure Lott... erm... Charlotte Maybury is a perfectly nice woman.'

'Well, no matter what she went through, that certainly wasn't my experience of her,' my mum sniffs.

I throw an exasperated sidelong glance at Cat, who quickly changes the focus of the conversation. 'Mrs Blake, your garden is looking beautiful.'

'Why thank you, Cat.' My mum tucks her bottle blonde bob behind her ears and beams at Cat. 'Between you and me, I think it's the best in the street. It's such a shame how some of our neighbours don't put in any effort at all. Really lets the community down.'

Cat stifles a giggle as I pretend to throw my face into my brunch in despair.

~

Once we've cleared up and moved through to the living room with a fresh pot of tea, I give Cat the signal. She offers me the same encouraging look she did in the restaurant, and I clear my throat.

'So, I have some interesting news.'

My mum's ears instantly prick up. 'Interesting, how?'

Honestly, she should hire herself out as a sniffer dog.

'What is it, Ems?' asks my dad. 'Good interesting or bad interesting?'

'It's good news. Very good news in fact—'

'Oh, my good Lord, you're pregnant!' cries my mum.

'*What?*' Why do people keep thinking that?

'That selfish man has disappeared off the scene and left you a single mother,' she gushes, like a river that's burst its banks. 'Well, you're right, it's terrific news. Not that there's no father on the scene, but a baby will give you some focus in your life.'

Cat is once again trying not to laugh. I look at her helplessly.

'You can move back here,' my mum goes on. 'And I'll help you so you can keep working. You can't be throwing your career away—'

'*Mum, stop.* I'm not pregnant.'

Poor Cat is now struggling so much that little snorts keep escaping from her mouth.

'Mum, please do me a favour and keep quiet until I'm finished.'

'Let our Ems speak, June.' My dad puts a calming hand on her shoulder. 'You'll get your say once she's done.'

My mum pulls a dissatisfied pout and grudgingly sits back in her seat.

'OK, here goes...' I take a deep breath, then hurriedly tell them everything from the cruel way that Dave broke up with me and being conned into buying a lottery ticket I didn't want, to my discovery of my big win and quitting my job after my run in with Karla. 'Can you believe it?' I say, once I'm done. '*I won the lottery.* I'm like a new woman, and it's totally helping me get over Dave.'

My parents gawp at me. For once, my mum is shocked into silence.

As my brain catches up with what I've just shared, I realise that, for a second time, I've failed to successfully execute my planned 'breaking news' speech – which means that I haven't censored things as much as I perhaps should have for my parental audience. But what else is there to focus on other than my win? I wait for them to gather themselves. This really isn't like them, and not at all what I expected.

'Dad, Mum, isn't that exciting? It had me speechless too.'

My mum recovers first, taking my surprise to new levels. 'You should know better than to wander around the city on your own at night. Also, why were you trying to buy a bottle opener? I really hope you weren't drowning your sorrows with alcohol, young lady. And don't even get me started on you quitting your job. Have you lost your mind? You had a nice secure position with a reputable company, and you've thrown it away for what? An early mid-life crisis?'

I'm so gobsmacked that I can't find a response. I turn to my dad in the hope that he'll be the rational one.

He shakes his head as if coming out of a trance and fixes me with a concerned look. 'Quitting your job like that wasn't a smart move, Ems. Although, if you've been bullied by your manager, I'm not surprised you've felt backed into a corner. Now don't worry, we can fix this. A strongly worded letter to your HR department to record that you had no choice but to resign should do it. This is constructive dismissal, nothing less.'

This has gone beyond ridiculous. I've just told my parents I've won several hundred thousand pounds and all they hear are what they consider to be my mistakes. They've not even acknowledged the money.

I shoot another hopeless look at Cat, who's looks so stunned by their response, it's wiped the smile off her face. She shrugs, obviously at a loss as to where to go next with this.

'Are you *kidding* me' I throw my hands up in frustration. '*That's* what you got from what I said?'

My parents stare blankly at me.

'Nothing else? You didn't get *anything* else from it? No exciting news?'

They look at each other.

'Oh, you mean the money you've "won"?' My mum adds air quotes to this statement.

'What do you mean the money I've "won"?' I replicate her gesture.

'For goodness sake, Emma, we weren't born yesterday. You've always been creative when it comes to sharing news that we won't like.'

'Wait a minute...' I try to compute what she's said. 'You think I made up winning the money to make you less annoyed at me for quitting my job?'

'Of course, you did.' My mum sips at her tea smugly. 'That's been your way ever since you were a little girl. You have an amazingly colourful imagination. You should really put it to some constructive use.'

Once again, I turn to my dad, desperate for him to show some confidence in me.

'Ems, you have been a wee bit economical with the truth in the past when you've gotten yourself in a scrape. But we realise you've been under a lot of pressure. Don't you worry, you'll get your job back and that dreadful woman will be dealt with.'

'But I'm not—'

'*Enough, Emma.*' My mum silences me, casting a thin-lipped look at my dad. 'We'll help you out. Of course, we will. We also need to have to have a chat about your impulsiveness. You must learn some self-control, because you can't be turning to alcohol or packing in your job every time things get a bit challenging. Behaviour like that that can be the beginning of a terrible downward spiral.'

Great. Now my parents think I'm a self-destructive waste of space. I'm so frustrated, I'm about to give up and signal to Cat that it's time to go, when I realise that I have the solution to hand.

I nip through to the kitchen where I've left my handbag and log into my banking app on my phone.

'Here, look at this.' I thrust it into my dad's hand when I return to the living room.

'Emma...' My mum sighs. 'The lengths you go to—'

'*Hang on*, June.' My dad, who's scrutinising the information on the screen, cuts her off. He clicks in and out of a few menu options, each time coming back to the home page of the app where my name and the balance of my newly opened savings account (which is temporarily housing the bulk of my win) are clearly displayed. 'Good god... Our little girl's struck it rich.'

'*Finally.*' I let out an exasperated sigh. 'It's incredible, isn't it?'

'It really is.' He's still a bit dazed, but he gets to his feet and envelops me in a bone-crushing hug.

'Couldn't happen to a nicer person, I reckon,' Cat pipes up and I flash her a grateful smile.

'*Excuse me.*'

We've all forgotten that my mum hasn't quite made it to the same place as us yet.

'Eric, kindly fill me in. *Please.*'

'Well, June, it's fairly straightforward,' my dad says, as if he never doubted me in the first place. 'Our Ems has indeed come into quite a lot of money. Have a look. It's there in her savings account.' He hands my phone to her.

The colour drains from my mum's face. '*What?* Well... *how?*' she splutters.

'It's not rocket science, June. She bought a ticket. Her numbers came up. She won.'

'Oh, I know that, Eric, I'm not daft. It's just... *so exciting.* Emma, come and sit, and we'll get another cup of tea on the go. I want to hear the whole story, every last detail.'

I grit my teeth to avoid saying something I regret – or another telling off. This is so typical of my mum. One minute she'll be making snap judgements about me and how I live my life, and the next she's trying to be my best friend. There's never an apology.

I give Cat a look I hope she interprets as *this is going to be a long day*. She simply grins back at me and makes herself comfortable on the sofa.

Chapter Fourteen

An hour and a half later, I've been through the whole story twice, and my mum has analysed it to death; from the shopkeeper's questionable sales tactics and my alternative approach to picking my numbers, to the moment I realised that I'd won and seeing the money there in my account. She has also – backed by my dad – given me a rather painful and lengthy lecture for tanking a bottle of wine on my own in The Meadows the moment my relationship went sour (I'm well aware it wasn't my finest moment and of the safety issue that created), and an even bigger one for quitting my job like I did. I did, however, receive some brownie points for saying no to a stranger (James, the arrogant twat from the shop) and the excited buzz that's been in the room since they discovered I was telling the truth is still burning big and bright.

Eventually, though – as I was dreading – the conversation steers in the direction of what I'm going to do with the money.

'You'll need to be very careful with it,' says my mum. 'It's not enough for you to go wild. And you'll still need to work, so I don't know what you were thinking packing in your job. I know you've mentioned some nonsensical idea about finding your dream career, but that's codswallop. Perfect jobs do not exist. Your father can help you get your job back, so you don't waste lots of money being unemployed.'

'Agreed.' My dad nods. 'And you need to look at how to get the most from your winnings. We'll take you to see a financial adviser and we can work through the best options together.'

'There's also your pension to consider,' my mum chips in again, as if she's part of an official tag team. 'You should top that up. You may have been earning a good salary, but these days you need to put a lot more in to have a reasonable income when you retire.'

'That's a good point, June. There really is a lot to think about.'

Here we go. This is exactly what I expected. I channel my inner calm as best I can before opening my mouth.

'Mum, Dad, as ever, I love you and I appreciate your support, but... I'm a grown woman, and I'd really appreciate it if you would leave me to manage my own money.'

'With the greatest respect, Emma...' My mum waggles a finger at me. 'What do you know about investment options and pensions? You need someone to guide you and help you make good decisions.'

I bite my tongue to halt the retort that's ready to leave my lips. I'm so glad I took the action I did on Thursday afternoon, otherwise this is the point where I'd have run out of a defence.

'*With the greatest respect, Mum,*' I mimic her in response. 'I know more than you think. I've already been to see a financial adviser.'

'Emma, don't speak to your mother in that tone,' my dad scolds me for the second time today.

Hurt clouds my mum's face and I feel a little guilty.

'Look, I'm sorry.' I soften my tone. 'But I have thought about that stuff, and... I want you to be proud of me for taking some sensible steps.'

'We *are* proud of you, Ems, aren't we, June?' My dad grabs my hand in an almost instantaneous turn around.

'Of course we are, silly.' My mum reaches over and ruffles my hair.

'I guess we have to accept that our wee girl's growing up,' my dad teases.

Oh, if only they would.

I spend some more time talking my parents through the conversation with the financial adviser and my initial thinking about how I'll manage my money, while conveniently omitting the bits I know are guaranteed to start an argument. My plan to have some fun, and where it came from, is my business. They don't need to know everything. Even Cat doesn't know about it yet. My mum and dad protest here and there and try to push their views, but as I've spoken with a professional, I'm able to bat back the parts I don't agree with. The fact that I'm also planning to gift them some money helps too, despite them making out that it's a 'completely unnecessary, but *very* generous gesture'.

~

I feel much lighter during the drive back to Edinburgh in the late afternoon. That's the difficult bit over. *Thank god.*

'That went better than I thought it would,' I say.

'Definitely,' Cat agrees. 'Good move going to see a

financial adviser first. It could have been a very different experience. Although, as I said on the way over, I don't think your parents are totally unreasonable, honey. They just really care, and unfortunately it comes across a bit over the top.'

'*A bit?*'

'OK, a lot.' She giggles. 'But you did really well. Especially when your mum started going on about Lottie like that. And now that's ticked off, you can look forward to some Saturday night fun with me and the girls. I can't wait to hear about this secret plan you were cooking up last night.'

Not long after we get back to Cat's, we're on our way out again, and as we enter Ruan Sabai – our favourite Thai restaurant and a beautiful little haven of peace and tranquillity, tucked away down a narrow close in the Old Town – our senses are engulfed by enticing aromas of lemongrass, coconut and lime. We order some wine and are toasting my successful encounter with my parents when Amber wanders in, closely followed by Sara.

After ordering our usual banquet for four and some general chit chat – which once again includes Cat ducking questions about her new bloke – I fill them in on my challenging parental visit.

'They sound like a mare,' says Sara. 'It's your money. You can do what you want with it.'

'Exactly.' I nod. 'But I guess having overbearing parents is better than having ones who don't give a shit.'

'For sure,' Cat gives my arm a supportive squeeze. 'By the way, honey, in case it's on your mind, no one's expecting you to pay tonight. That was really generous of you the other day, but it was a one-off.'

Sara vigorously nods agreement, indicating that I'd be mad to think anything else.

'*Oh, what?*' Amber feigns outrage. 'I figured it would be dinner on you for the next ten years.'

I arch an entertained eyebrow at Cat and she laughs. This particular issue had crossed my mind – whether there would be any expectation on me – so I'm relieved that my friends have addressed this. And anyway, I'm planning to treat the girls to something way better.

Our starters arrive and we're temporarily distracted as we pass the food around, 'oohing' and 'aahing' over the delicious smells coming from the dishes.

'Can I tell you what I'm planning to do with my win?' I say, as we tuck into our platefuls like a flock of ravenous vultures. 'Well, a couple of the things I'm planning. I haven't got it all sorted yet but I do have something exciting to share.'

I instantly have their attention, and I'm about to elaborate, but Amber beats me to it.

'You're getting a boob job.'

'No, but thanks for making me wonder if I need one.'

'How many people who get boob jobs actually need them?' Sara offers, and our eyes involuntarily fall to her generous, tanned cleavage, framed perfectly by her burnt orange (no doubt, designer) wrap dress.

'*Hey, they're real.*' She pushes her chest out further as if to prove it.

'If you say so,' Amber mutters, mouth full of chicken satay. 'Emma, go for it.'

I start by filling them in on my plan to gift money to my parents and make the two charity donations in memory of Lottie's late family members.

'Aww that's such a lovely gesture.' Cat puts a hand to her chest. 'Lottie must be really touched.'

'She is.' I nod. 'She seemed quite overwhelmed, but it was so important to me to do something for her.'

'*Yeah, yeah*. We know, you're a saint and all, well done.' Amber's patience appears to be wearing thin. 'Will you fast forward to the good bit. There had better *be* a good bit.'

'I was *getting there*.' I give her a look that I hope loosely translates as 'shut the hell up' and she offers me a withering stare in response. 'So, the exciting part...' I pause for effect. 'Is that I'm going to live like a millionaire for a week.'

Chapter Fifteen

Instead of the excited faces I had expected, my friends stare back at me blankly.

'What does that actually *mean*, Emma?' Sara asks.

I tell them about Lottie's request, and this time, even Amber seems a touch moved by it.

'That's so sad,' says a glassy-eyed Cat. 'To think that she punished herself for so long. And for something that was completely beyond her control.'

'It is,' I say, my tone sombre. 'So, of course, I agreed to it, on the basis that she would have input to what kind of fun I have – you know, so I could kind of do it *for her* – but she was very vague. She did give me something, though.' I pick up my phone and read aloud from the notepad app. 'She said she would do something relaxing, something fun, something indulgent, maybe something practical – as long as it was enjoyable – and something outlandish. I also tried to get her to join me for it, but she flat out refused. Says she hasn't got the stamina.'

'That's a shame. It would have been nice to get her out

and about, having some of the enjoyment she's missed out on.'

'My thoughts exactly, Cat, and I'm not letting her get away with it. That's continuing the self-denying behaviour she says she regrets, so I'm going to line up a few surprises to make sure she's involved.'

'Come. *On.*' Amber's patience finally depletes.

'Sorry, sorry.' I shoot her an apologetic look. 'Basically, I've earmarked a sizeable figure to spend this coming week.'

Amber just about spits out her wine. '*Awesome!* Can we go to a male strip club and shove tenners in their g-strings?'

'Trust you to come out with something like that. Actually, the money is already allocated and my plans are in place.'

'*What?* You *are* kidding. This sounds like the most boring week ever.'

'Amber, sweetie.' Sara puts a hot pink taloned hand over hers. 'Do us all a favour. Sit on yourself and let Emma speak. You're acting like a toddler.'

'Thank you, Sara.' I give her a little wink to express my gratitude, while Amber slumps back in her chair, pretending she's lost interest and isn't listening.

'What's the plan then, Emma?' Cat asks.

'Well... it's not quite a full week. More of a working week in that, officially, things will start on Monday and finish on Friday.' I quickly pop a forkful of Thai fish cake in my mouth, chew and swallow it. 'Most people have probably daydreamed about what they'd do if they won a huge sum of money, right?'

'Yes, indeed.' Sara looks dreamy. 'I for one would *live* in Harvey Nics.'

'Sounds about right.' I smile at her. 'Well, because Lottie didn't give me much of a steer, I decided to take inspiration from my own well-worn, I've-just-come-into-a-huge-sum-of-money themed daydreams, which line up quite nicely with her rather ambiguous criteria. She certainly seemed happy enough with my plan when I called her to road-test it on Friday evening. So, from Monday I'll be doing something different every day. And before you get too excited, I'm not going sky diving, bungee jumping, white water rafting or any of that—'

'Now that I'd pay good money to see,' Amber hoots, betraying her fabricated demeanour of non-participation.

'So...' I continue, ignoring her. 'On Monday, I'll be checking into a suite in the Charrington Grand Hotel for four nights.'

'Oh, wow, that's a five-star hotel.' Cat's eyes light up. 'I'm so jealous.'

'Cool, huh?' I waggle my eyebrows at her. 'I can't wait. Monday also involves the three of you...' I deliberately add an air of mystery.

'Ooh, how?' asks Cat.

'Because I'm hoping you ladies will be able to finish work early... so we can go to Archer & Crombie, the luxury travel agency on George Street, and book an all-inclusive holiday to somewhere exotic—'

'*Oof, yes! Now you're talking!*' Amber whoops.

'I'm probably most excited about this bit.' I rub my palms together in anticipation. 'I've never been anywhere tropical before. Would be great if we could go as soon as possible – obviously depending on whether you can all get time off work at short notice.'

'I've got next week off already,' says Amber. 'And I can extend it if needed. Rich and I were just using up some annual leave. Now it's *party time*.'

'Emma, hold on...' Cat appears uncomfortable. 'That's

too much. It'll cost you a fortune. Remember what the woman from the lottery said. Maybe you should take some more time to think about it.'

'I've already thought it through.' I give her a sincere look. 'Very carefully. I want to do it—'

'But, honey, you're still on a high. This only just happened. You need time to come back down to earth and think about what you really—'

'*Shut up*, Cat,' Amber, who's been watching this exchange like a tennis spectator, suddenly interjects. 'Are you seriously trying to talk Emma out of this? This is *exactly* what she needs. She gets to kick off her new life with a bang, and we get to be there with her.'

Cat starts to protest again, but I shut her down. 'Cat, I love you and as I said, I appreciate your concern, but this is not negotiable. You guys are my best friends. You've propped me up through every crisis and drama in my life for as long as you've known me. Am I right?'

'Well yes, but—'

'No buts. It's settled. All you need to do is sort out some time off work, turn up on Monday and I'll see to the rest.'

Cat still looks uncomfortable, but she gives in. 'I guess I am due some time off, and I can get one of my team members to deputise for me, so it shouldn't be a problem. Thanks so much for this, honey. You're such an amazing person, sharing this with us. It really is more than—'

'Quit the gushing.' Amber playfully bats her on the back of the head. 'But Emma, she's right. This *is* awesome, you totally rock. One question though: why do you want to go to an actual travel agency when we could book the trip online? It would be easier and probably cheaper too.'

'I thought you might ask that,' I say. 'Lottie also talked about how us "youngsters" miss out on life through being glued to our phones. She suggested that I make sure I live every moment of this experience, which is why we're going to a bricks and mortar shop. The holiday idea has been floating in my mind since my win was confirmed and I noticed there was a nice-looking travel agency on George Street when I went to the bank on Thursday.'

'OK, fair enough.' She seems to respect this, which I'm relieved about. Amber may be intolerant, but she's not inhumane, and I know she has a softer, more reasonable side in there somewhere.

There's a momentary silence during which something dawns on me. Sara hasn't said a word. Cat and Amber must come to this realisation at the same time, because our three pairs of eyes simultaneously land on her. Sara smiles her stunning, not a care in the world smile, but at the time, shifts in her seat.

'Sara, are you OK?' I ask.

'Yes, fine, sweetie.' Her tone is dismissive. 'It's... well... it's a fantastic offer, thank you, but there's no way I can take a holiday any time soon. My boss is in the middle of the biggest strategic negotiation the company has ever been involved in, and the demands on my time are huge.'

'*Oh no*, Sara. That's so rubbish.' I feel really vexed for her. No wonder she didn't get excited like the other two.

'It's fine, honestly.' She inspects her nails, her lack of eye contact making it obvious that she's disappointed. 'These things happen. You girls go ahead.'

'How about we delay it?' I suggest. 'We don't have to go so soon. We could plan it for two, maybe three months from now.'

'Yeah, we can totally do that,' says Cat.

'No way.' Sara holds her hands up to halt any further discussion. 'We all know that the time for this holiday is now. Anyway, I've been told to forget any extensive annual leave for the next six months until the project is completed.'

'*What?*' Cat's face brims with shock and concern. 'That's nonsense. You'll burn out.'

'Tell them where to go,' says Amber.

'Ladies, relax, please.' Sara sits back in her seat. 'It's no biggie. Yes, it's disappointing that I'll miss out, but I'm getting loads of overtime pay, and I'll also get a bonus for my extra effort.'

Cat, Amber and I collectively sag. It seems that we're the ones feeling the pain she claims not to.

'Please, let it go.' She laughs, taking in our faces one at a time. 'I'm absolutely fine with it.' She blows us air kisses as if to reinforce her message.

'OK, sure. Sorry, Sara,' I say when it's clear we're making things worse. 'We'll say no more about it, except that we'll miss having you with us. How about we all do something together when you eventually get some leave?'

'That would be fabulous.'

Although we've accepted Sara's situation, it's thrown the conversation off. There's a short silence, during which the waiter appears to clear away our starters, and when he walks away with our plates, Amber, who's become distracted by something on her phone, suddenly looks up.

'Hey, that was only Monday. What happens the rest of the week?'

Relieved by the opportunity to lift the mood, my smile returns. 'I'm glad you asked. On Tuesday, I'm going to buy myself some wheels.'

'*Ooh, exciting,*' Cat claps her hands together. 'What are you going to get?'

'To be honest, I have no idea. I've never had my own car. Couldn't afford one when I was living in flat shares, and when I moved in with Dave, he drove us everywhere. But it makes sense to have one now – especially for visiting Lottie. It takes ages to get to Ratho on the bus. I'll have a look online tomorrow and arrange some test drives. It won't be a supercar or anything, but I'm hoping with my budget, I can get something compact and top of the range.'

'Small cars are boring,' says Amber. 'You should get a four by four. They're much more stylish.'

'Thanks for the advice. But have you seen me parallel park? It would end up being a rather obscene ornament.'

Cat and Sara laugh, clearly understanding my issue, while Amber simply shakes her head in disapproval.

'Anyway, moving on... For Wednesday, I've booked the spa day to end all spa days at the hotel: a full day of treatments – manicure, pedicure, body wrap, everything I can have massaged, massaged, facial, you name it...'

'That sounds incredible.' Cat sighs and angles her face upwards as if imagining how it would feel.

'It so does,' Sara follows suit.

While we're contemplating my day of Zen, our main courses arrive – a seemingly endless spread of colour, textures and yet more tantalising smells. Within seconds, we're happily digging into mountainous platefuls, comparing and commenting on the different dishes.

'Thursday?' Amber prompts me, her patience eroding once more from all the distractions.

'Yup.' I quickly chew and swallow a mouthful of food. 'Thursday is shopping day – and again, in bricks and mortar stores, not online, so I get the full experience as Lottie requested. I'm going to completely reinvent my image – and shed the "trophy wife" clothes and accessories that Dave bought me. Emma 2.0 is going to be stylish and understated.'

Amber snorts at this.

I narrow my eyes at her and continue. 'Then on Friday... This one's a bit daft, but it's something I've seen in films and always loved the idea of. And it definitely ticks Lottie's "outlandish" box. The best way to end my big week is with a celebratory night out, right?'

'Definitely,' says Sara, while all three of them nod enthusiastically.

'So, I want to go to one of our favourite bars – it needs to be a small one – and buy champagne for everyone.'

There's another stunned silence.

'When you say everyone, do you mean everyone in the bar?' asks Cat.

'Exactly that.'

'Oh, now *that* is good.' Sara seems impressed.

Amber, however, doesn't share her enthusiasm. 'Why do you want to buy expensive booze for strangers? Sod everyone else. Just buy us champagne. It'll cost you less.'

'I was planning to do that anyway. Though, as you're such a lightweight, I can afford to buy it for everyone else too.' I give her a cheeky wink and she extends her middle finger at me. 'So, that's it. That's my plan.'

'It all sounds amazing,' says Cat. 'Which bits are you going to get Lottie involved in?'

'I haven't quite sorted that yet. But I'm thinking – because of what she said – it needs to be things that won't require too much energy. I'll figure it out. *Roll on next week!*'

We clink our glasses together excitedly and the rest of the evening is taken up with lots of excited chatter about the week to come. The night ends on a real high and I find myself thinking that right now, this is the happiest I've ever been. As long as I can keep thoughts of Dave from my mind.

Chapter Sixteen

It feels like another excruciatingly long wait from Saturday night until I can start the most exciting week of my life. I'm restless, like a child waiting for Christmas.

Thankfully, I still have some planning to do, so I distract myself with that on Sunday afternoon.

Armed with my phone and my laptop, I park myself at Cat's breakfast bar and type out a list of possible stores for my shopping spree. It doesn't take long, because I quickly realise that I don't want to end up a sweaty mess from lugging loads of heavy bags around town – it probably wouldn't even be possible with the amount I'm planning to buy. Really, my only option for this planned experience is a mid-level department store, because the high-end ones would only laugh at any attempt to buy a whole new wardrobe (including makeup) with my reasonably generous but not outrageous budget. I expect some of their handbags alone would cost what I'm planning to spend. Left with only one choice, I mentally tick that item off my to-do list, and move on to looking at cars and car dealerships online.

Two hours later, after a lot of mind-numbing research and several phone calls, I'm more clued up than I was and have four test drives arranged. I've also worked out how to weave some surprises for Lottie into my week. Mission completed, there's just one final thing I need to do.

'Hi.' I grin manically as Lottie's smiling face appears on the screen of my phone.

'Hello, my love. Golly, you seem in good spirits.'

'That's because I am. I'm calling as part of the official run up to my week of creating amazing life-long memories, for which everything is now in place. I'm ready to roll – and I'm so excited.'

'Brilliant. This is exactly how I want it to be for you. A week that you never forget – not for the money you spend, but for the experiences you have along the way. I'm certainly looking forward to hearing how you get on.'

'I'll give you regular updates.'

'Oh, there's no need for that,' she says. 'Come and tell me all about it at the end.'

'*No way.* You're the reason I'm doing this. I want you to experience it with me – as much as you can anyway. *Bringing you the news... as it breaks.*' I put on an exaggerated journalistic voice.

Lottie laughs again. 'You really do brighten my life, Emma. What would I do without you?'

I respond with nothing but a beaming smile.

∽

My week of living like a millionaire finally arrives, and it's a different start to the usual Monday morning. Normally, I'd drag myself out of bed after hitting the 'snooze' button five

Lucky Number

times. Then I'd grump and curse my way around Dave's apartment, while discovering I'd forgotten to iron my trousers, run out of milk or misplaced my work pass. I was the epitome of disorganised at the start of every single week.

Today is the complete opposite. My eyes ping open at 8.30 a.m., and I lie there feeling blissfully relaxed while listening to the urban gulls mewing outside my window. A huge smile spreads across my face.

Jumping out of bed, I skip to the shower, where I daydream about the week ahead. So many things to look forward to – a real once-in-a-lifetime experience.

Unfortunately, this carefree state doesn't last long, and by the time I'm massaging the conditioner through my hair, my mind has wandered to not-so-happy thoughts – of Dave. Thoughts that had been so pleasantly absent these last few days: what he's doing, whether he thinks about me or regrets his decision, whether he's met someone new. Scowling at this intrusion, I shake these unwelcome questions from my mind. There's no way I'm letting him ruin this. My life is back on track, better than it ever was.

I force my mind onto a more positive topic: the multitude of WhatsApp messages flying back and forth yesterday, between Cat, Amber and myself – all in anticipation of our trip to paradise. Although we're still disappointed about Sara not joining us, we agreed not to let that get in the way. I mentally flick though the possible destinations we discussed, all palm trees, white sands and aquamarine waters, and in no time the giddy feeling of delirium comes flooding back, and I'm raring to go again.

I spend the morning and early afternoon packing and making myself suitably presentable for my luxury hotel stay (I want to fit in, not stand out like a sore thumb). Then, shortly before three p.m., I leave Cat's flat, wheeling the small case I use for minibreaks behind me, and amble along Fountainbridge to Festival Square.

On walking through the automatic doors of the Charrington Grand Hotel, I'm welcomed by a pristine porter, who takes my case and ushers me to the grand reception desk.

'Good afternoon, madam, how may I help you?' a friendly male receptionist called Nazim greets me.

'Hello. I, eh... have a reservation in the name of Blake.'

'Of course, madam. One moment, please.'

He taps away at his computer, leaving me to take in my surroundings. The elegant marble floor echoes with the footsteps of the hotel guests and staff milling around, while magnificent sparkling chandeliers twinkle invitingly. A few strategically placed white pillars add to the sense of grandeur and appear be holding up this vast chasm of a room. It's an impressive sight; a playground for only the most privileged in society. I had a few experiences in similar places with Dave when he was still at the stage of trying to impress me (or show off, more likely).

'OK, here we are...' Nazim is still tapping. 'You're staying with us for four nights... bed and breakfast... in one of our classic suites. Is that correct?'

'It sure is.' I go for a casual tone to avoid giving myself away as the overexcited imposter that I am.

'You also have some bookings in the spa on Wednesday...' He peers at the screen and his eyebrows lift. 'All day. Looks like you'll be having a relaxing time.'

'I hope so.' I smile, amused by his reaction.

Nazim completes my check-in and summons a colleague from concierge to take me to my room. I follow the man into the lift, which takes us to the top floor of the hotel. He leads me down a long corridor, before opening the door to what must be my suite with an electronic keycard.

The moment I step inside, I'm completely mesmerised. It's dripping with style: original art on the walls and a very modern but neutral style of decor. There's a large, swanky bedroom with a bed so big, I didn't even know they made them that size. I also notice that my suitcase is already waiting for me on the luggage shelf within the open wardrobe.

The man shows me around the rest of the suite, which has a separate living area hosting a huge flat screen TV, two small sofas, and a couple of stylish sculptures. The bathroom is so beautiful, I could spend all day in it. It has twin marble sinks, a large walk-in shower and a bath. This is the epitome of luxury.

As soon as I'm alone, I unpack my case, grab the remote for the bedroom TV and sink into the enormous bed, relishing the feeling of being in such incredible surroundings. I'm in my element, without a care in the world. That is, until unwanted thoughts of Dave creep back into my mind, along with (who knows why?) an equally unwelcome memory of meeting that arrogant guy, James, in the bank queue last week. I mean, why do even care about him? Maybe it's because he and Dave seem so similar and they've both inflicted mental pain upon me.

While I'm wrestling with my renegade brain, my phone buzzes with a message from Cat.

Hi, honey, are you at the hotel? How's your suite? Can I can come and see it after we've been at the travel agent? Cx

I quickly tap out a response.

I am and it's more amazing than I even imagined. Yes, please come see it after. We can order room service. See you in a bit. xx

Perfect. Cat's company is exactly what I need to keep my mind off arsehole men.

Chapter Seventeen

Just after 4.30 p.m., I meet Cat and Amber outside Archer & Crombie, the luxury travel agency on George Street.

'You're late.'

'Nice to see you too, Amber.' I playfully flick her hair. 'I'm only five minutes late, and good things come to those who wait. You both ready to book the holiday of a lifetime?'

'*So* ready.' Cat claps her hands together excitedly.

'OK, let's do this.'

'Hang on.' Amber suddenly stops us. 'Emma, I know you're in the money-is-no-object camp right now, but let's make sure you get a good deal on this. I don't want them to see you coming. It's also worth trying to get a few perks thrown in.'

'Wow, Amber...' I laugh. 'Are you feeling OK? You're not normally so helpful.'

'Whatever. Look, if you walked into my shop, I'd be sizing you up straight away, so just listen for a minute. We tell whoever serves us that we're shopping around, and let's take some time out before we commit to anything. There's a Starbucks over there we can grab a quick coffee in to weigh up our options.' She points across the road.

'All right, great. Thanks for looking out for me.'

'You're welcome. Now don't cock it up.'

Pushing open the door, we walk inside. There are a handful of desks at the back of the shop, but the main feature is two spacious lounge-style seating areas, each decked out with expensive looking leather sofas and a swanky glass coffee table sporting a vase of tropical-looking flowers. It doesn't really look or feel like a typical travel agent, which, given that everything is about experience these days, I expect is what they're aiming for.

'Good afternoon, ladies. How may I help you?' comes a voice from our right.

Lingering to admire a picture on the wall of some stunning tropical destination, I don't see who's greeted us at first. However, I do catch a fleeting exchange of looks between Cat and Amber, which suggests that they think he's easy on the eye.

Curious, I turn in the direction of the voice and stop short.

'Well, hello, *again*...' He grins at me.

To my dismay, the voice belongs to James. *The* James, who has succeeded in winding me up in public – not once, but twice. *Oh, why did it have to be him?*

'Well... isn't this a surprise?' I try to sound nonchalant, so that I come across as the balanced, sophisticated woman that I am (or at least, want to be). 'Three times in a matter of weeks. You'd forgive me for thinking you're stalking me.'

'Yes, I would.' His lips curl in amusement. 'If it weren't for the fact that *you* walked into my shop.'

Amber snorts in amusement.

OK, not quite the clever quip I was aiming for. I can already feel myself turning beetroot.

'Do you two know each other?' Cat asks.

'Our paths have crossed,' says James, who, to my immense annoyance is playing it super cool, and making me look like an even bigger tool in the process.

He gives give a Cat sparkling, white-toothed smile, and she visibly melts.

'So, how can I help you today?' He turns straight back to me and I swear the bastard is gloating. 'Are you perhaps here to book a holiday?'

'Erm... yes... that's right.' I clear my throat, which suddenly feels choked. 'That's... ahem... why we're here.'

Amber swiftly kicks me in the back of the leg, nearly flooring me in the process.

'*Hey*,' I snip at her, then turn back to James. 'Sorry, what I meant is, we're shopping around for a late deal, and... we'd like to explore some options with you.'

'I *bet* you would,' Amber mutters under her breath.

I try to subtly kick her back, but only succeed in doing what looks like an awkward curtsey. Straightening up slowly, my face on fire, I pretend that I'm suddenly interested in my surroundings, while out of the corner of my eye, I can see James surveying us with a bemused look. Clearly, he wasn't expecting to have to deal with a group of twenty-something teenagers today.

'No problem at all.' He signals for us to take a seat at one of the desks, and we obediently oblige. 'I can certainly get some quotes for you. And for the two ladies who haven't already had the pleasure of meeting me – *formally* or *informally*...'

I blanch, recognising this as a reference to our excruciating conversation in the bank queue.

'I'm James. And you are…?'

Cat and Amber introduce themselves.

'Pleasure to meet you both.' Once again, he returns his focus to me. 'Have you had any thoughts on a destination?'

I go to speak and somehow manage to choke on my own saliva. Coughing uncontrollably, all I can do is point helplessly at my friends and grudgingly accept the water that James fetches from the cooler in the seating area (of course he does).

Amber gives me her 'are you shitting me?' face, but I can't seem to get a hold of myself. *What the hell is wrong with me?*

'We've landed on Antigua, St Lucia or the Seychelles.' Cat comes to my aid, but also a little too enthusiastically. She clocks a look from Amber and tones it down. 'But there are so many different options and providers, we're really just at the comparison stage.'

'OK, great.' James unlocks the screen on his laptop. 'That's a good start. And when were you thinking of going?'

'Monday,' says Cat.

'Monday the…?' he asks, as he types.

'Next week.'

'I see. A last-minute break to paradise.' He looks up at us, intrigued. 'Any special reason for this trip?' He meets my gaze and I look away quickly.

'Oh, um… You could say that…' Cat's clearly spellbound and I find myself wondering why. James is obviously good-looking in a conventional sense, with those espresso-coloured eyes, thick, dark hair and well-defined jawline, but he's way too cocky and confident for my liking – far too similar to Dave in that respect. I'd have thought she'd pick up on that straight away.

'There is a reason for this trip,' Amber jumps in before Cat can spill like she's taken truth serum. 'Emma here just got dumped by her boyfriend. We thought it might be good for her – to get over the wanker.'

WTF? I shoot her a look that loosely translates as 'thanks, now I look like a total loser'. I know she sees me, but she ignores my daggers and keeps her attention on James.

'I'm really sorry to hear that, Emma.' James gives me half sympathetic, half knowing look. 'He's obviously an idiot, your ex.'

'Thanks.' I sink down in my seat, wishing it would jet propel me through the ceiling to put me out of my misery. He's obviously twigged that our brief encounter over the bottle opener was the night of my breakup.

'OK, then.' James broadens his attention to the three of us. 'I've helped mend many a broken heart with a great holiday deal, so let's see if we can find you something special. Quick question: I can prioritise your shortlist, but as it's last minute you're looking at, the more open you are, the better. Is there anywhere else would you consider?'

We all look at each other.

'Well, perhaps any of the Caribbean islands?' Cat suggests, and we nod in agreement.

'Mauritius is also an option. Even the Maldives – at a reasonable price.' Amber emphasises this point.

'Sure.' James nods his understanding.

'Ooh... I saw a place that looked incredible on a YouTube travel vlog the other day,' I say, suddenly coming back to life. 'An up-and-coming holiday resort called... what was it again... ah, yes, Kerberos. That was it. It's meant to be really trendy, but still quite peaceful and authentic – and apparently, a few big celebs have been there recently. Maybe it would be good to go to somewhere like that, you know, rather than the mass market tourist resorts. James, you must have heard of it?'

Cat and Amber look at me blankly, then turn their attention to James for his response.

'I have heard of it, Emma, yes.'

'Great, so what do you think?'

'I... eh... don't think that's your dream destination.'

'Why not?' For some reason, I feel the need to defend myself and not allow him to outright dismiss me. 'The vlogger was really enthusiastic about it. The beach was stunning and the accommodation they stayed in was gorgeous. Kind of a... *rustic-chic*. We should at least take a look at it, eh, ladies?'

I've got no idea what rustic-chic actually means, but I'll be damned if he's going to get the better of me – *again*.

'Emma...' James says again, before the other two have the chance to reply. 'Can I perhaps recommend that you stick to what you and your friends have already come up with. You know... to keep some focus in your destination search.'

'Focus? I thought you wanted us to be openminded so that you could find us the best deal?'

James clears his throat. 'Well, yes... I did say that, but I think you have enough options to consider now.'

'Really? That seems like a bit of a U-turn.' I narrow my eyes at him and then twig. 'Oh, I get it, you don't sell holidays to Kerberos, and you're worried that you'll lose your sale if we decide we want to go there. Am I right?'

'Eh... yes. You're right. We don't sell holidays to Kerberos.'

'But why not? Surely if it's an up-and-coming destination,

this travel agency would want a piece of that pie.' I'm now getting frustrated, because I sense that James isn't being straight with me. He's never been backward in coming forwards before, so why now? Is it because Cat and Amber are here? 'James, do me favour, will you, and just tell me what the problem is with my suggestion of Kerberos?'

James puffs out his cheeks with the look of a defeated man and I sit back, satisfied that I've finally gained the upper hand with him.

'OK. Kerberos is not somewhere we sell holidays to, because... um... how do I put this... it's one of the moons of Pluto.'

Amber and Cat explode with laughter.

'*What?* No... I'm sure that's what it was called.' Heat creeps up my neck while I wring my hands anxiously.

'Emma, trust me, I'm a bit of a space nerd.' James gives a self-deprecating smile. 'Kerberos was the fourth moon of Pluto to be discovered. It was found in 2011 using the Hubble Space Telescope and it's named after a mythological three-headed dog. It's definitely not a holiday resort. Did you maybe mean Caicos, as in the Turks and Caicos Islands in the Caribbean?'

Amber and Cat are rather unhelpfully howling with laughter to the left of me, making it even harder for me to think straight.

'I... don't know.' I'm now desperate to change the subject.

James moves things along. 'All right, I have enough information to get started. How about you ladies relax with a tea or coffee while I work on finding you the perfect holiday?'

'That would be lovely.' Cat's already getting to her feet.

'Actually, before you go, there are a few things we haven't

covered,' he says. 'What duration are you looking for? Board-wise, are we talking all-inclusive? And how many stars?'

As I'm the one financing this adventure, it needs to be me who answers. I pull myself together enough to give him a coherent answer. 'Ten days all-inclusive would be perfect. And a five-star resort.'

Cat gently grabs my arm. 'Emma... I'm not sure... we can all afford to go five-star.' She's trying not to blow our cover, but she's clearly deeply uncomfortable with how much that would cost me.

Before I can respond, Amber – who's evidently more at ease with the idea – jumps in to close down Cat's protest.

'Cat, we need to do this for Emma. She's been through a lot. Surely, we can stretch to a five-star holiday if it helps her get over things.' She places her hand on mine in an Oscar-winning show of support and solidarity, then winks at me when James looks away.

Now, Cat has no choice but to back down or she'll seem hard-hearted.

'I guess you're right.' She tries to say it breezily, but I can detect the frustration in her voice. 'Though I was trying to think of Emma's financial situation too. Wouldn't want her to have money problems on top of everything else.'

'Oh, don't worry, I'll be fine.' I merrily wave away her concerns.

'That us sorted then?' James's attention is ping-ponging between us, clearly sensing that there's something going on and understandably curious as to what it is.

He sees us over to the sofas in the seating area and arranges our drinks, before getting to work at his desk.

'Thanks for that,' I say in a low voice, eyeballing Amber and Cat. 'You could have come to my rescue, or even changed the subject. I looked like a right muppet.'

'I'm so sorry, honey.' Cat's sincerity is unmistakable, but she still has to stifle a giggle. 'I really felt for you, but I couldn't stop laughing. It was *her* fault.' She points at Amber.

'Hey, what did I do?' Amber complains. 'By the way, you're totally welcome for me stopping you two dipshits from giving things away. You're as bad as each other.'

She raises her eyebrows as she looks from Cat to me, while I dig my heels in with my 'unimpressed' look.

'*Oh, come on,*' she practically yells, then lowers her voice. 'That was *hilarious* with the whole Pluto thing. You know me better than to expect a bail out in a situation like that.'

She has a point.

'How do you know James, Emma?' asks Cat. 'He's absolutely gorgeous.'

'Is he? I think arrogant with an overinflated ego is a more accurate description,' I huff. 'He's the guy from the shop on D-day night.'

'He's the guy you told to eff off?' Her mouth drops open in surprise. 'He doesn't come across that way at all. I thought he was very diplomatic over the whole Pluto misunderstanding. He actually tried to help you save face there.'

'Thanks, do you really need to bring that up again?'

'I'm sorry.' She puts a sympathetic hand on my shoulder while I sip my coffee morosely. 'I just think that maybe you've got him wrong. Amber, what do you think?'

She shrugs. 'I wouldn't say no.'

'That wasn't really what I was asking, but I guess it still proves my point. If Amber approves then surely that's a good sign.'

'No... see, you don't get it.' I vigorously shake my head. 'He was only "diplomatic" there because he wants to sell us a holiday. He has this kind of self-assured, knowing, superior way about him. Too reminiscent of Dave. Anyway, even if he wasn't a twat, I'm not ready for anything else yet. It's all still too raw.'

'Fair enough,' says Cat. 'Sorry, honey. But I will say, for the record, that I think James seems genuine. Confident, yes, but not like Dave.'

'Yeah, well, I'm sure that – like Dave – he's well practised in convincing people he's something he's not.'

We change the subject, and chat away lightly while drinking our drinks, until James joins us with his laptop.

'Ladies, you're in luck. I've found a few cracking deals for you.'

We murmur in surprise as the huge picture of a far-flung destination on the wall beside us is suddenly replaced by a duplicate of James's laptop screen. He knowledgeably takes us through some options, offering his own thoughts on each one. After quite a bit of bargaining – including me and Cat laying it on the line with Amber that we will *not* be paragliding or jet skiing with her – we've narrowed down to two options: Antigua or the Bahamas, which wasn't on our original shortlist, and I'm now wondering why, because it looks *incredible*.

I'm about to commit the ultimate faux pas in Amber's eyes, so we can just get our trip booked, but she obviously senses this and leaps into action.

'James, thanks, this has been useful. We'll need to look at these two options against some others we're considering.'

'That's right,' I say, falling into line while wondering if James is actually buying any of this.

'We'll let you know either way,' adds Cat, who still appears to be under his spell.

'No problem, ladies.' James smiles easily, while we all get

to our feet. 'It's been a pleasure. Just remember that there's limited availability because you're leaving it so late.'

He escorts us to the door, and we pile out onto the street, then make a beeline for Starbucks, aware that we have just over an hour until the shop closes for the evening.

Chapter Eighteen

'So, on balance, that went well,' says Cat, once we're settled at a table away from the window.

'If that's how you want to label it.' Amber scoffs. 'Don't think you two will be winning a BAFTA anytime soon. Or Mastermind for that matter.'

My mortification resurfaces as Cat and Amber start howling with laughter once more.

'In my defence... I was more focused on how beautiful the place looked rather than what it was called. And... well... I just malfunctioned.'

'You can say that again.' Amber raises an appraising eyebrow. 'I reckon you're into him.'

'I am *not*.' I purse my lips in irritation. 'I can't stand the guy, and he doesn't like me either. He just likes making me look stupid.'

'Aww... Amber, leave her alone.' Cat's clearly feeling guilty for laughing. 'I'm sure you've embarrassed yourself in front of a guy at some point in your life.'

'Nope. Never.' She adopts a smug expression. 'Rich knew he was onto a winner with me right from the start.'

Cat and I roll our eyes.

'Right, anyway...' I take a few quick sips from my flat white, aware of the time. 'What's it to be? Antigua or the Bahamas?'

'I'm fine with either.' Cat shrugs. 'They both sound wonderful.'

'Me too. It's your call, Emma,' says Amber. 'You're the one who's bankrolling this.'

'OK...' I silently chew over our options. 'Shall we go with the Bahamas? That resort with the private island sounds *unbelievable*. And from what James was saying, it seems to be the better option. Not that I care what he thinks,' I add quickly on clocking the sly smile that appears on Amber's face. 'But he is the one with the travel knowledge. That all right with you two?'

They nod.

'Great. Sorted. Let's go get it booked before we miss out.'

Abandoning our half-finished drinks, Cat and I start to get up, but Amber holds up a hand to stop us.

'*Wait*. As you're both incapable of functioning normally around this bloke, I'm taking over. And I'm going to try something before we head back there.'

Intrigued, we settle back in our seats while she pulls out her phone, looks something up and then holds it to her ear.

'Hi, James, I was just in your shop with my two friends... that's right, the one that wanted to go to outer space...'

I attempt to cuff her across the back of the head, but she ducks away from me.

'So, we're down to two options – yours and one we saw online... yup, really good price it is. If you're able to throw in a perk or two for the Bahamas, we'll come back and book right now... sure, I can wait.'

Cat and I are totally gripped, waiting to hear the response.

'OK... I see... yup,' Amber continues her conversation. 'So, you can offer us a free luxury travel kit each... worth two hundred pounds.'

Cat and I high five.

'Let me check with the girls...' Amber hits the 'mute' button her phone. 'Shall we ask him to chaperone us to the airport, Emma?' She gives me a wicked look.

'Eh... *no*. Don't you dare, Amber.'

'Only kidding. I've got a better idea.' She returns her attention to the call. 'So, James, the travel kit we like, but there's one more condition... you take Emma on a date when we get back...'

What the hell?

I'm momentarily paralysed with shock, but I quickly recover and dive for the phone, desperate to stop Amber from saying any more. She swiftly dodges out of my way.

'I see...' she says to James. 'I suppose that's fair enough. OK, we'll see you shortly.'

I stare at her incredulously when she's ended the call. '*What have you just done?* I can't go back in there now. That guy thinks I'm an airhead as it is, and now he gets the pleasure of rejecting me too. Amber... I could *kill* you.'

'Chill, would you?' Amber sits back in her seat.

'*No, I will not chill.* We only have a few days to get this holiday arranged.'

'Yes, and it's sorted. I repeat... *chill*.'

'How can it be sorted if I now refuse to go back in there, and I'm the one putting it on my credit card?'

Amber sighs. 'It's sorted because he said yes. To both requests.'

'*What?*' Cat and I say in unison.

'You heard me. He's going on holiday himself while we're away, but he said he'd happily take you out on a date when he gets back.'

'*Really?*' I'm momentarily distracted by the ego boost this provides. 'You're not messing with me?'

'No, I'm not *messing* with you. I could tell he liked you the second he clapped eyes on you. You may have made an arse of yourself, but some guys love that type of thing. There was never a doubt in my mind he'd say yes.'

'Gosh.' I lap up Amber's backhanded compliment, then realise what I'm doing. 'Actually... no. I don't want to go out with him. I don't even like him.'

'Emma, what's your actual issue with this guy?' Amber asks, seeming to lose patience with me. 'He's nothing like Dave. Cat thinks so too.'

'I think he seems really nice,' she says. 'He did tease you when we first arrived in the shop, but more in a flirty way.'

'Well, maybe you're not the best judge, Cat,' I fire back, instantly aware that I've overstepped. 'Sorry, I was feeling cornered. I don't mean that.'

'No problem.' She looks slightly wounded.

'Well, *I am*,' says Amber.

'Huh?' I'm confused.

'I said, *I am*... the best judge. And I say he's way better than that self-obsessed wanker you used to date. Perhaps you not liking him is the best possible sign.'

Now it's my turn to feel hurt. 'What... do you mean?'

She takes a mouthful from her cup. 'You were hardly wise to Dave's nonsense. You make out that Cat's not got a good picker, but she saw Dave's flaws way before you did.'

'But I was the one—'

'Yeah, I know, love is blind,' she mocks me lightly. 'Which brings me to my second point. You're so busy trying to make out that you hate this guy, when it's glaringly obvious you fancy the pants off him. You just won't admit it. If you didn't like him, you wouldn't keep behaving like a dumbass in front of him – and you wouldn't care what he thinks. Case and point.' She mimics a mic drop and folds her arms while I sit there, speechless.

'I... don't... *fancy* him, Amber,' I manage eventually. 'As I said, I don't even like him.'

'So, prove it.'

'*What?* How can I *prove* it?'

'Go on a date with him, and if you still don't like him, then I'll accept that.'

'Amber, that's ridiculous.' I take in her I've-so-won-this-already face. 'OK, fine... I will. And you'll find out that you're wrong.'

'Great,' says Amber. 'I look forward to that. Now, shall we go get this booked?'

'Yes, please,' Cat pleads.

'I guess so,' I reluctantly agree, still dreading the idea of facing James, given my friend just asked him out for me – and I'm not twelve.

We head back over to the travel agency, where James greets us as we walk through the door.

'Hello, again.' He gives me a little wink, which only increases my resentment and further fuels my sense of him having too big an ego.

Forty minutes later, our luxury all-inclusive break in paradise is successfully booked with the cover story of it all being put on my credit card for insurance purposes. I've also managed to get through the experience without making an idiot of myself again, which I guess is something.

As we're getting up to leave, a smiling James hands me his business card. 'I expect you'll be needing this.'

'Ah... erm... yes. In case we need to check on any last-minute details...' I turn the card over and see that he's scrawled his personal mobile number on the back, complete with smiley face. 'Or... anything else that might come to mind.'

'I recommend the latter.' His eyes lock on mine, and I flush with embarrassment. 'I'll email you when your travel kits arrive. I should be able to post them out to you in time for your departure. Have a great holiday.'

We step out into the fresh air, where we chat excitedly for another couple of minutes before Amber has to head off to meet her husband.

'Cat, I'm really sorry about that comment before in Starbucks.' I say, as we wander along Rose Street together in the direction of the hotel. 'That you're not a good judge when it comes to men. I don't know where that came from.'

'That's OK, honey.' She puts her arm around me. 'Amber had you backed into a corner, as you said. I know you didn't mean it.'

'She did, didn't she, the little minx. All this talk about me supposedly liking James. It's complete nonsense. I'm *so* going to prove her wrong.'

'Of course, you are.'

As she says this, I catch what looks like a knowing glint in her eye. But it's gone in an instant, leaving me wondering if I even really saw it.

Chapter Nineteen

The next morning, my awakening is even dreamier than the day before. I feel like a movie star, lazing in my enormous bed in my fabulous suite. God, am I living the life right now.

I smile as I think back to Cat's reaction to it all the evening before.

'*Wow! This place is amazing!*' she declared, charging from room to room like an overexcited toddler.

'I take it you've never been in a suite before either?' I chuckled.

It turned out that she had never stayed in a five-star hotel full stop, and it gave me a warm glow knowing that will change when we head to paradise next week.

Throwing back the covers, I leap out of bed, my smile growing even wider when I open the curtains to find that it's a beautiful sunny day to perfectly match my mood.

'What is today, Emma?' I ask myself in the full-length mirror on the wall. 'It's Tuesday, which means... *it's new car day!*' I do a little dance on the spot.

After I've showered and been for the hotel breakfast to

end all hotel breakfasts, I return to my suite to get ready for my outing. I want to look confident and credible for my test drives so I packed one of my well-worn work outfits for today: a pale green chiffon blouse and a black trouser suit, but it's a bit overkill so I ditch the suit jacket to tone it down. My weather app is showing that it's unseasonably warm so I should be fine like this.

My first three test drives fortunately go without a hitch and I commend myself on the swotting-up I did on Sunday afternoon. It meant I was able to talk knowledgeably with the car salespeople and avoid being taken for a metaphorical ride. Having now had three similar conversations, I'm well-versed on the process, and I've been offered some pretty good deals (I think so, anyway).

On my way to my final test drive – I've saved my first choice for last – I see the pleasant day that started out, has been replaced with a dark and gloomy sky. Huge, menacing clouds roll across the horizon and a chill breeze has picked up, which immediately cools me.

I should have known better than to trust the Scottish weather to stay pleasant.

I pick up my pace, but only make it halfway from the bus stop to the car dealership, before huge fat raindrops are pounding the ground like missiles around me. Realising that I've only got seconds to find cover, I scan my surroundings in desperation, but there's no shelter nearby and the car showroom is still a couple of minutes' walk away.

The heavens open with a torrential downpour, creating almost instantaneous rivers down the sides of the road. I make the best run for it I can in my heels, but by the time I reach the Newbridge Luxury Car Collective, I'm soaked through. I launch myself through the door, discovering too late that there's a step, and I – and the contents of my handbag – sprawl across the floor like scattered rubbish.

Wiping my rain-soaked face with my hand, I slowly look up. Two car salesmen and a handful of customers have witnessed my grand entrance, but not a single one of them comes to my aid. I get up and start shoving things back into my handbag, and while I'm sorting myself out, I overhear a churlish remark muttered by one salesman to the other.

'This one's yours, mate. Get some practice in. No way she's here to buy one of our motors today.'

Feeling stung, I watch the older of the two salesmen walk away into the staff office.

The younger man finally comes to my aid, picking up the bits and pieces that have strayed the furthest and handing them to me. To add to my humiliation, one of them is a super-plus tampon.

'Are you OK, madam?'

'*I'm fine.*' My response comes across more vicious than intended, causing him to back off nervously.

Standing up, I straighten my outfit and take a proper look at him. He's younger than I first thought; probably only about nineteen or twenty, with bad skin and thick glasses. He's also shifting from one foot to the other, clearly at a loss as to how to handle this situation, and I actually feel sorry for him – especially as it wasn't him who made the comment.

'Sorry for being rude.' I give a weak smile. 'My day was going well until that downpour. I'm Emma Blake. I have an appointment for a test drive. You're my fourth today, in fact.' I feel the need to prove myself a worthy customer.

'I'm Grant. Nice to meet you, Ms Blake.' He holds out a tentative hand and I shake it. 'If you have your driver's licence handy, I'll go and check your booking.'

I hand it to him and he disappears into the office, leaving

me to have a nosey around. With it being a franchise that offers a few different car makes, it's really quite vast, with different sub-showrooms.

Wandering around, I admire the different models, which include the car I'm here to test drive – a small Mercedes hatchback – and while I'm taking a good look at it – inside and out – something catches my eye. A sporty hardtop Mercedes convertible, with stunning curves, sparkling silver paint and stylish alloy wheels. Drawn to it like a moth to a lamp, I drift across and walk around it, tracing the perfect angles of its bodywork with my finger. I bend my head inside the driver's door and take in the pristine, beautifully styled, dark interior, all the time imagining myself taking a leisurely spin on a bright summer's day with the top down.

'It's nice, isn't it?' Grant appears out of nowhere, the shock causing me to bang my head on the door frame.

'*Ouch*. Yes, it's lovely. Really lovely.' I stand up, rubbing my throbbing head.

'You should see it with the top down, it looks even better. Anyway, we're all set.' He dangles a key in front of me with a lop-sided grin. 'If you'd like to follow me, we'll get started with the test drive.'

'OK, sure...' There's something swirling in my brain that I'm finding impossible to ignore. 'Only... I'm wondering... could I maybe test drive the convertible first?'

This isn't part of my plan, but it's just a bit of fun – when in Rome, as they say. I expect Grant's eyes to light up, but it has the opposite effect.

'Ah, right...' His shoulders slump. 'I'll need to see if there's one available, but I'm sure that won't be a problem.'

For some reason, I'm left feeling like I've kicked a puppy. Having agreed to act on my request, Grant doesn't take any action that would indicate he's going to sort it out. Instead, he hangs by my side, pretending to polish a non-existent smear off the paintwork of the convertible.

'Eh... Grant? Will you check that for me, then?'

He stops polishing. 'Sorry, yes, I'll go sort that for you.'

He skulks off, hands in his pockets, while I stare after him, wondering what's caused this unexpected change of mood. Shrugging to myself, I turn back to the car and start admiring it again, and I don't have to wait long to find out what's wrong.

'Ms Blake?' A voice booms from behind me, giving me my second near heart attack of the day.

'Yes?' I turn and find myself face to face, not with Grant, but with the older salesman who made the comment when I first arrived.

'I hear you want to test drive the convertible instead. Little beauty, isn't she? She's getting fantastic reviews. I'm not surprised you're tempted.'

'Yes... that's correct.' I look around for Grant.

'Right then, follow me, and we'll get this baby on the road. I'll take you on some open stretches, so you can feel her purr.' He says this last bit with such a sleazy tone that I gag a little.

'Where's your colleague? I thought he was going to do the test drive.'

'He's in the back.' He jabs his thumb towards the office. 'Got some admin to sort.'

'OK, no problem... I guess.'

The salesman, in his misguided charm offensive, has neglected to introduce himself. He continues his sleazing, while I reluctantly follow him towards the showroom exit. Now dreading the test drive I was looking forward to only moments ago, I'm angry at myself for letting him take over like that. Why am I just accepting this?

'Come on, then. *Chop chop.*' He beckons me through the door.

Although he's making a joke of it, it's clear he's getting impatient. Am I really going to trot along behind him like a little dog? Like I apparently did with Dave all that time? I barely made it through the door before this man wrote me off.

He beckons me again, making me feel like a naughty pet and something inside me snaps. This is *exactly* the type of situation I thought I was done with since my win.

Sleazy Steve, or whatever his name is, has clearly used his authority to swoop in and steal Grant's sale now that I'm looking at a more expensive model. And Grant obviously knew this would happen. I can make an excuse and leave, meaning he'll think he was right about me all along and my plan for today will be scuppered, or I stand up for myself, and poor Grant.

'Excuse me, Mr...' I make sure he realises I don't even know his name.

'Oh, sorry, sweetheart. Steven Wade. Call me Steve.'

I suppress a smirk at my accuracy in guessing his name. 'OK, *Steve*. I'm afraid I have a problem.'

'Changed your mind already?' He regards me with a bored look and checks his watch.

Feeling intimidated by his behaviour, any courage I've mustered deflates immediately. 'Actually... yes... yes, I have. Apologies for wasting your time.'

Head down, I turn and start to walk away, disappointed in myself for avoiding yet another difficult interaction.

'No problem. Figured it was a bit pricey for you.' He tries and fails to hide a sneer.

This time he really hits a nerve. *How dare he?* Why on earth am I letting this misogynistic prick stop me from doing what I want to do? I'm so outraged that I become stiff with tension. He's another bloody Dave, thinking he's above everyone else. Well, he's damn well not and I am so sick of men treating me like this. *Nothing* is going to get in the way of me ending my day with a new car.

I take a deep breath and walk back towards him. 'Actually, no... sorry. I should have been clearer. I've not changed my mind about the test drive... I've changed my mind about doing the test drive with *you*.'

Sleazy Steve is shocked into silence.

'Now... if this dealership wants a chance at making a sale from me today, as well as avoiding a complaint for sexist behaviour and blatant rudeness – yes, I heard your comment when I arrived – I suggest you go and get Grant.'

I'm shaking inside, but he doesn't know that, so I simply fold my arms and let the silence do the work. For a second, I wonder if he's going to back chat me again or even try sweet talking me, but instead he raises his hands in defeat and heads off towards the office without uttering a word.

Once he's out of sight, I let my arms fall, panting a little as I take in what's happened. I did it. I stood up for myself – and this time there was no alcohol involved. My newfound wealth is totally working for me. I allow myself an inner high five.

Moments later, Grant comes bounding out of the office, his lop-sided grin back firmly where it should be. He leads me to a covered area outside where a Mercedes convertible, pretty much identical to the one inside, is sitting with its roof retracted. Its silver metallic paint shimmers in the sunshine – which has thankfully made a reappearance. I open the door and slide into the driver's seat, where the solid feel of the steering wheel and the coolness of the dark grey leather upholstery send an excited shiver through me. I run my fingers along the dashboard, then down towards the automatic gear selector, circling the various buttons as I go. I can already imagine what it would be like to experience this luxury every day.

Grant jumps in beside me, and after giving me a slightly hesitant tour of the controls – which was more like us figuring things out together – we're on the road, top down, with me behind the wheel. It's even better than I imagined. I already feel at one with the car, the drive being smooth and effortless.

'So, Grant...' I manoeuvre my way onto a long stretch of tree-lined country road, enjoying the roar of the engine and the pull of the car as I hit the accelerator. 'What's the deal with you and Steve?'

'What do you mean?' Grant appears thrown by the directness of my question.

'You know exactly what I mean. If I hadn't made it clear I didn't want to do the test drive with him, you'd have missed out on this sales opportunity. Does he do that to you all the time?'

'Um... no. He's... good to learn from. He's my boss. That's just how things go.'

'It might be how they go, Grant, but it's not how they should go. I respect that you're trying to be diplomatic, with me being a customer and all, but I've seen enough to know that you're being treated unfairly.'

Grant says nothing, but I sense my observations have hit the mark.

'I know it's none of my business,' I continue, unable to let this go. 'And I won't pry any more, but I will say one thing. Until recently, I was in a similar situation to you—'

'No way.' He eyes me sceptically.

'I was, honestly. I was lucky enough to find an easy route

out of it, but it's made me realise a few things. People like Steve and my old boss are bullies, and they're not nearly as tough as they make out. The minute I faced up to my own boss – and believe me that was not easy for me – she backed right off. Don't do anything that will get you in trouble. But *do* believe in your potential, and don't be afraid to stand up for yourself.'

'Won't that make things worse?'

I shake my head. 'I really doubt it, Grant. As long as you don't go too far with it. Politely hold your own with Steve, and I bet he'll respect you, even if he doesn't like you. Respect goes a long way.'

'Gosh, thanks, Ms Blake.' Grant gives me a toothy grin. 'I've never really thought about it that way. I'll give it a try.'

'Good for you. It's Emma, by the way. And if what I'm suggesting doesn't work, a left hook to the gut works wonders.'

We both laugh, and I'm pleased to see him loosening up. I cross my fingers that things will go better for him in the future.

'How much does one of these cost, then?' I move the conversation back to business.

'It depends. There's a quite a difference between the starting price and the top of the range model. I can talk you through all that when we get back.'

'Sure, sounds good.'

Cruising through the countryside, I'm so lost in the experience that I fail to notice the darkening sky. Unfortunately, Grant also misses this, and before we know it, we're caught in another torrential downpour.

I squeal as the torpedo-like raindrops pelt my face.

'*Oh, heck!*' I can hear Grant panicking over the thundering rain, frantically searching for the controls to put the roof up, but he's taking too long and we're getting soaked.

'*What are you doing?*' I shriek. I'm trying desperately to peer through the windscreen, but it's almost impossible to see anything, even with the wipers on full. I can't even see a safe opportunity to pull over, so I have no choice but to tail the blurry lights of the car in front of me.

'I can't... I don't know how to put the roof up.'

'Are you *kidding* me?' I stare at him in disbelief. 'Well, you need to figure it out... *now*.'

'*Oh no, oh no.*' His panic rises further while he scrabbles around the controls. It's clear that all sensible problem-solving logic needed for this situation has evaporated.

'*Grant!* For goodness sake. Will you do *something*.'

We're both now soaked through, as is the interior of the car. Grant looks around him wildly, eyes wide like a hunted deer, then he spots something, turns and grabs it from the back seat.

Seconds later, the rain is no longer pummelling me, allowing me to focus fully on the road. I exhale with relief, then glance across at Grant and do a double take. He's holding a huge, bright red golf umbrella over our heads. He offers me a sheepish smile, causing me to burst out laughing.

'I suppose I have to give you points for effort – and creativity.' I slap the steering wheel in amusement.

Eventually the worst of rain subsides, and as the visibility improves, I realise how ridiculous we look. A few pedestrians point and laugh, even shout things at us, as we pass through a small village, but I really don't care. Grant has made my day with his ineptness and I find myself feeling quite protective of him. He obviously hasn't been trained properly, which isn't his fault.

'Right,' I say. 'Let's stop and figure this out.'

NINA KAYE

I pull into a layby and we use the manual from the glove compartment to work out how to put the roof up. With the hilarity of the moment having passed, Grant is overflowing with apologies, no doubt beside himself with worry about his job.

'Hey, come on,' I attempt to soothe him. 'This isn't the end of the world. The interior will dry.'

'I know it will... but when Steve finds out how useless I am, he'll fire me for sure. How can he not? I've never been allowed to do a test drive in one of these before... that's why I didn't know how to do it.'

'Well, there you go. That's a good enough excuse.'

'You don't know what it's like,' he says, the brief carefree moment having well and truly passed. 'Steve's got it in for me. He'll use this to his advantage.'

Taking in his forlorn expression, and sincerely hoping this will not spell the end of Grant's job – not least because I would feel part responsible for if he did get fired – I suddenly have an idea.

'Maybe not... Maybe nobody needs to know. Listen to me very carefully...'

Chapter Twenty

An hour and a half later, I drive out of the dealership parking lot in the convertible I just test drove. Deliriously happy, and unfazed by the seat squelching beneath me, I hoot with joy as I remember the look on Sleazy Steve's face when Grant told him – having been briefed by me – that I wanted that car, there and then, or no sale. It seems Steve was fully convinced by my earlier threat to report him to his superiors, because he didn't put across even the slightest objection. It was win-win, because I was able to help Grant improve his sales stats and cover up his faux pas – and I got an amazing deal on the car with it being a demonstrator model.

On arriving outside Cat's apartment block, I park in one of the visitor's spaces and run inside to change into some dry clothes. I then grab a towel and some plastic carrier bags, and head back out the car. I'm in the middle of mopping up the puddles in the leather seat seams when Cat arrives home from work. She rushes over to me, her face a conflicting mix of excitement and concern.

'I thought you weren't getting a sports car. What happened? That must have cost a packet.'

'Au contraire...' I give a sly smile. 'It's one of their demo cars, which knocks a whack off the price ticket, and I managed to negotiate an extra discount too. Oh, and it's a hybrid engine, so I can kick about mainly on electric, saving myself money on petrol.'

'*Amazing*. Well done, you.'

'Thanks... I have to admit, I'm feeling pretty pleased with myself. Anyway, I must go, or I'll be late.'

'You heading back to the hotel?' she asks.

'Nope. I'm taking Lottie out for dinner.' I jump into the driver's seat and start the ignition. 'Not that she knows it yet.'

'Oh, that's lovely. Have a great time.'

I give her a little salute and pull out of the space.

~

A short time later, I pull into Lottie's driveway in Ratho. She must hear the wheels on the gravel, because she comes to the front door, gaping in astonishment.

'You've obviously had quite a day,' she says as I'm getting out of the car.

'Yup.' My grin is so wide, it's probably visible from the moon. 'It was *incredible*. I'm so glad you suggested I do this.'

'As am I. That's quite a machine. You'll need to take me for a drive in it sometime.'

'How about now?' I waggle my eyebrows mischievously. 'I've booked us a table at McArthur's Larder in Bruntsfield.'

Lottie looks a little taken aback. 'You've booked a restaurant for dinner? My love, I didn't even know you were coming. Have I forgotten? I know I'm getting old, but—'

'You haven't forgotten anything.' I usher her back inside. 'I wanted to surprise you. Now go and put on something nice.'

'Oh... all right. Give me a few minutes, then.'

I watch her slowly climb the stairs, using her stick to help her. It's obvious that she's finding it a challenge, but from the ticking off I've now had on several occasions, I know better than to try and help her. I wait patiently until she's ready, and on opening the passenger door for her, Lottie clocks the plastic bags on the seat and regards me quizzically.

'It's a long story,' I say. 'One I'll very much enjoy sharing with you over dinner.'

I help her into the car, and then get into the driver's seat.

'Emma, this is all very unnecessary. A FaceTime call would have been more than enough.'

'Not for you, it wouldn't.' I help her with her seatbelt. 'As you refused to join me on my little adventure, you can at least let me take you for a nice meal.'

'I suppose it's difficult to argue with that,' she concedes with a light frown.

We leave Lottie's cul-de-sac and drive to the edge of the village, where I pull over and apply the foot brake.

'Watch this.' I hit the button to retract the roof.

Lottie looks flabbergasted as it folds away behind us, and the early evening sun bathes us in a warm glow. 'Good grief. I don't think I've ever been in a car this smart.'

'Well, hold on to your hair. Because it's about to get windy.'

I pull out onto the open road, hit the accelerator and give Lottie the drive of her life. She laughs more than I've ever seen her, as we tear along the road, our hair flapping around our faces.

~

Later, as we're eating, I fill Lottie in on my day and I can see that she's enjoying this experience immensely. Having spent so many years physically and emotionally locked away in her makeshift prison, it warms my heart to see her finally getting some real enjoyment from life. Though it also tugs at me that she's missed out on so much. I decide we need more outings together in the future, regardless of what she says.

'That was very shrewd and kind of you negotiating that deal on the car,' says Lottie, when we've finished our meal and she's sipping her decaf coffee. 'I'm sure that young man appreciated your support. You're a good girl, Emma.' She pauses reflectively. 'You really have had quite a day.'

'I have.' I chew on one of the petit fours that's been served with the coffee. 'And it's all thanks to you.'

'Nonsense. I simply steered you in the right direction. It's you who is creating the experiences and the memories.'

'I suppose. Have you enjoyed your meal?'

'I have indeed. Thank you ever so much.' She dabs at the corners of her mouth with her napkin and pops it down on the table. 'The food was quite exquisite. You've made an old woman very happy.'

'Exactly what I was aiming for.' I blow her a kiss and then signal for the bill.

~

After dropping Lottie off at home, I park in the hotel's underground car park and return to my suite. I want to feel nice and refreshed ahead of tomorrow's spa marathon to get maximum benefit from the experience, so an earlier night than usual is exactly what's needed.

Just as I'm snuggling down under the feather duvet, my phone alerts me to a new message. Lifting it from the bedside table, I'm expecting it to be from my mum or one of the girls, but when I see the notification on the screen, I freeze. It's from Dave.

Hey, Dimples. Long time no speak. I've been wondering how you're doing. Meet me for a drink tomorrow after work? xx

I stare at the message, unable to form any rational thought, but it's not long before the floodgates open.

What the hell? He made it clear he wanted nothing to do with me. What's changed? Does he want to get back together? Does he know about my win? And what's with the two kisses at the end of his message? That was our thing when we were together but it's hardly appropriate for where we are now. I suddenly remember what Vivienne said – to be wary of people turning up unexpectedly. But how could Dave know? We don't have any mutual friends and I've only shared my news with a handful of people. Has he bumped into one of the girls? Surely they wouldn't give him the time of day.

My shock morphs into anger.

He has such a nerve. Not a peep out of him all this time. And now he's messaging me like we're old pals. Worse, he's used my pet name. What makes him think I'm going to drop my plans and meet him at such short notice? After all that's happened. He can get lost. I'm so over him.

Then my old habits take over.

Though, what if he's recognised how badly he treated me? Maybe he wants to apologise. Or he's realised that he's made a mistake. People can change, especially when they have a wake-up call, like at the end of a relationship. I should at least meet him and hear what he has to say.

Conflicted, I decide I should sleep on it, so I wait half an hour before sending him a tentative reply, making sure I come across as happy and busy – which I am. I also add just one kiss, because two feels wrong, and I can't bring myself to be so cold that I don't add any at all.

Hey, I'm good thanks. Not sure about tomorrow. Got a lot on this week. Text you in the morning if I can. x

My phone buzzes almost immediately with his reply.

OK. Let me know. xx

I switch off the vibration mode on my phone to avoid any more unwanted interruptions and throw it onto the chair in the corner of the room in frustration. Then, I slide under the covers with the unfortunate knowledge that, despite my incredible surroundings, and this being the most comfortable bed ever, it's now going to be a sleepless night. Dave has always had the knack of getting in my head at the worst times.

Chapter Twenty-One

At eight a.m. the next morning, my alarm sounds its gentle, ascending melody. I wake groggily, and for a second my brain is tricked into thinking it's time to get up for work. I'm about to hit the 'snooze' button, but then I remember where I am.

Exhausted from a night of tossing, turning, overthinking and overanalysing – all thanks to Dave's message – I drag myself out of bed and stand under the rainfall shower head, allowing the warm water to douse me therapeutically until I feel more human. I then make myself as presentable as I can and head down to the swanky hotel dining room.

Over a delicious breakfast, served to my exact specifications (they asked, I wasn't being entitled), I read and re-read Dave's message, agonising over every word, every punctuation mark, trying to find a hidden meaning that's simply not there. He said he's been wondering how I'm doing, but that sounds more like an empty platitude borne from a guilty conscience than anything else. I don't want to give him the satisfaction of being at his beck and call, nor do I want to set myself back after the progress I've made, but if I don't meet him, my mind will be tortured with a never-ending stream of unanswered questions and 'what ifs'.

After an inordinate amount of toing and froing, I decide I'll see him, but only briefly. That will give him enough time to say what he wants to say, and then I can get away quickly, without giving too much away.

I send him a short message.

Hey there. I can meet you later, but only for half an hour. I have plans straight after. Chambers Bar in the Charrington Grand Hotel at 6.30pm. x

He replies straight away.

Brill. See you there. xx

'OK, that's enough of that,' I murmur to myself, placing my phone face down on the table.

I need him out of my head if I'm going to get any enjoyment out of today. I'll get my answers when I meet him, and until then, I'm keeping this strictly to myself. I certainly don't need the additional pressure of people telling me what I should and shouldn't do. Whatever the outcome, it has to be on my own terms.

I'm pouring myself a final cup of tea, feeling grateful that all I have to do today is sit and be pampered, when a member of the breakfast staff appears at my table.

'Ms Blake?'

'Yes?' I look up at her and smile.

'I've just had word from the concierge desk that your companion will be arriving in five minutes. I gather you would like to go out and meet them?'

'Fantastic. Yes, I would.' My enthusiasm finally returns.

I throw back the last of my tea, and make my way out the back entrance of the hotel. A couple of minutes later, a sleek black limousine pulls up in front of me. The concierge steps forward, opens the rear door and assists the passenger out of the car.

'*Emma.*' Lottie gives me a faux scolding look as she makes her way slowly towards me, her walking stick supporting her on one side and the concierge clutching her arm protectively on the other. 'What *have* you been up to? Such a shock I got when *this* turned up in my little driveway.' She waves her free arm towards the car.

'It's a complimentary service the hotel offers.' I grin at her incredulous face. 'I wasn't going anywhere, so thought I could make use of it some other way. Nice surprise?'

'Well, yes of course, my love. Other than I wasn't ready to go anywhere. The poor driver had to wait for me to sort myself out.'

'Don't worry, he knew he'd have to wait a bit.'

'He was ever so patient. A charming young man. But, Emma, why am I here?'

The concierge transfers Lottie to me, making sure I have a good grip on her arm, and I nod my thanks.

'Today, Lottie...' I beam at her. 'We're going to have a day of rest and relaxation in the spa together. I've booked you a range of treatments – and before you say anything, it's all perfectly tailored to you. They'll also do a double check with you around your health issues.'

'Oh, dear girl. You really are an angel.' She seems genuinely overwhelmed. 'This is so unnecessary, and it must be costing you a lot of money. You shouldn't be wasting it on an old lady like—'

'*Hey,*' I silence her. 'Don't you be talking about my Lottie like that. This is *exactly* what you deserve. And anyway, I'd be lonely doing it by myself.'

'Fair enough.' Lottie brushes down her outfit, as if checking whether she's respectable enough for such an establishment. 'In that case, I am very much looking forward to spending the day with you.'

'Me too.' I give her a side hug and a kiss on the cheek.

With the initial excitement having passed, Lottie scrutinises my face. 'You look tired, dear. Did you not sleep well?'

'Not as well as I'd hoped. You look nice today.' I quickly change the subject and steer her inside towards the lifts.

On reaching the top floor of the hotel, we're treated to an impressive view of Edinburgh castle and the city centre before entering the plush spa, where the waft of aromatherapy oils and spiritual, meditate-in-a-rainforest music creates an inviting ambience. A day in this place is exactly what I need to forget about my impending meet up with Dave.

'Hello, there,' says a voice from behind us.

We turn to see a young, fresh-faced beautician beaming at us.

'You must be Emma and Lottie.'

'That's right. Hi.' I suddenly feel self-conscious in front of this doe-eyed woman who must be a five years younger than me. Goodness knows how Lottie must be feeling if that's the effect she has on me.

'Perfect,' she chirrups. 'Lovely to meet you. I'm Sammy. Let's get you both nice and relaxed, and then we'll start your treatments. Emma, you're with me today. And Lottie, my colleague, Anika, will be looking after you.'

She gestures to another immaculately made-up young

woman who has appeared beside her, then hands us our robes and slippers.

After a quick change and some wind down time, which includes drinking a green concoction that looks like it belongs on the set of *Ghostbusters* (but actually tastes delicious), Lottie and I part company to begin our treatments.

'See you in a while,' I call after her, as I follow Sammy out of the reception area.

The treatment room is decorated in easy-on-the-eye light pastel colours, with a tiled floor to match. The same relaxing music from reception floats down from a speaker above, while a pleasant aroma of fruity, spicy essential oil hangs in the air. Standing alone with beautiful, youthful Sammy, my feeling of self-consciousness returns.

'I think I'm in need of some intense maintenance.' I hear myself saying. 'I don't normally look this washed out.'

'Don't worry at all.' Sammy surveys my puffy, sleep deprived eyes and ashen complexion. 'You're in absolutely the right place. By the time we're done, you'll be looking and feeling better than you ever have. We'll start with your full body massage to get you super-relaxed.'

She instructs me to strip down to my knickers and lie on the massage bench face down, then leaves me to get sorted. Feeling exposed in just my underwear, I quickly hop up onto the bench, which actually looks more like a single bed, and wriggle into position while pulling the cosy feather duvet up over my back. It's so lovely and snug that I already feel better.

Sammy enters the room and asks me about any specific areas I'd like her to focus on, then checks on the pressure she's applying initially. She works silently on my tension-wrought body, allowing me to focus on nothing but relaxing and enjoying the experience. As she kneads my aching muscles, I feel myself begin to unwind. It's painful at times, but a good, replenishing pain, and before I know it, the deliberate, rhythmic movements have washed away all negative thoughts and worries, causing me to drift into a state of deep relaxation.

～

A couple of hours later, I join Lottie in the hotel restaurant for afternoon tea. We're welcomed by three mouthwatering tiers of sandwich fingers, savoury snacks, scones and cakes.

'This looks amazing.' I sit down at the table. 'How's it been so far?'

'Simply divine,' she says. 'I've had a manicure, a facial and an aromatherapy massage, and this spread looks delicious too. Thank you ever so much for this experience, Emma. Your generosity is quite humbling.'

'You're so welcome.' I pour her a cup of tea, pleased to see that she looks genuinely relaxed and rejuvenated. 'And enough of that chat. You've more than earned it after years of me chewing your ear off about my parents... my jobs... men... you name it. I'm so glad you're enjoying it. Oh, your nails are fabulous.' I grab Lottie's hand, admiring Anika's work.

'I wondered if the colour was a tad young for me, but Anika insisted that was not the case.'

'It totally works. You're like a glam gran.' My hand shoots to my mouth in horror on realising what I've said. 'Oh, I'm so sorry, Lottie. What a stupid thing to say.'

'Nonsense.' She picks a smoked salmon and cream cheese sandwich finger from the bottom tier of the cake stand. 'What have I told you about not tiptoeing around me? I *am* a grandparent. Sophie is still with me every day – in here.' Her hand goes to her chest.

'I know she is.' I nod solemnly. 'Sorry for the tiptoeing... again. Actually, I was wondering if you'd had any thoughts on which charities you'd like to donate the money to?'

'I have. It wasn't difficult. There's one that provided support to Caroline when Sophie was ill. And I've been giving some regular small donations to a suicide prevention charity for some time. I thought they might be a good choice.'

'They sound like just the right beneficiaries for the money.' I take a bite from my egg and watercress sandwich.

'I think so.' Lottie smiles wistfully.

'I'll arrange the donations as soon as I'm back from my holiday with the girls. And actually, I wondered...' I stop, unsure whether to continue.

'You wondered what?'

I put down my sandwich. 'Um... I wondered if you might want to visit the charities in person to tell them about the donations. With me. It might be good for you to talk to them a bit about what happened to you...' I chew my lip, unsure how Lottie will respond to this suggestion.

She sits quietly for a moment, then looks at me. 'I think that's a lovely idea, and I think I am ready. Caroline and Sophie would want it too. Thank you, my love, this means a lot to me.'

Saying nothing, I reach over and squeeze her hand, suddenly caught by a swell of emotion – partly for Lottie and partly because I'm struggling to suppress my own mixed-up feelings about Dave getting in touch. It's no use. I can't hold them in anymore.

'Lottie, Dave's been in touch.'

'He has?' She sips at her tea, giving nothing away.

'Yes, he wants to meet me tonight. I've said I will, but only for half an hour. I know I shouldn't, but I need to hear what he's got to say. I feel so conflicted.'

'I'm sure you do. And that is natural.'

'Do you think I'm an idiot for meeting him?' I search her face anxiously.

She shakes her head. 'Not at all. Emotions are complicated. I understand that you want to follow your instincts, but do be vigilant.'

'I thought you'd tell me I shouldn't go.'

'I never tell you what to do, Emma, you know that. I will only ever suggest what to bear in mind while making your decisions.'

'Of course.' I fidget with the teaspoon on my saucer. 'That's good advice about being vigilant. Vivienne from the lottery said something similar. I need to protect myself from being manipulated, especially if he's found out about my win. I hope it's not about that, but I also don't know what I want from meeting him.'

'It's also important to protect your heart.' Lottie plucks a fruit scone from the middle tier of the stand and cuts it in half. 'Whatever comes of this conversation, just be sure that it's what's best for you, not for Dave.'

'That makes perfect sense. You are a wise one, Lottie.'

Chapter Twenty-Two

Once we've filled up on delicious afternoon tea treats, Lottie and I return to the spa for the rest of our treatments, including having side-by-side pedicures, while laughing and chatting away. It's such a companionable experience. We're two ladies of vastly different generations – but with so much that connects us.

Later, as I'm helping her back into the limousine, I can't help thinking that Lottie looks paler and more tired than when she arrived. Concerned that the day should have had the opposite effect, I ask if she's all right, but she waves my worries away.

'I'm just old, my love. This has been one of the most glorious days in my lifetime. I will treasure this memory for the rest of my days – however many I have left.'

'Oh, *stop it*,' I squeal, starting to well up. 'Don't say things like that. I'm so glad you enjoyed it, though. Safe journey home and I'll call you tomorrow.' I close the door and the car pulls away smoothly.

Returning to my suite, I spend the next ten minutes marvelling at how, as Sammy promised, I'm looking and feeling better than ever. The combined therapeutic effect of my treatments and opening up to Lottie about Dave has caused all my tension, aching exhaustion and stress to dissipate, leaving me relaxed and revitalised. My previously puffy eyes now look healthy and hydrated, and my skin – which smells all zingy and wonderful – is almost luminous. I also can't stop looking, in delight, at my hands and feet, so youthful and beautiful, sporting matching nude gel nails. And it might just be me, but I think I do look slightly slimmer after my body wrap.

Deciding that I want Dave to see what he's been missing out on, I put on some makeup (my current signature evening look, which I'm hoping to refresh on my shopping spree tomorrow), the best cleavage enhancing top I have and the designer jeans he bought me (which will soon be destined for a charity shop), then I fluff my hair up with some of my styling product.

Appearance sorted, I chill out watching TV for half an hour before taking the lift to the ground floor, all the while retaining my Zen state. Nothing is going to rile me now. Not even him.

On entering the tasteful, seductively lit bar – ten minutes late, to let him sweat a bit – I can see Dave sitting at a table in the far corner, facing the window. My pulse quickens, making me hesitate, and I'm annoyed that, even after the way he's behaved, he can still have that effect on me.

Come on, Emma, you've got this. He's the one that asked you here and he has no power over you anymore. Keep an open mind. Hear him out. But protect your heart, as Lottie said.

Unfortunately, this impromptu pep talk only half works, because the problem is, I'm so mixed up and confused by this unexpected liaison, I don't know whether I love him, hate him, want to fall into his arms or kick him in the balls.

On that basis, I decide that saying as little as possible is the way to go. I need to be cool and indifferent.

Dave must sense my entrance, because he shifts round in his seat, eyes following me as I self-consciously approach the table and sit down. This is even more awkward than I imagined it would be.

'Hi,' I greet him as casually as possible, while noticing that he's already bought us drinks: a red wine for me and a beer for him.

'Hi, Emma. You look... great.'

'Thanks.' I touch my cheek shyly. 'I fancied some proper pampering at a beauty salon and it's done me the world of good.'

'It was clearly worth the money.' His gaze lingers on me, and I feel an involuntary flutter in my stomach. 'Do you still need to go at seven? It doesn't leave us much time to talk.'

'It's fine. My plans have shifted. I have an extra half-hour.'

'OK, good. Cheers.' He lifts his glass, tilting it towards mine.

'Is this really a "cheers" moment?' I fix him with a questioning look.

'Why not? For old time's sake? I've missed our little rituals.'

My heart nearly stops. *He's what?* Is that code for he's missed *me*?

'I suppose.' I clink his glass, remaining outwardly calm and collected, while my insides are riding a roller-coaster.

'So, how have you been?'

'Fine. You?'

'Just "fine"?' He gives me a searching look.

'Yeah. Just fine. And you?'

There's no way I'm telling him anything about the last

month; no need for him to know what a state I was in after we split up. And I definitely don't want him knowing anything about my lottery win, particularly as he hasn't yet shared his motives for being here.

'Well, I guess I've been "fine" too,' he says. 'But I've also missed having you around.'

There it is again. He's missed me. There's no way that can be misinterpreted. The question is, has he missed me for real, or because he's somehow heard about my overnight wealth?

'Is that actually true?' I raise a sceptical eyebrow.

'Of course.' He looks at me like I've gone mad. 'You can't be with someone all that time and not miss them when they're gone. I realised... I'd been selfish towards the end. I didn't appreciate all the good stuff until you weren't there anymore. I'm sorry for that, Emma. I shouldn't have treated you like that – especially making up the trip to France. That was cruel.'

I'm shocked into silence, but my mind is whirring like a hard drive. Dave, who has never once apologised to me, has just said sorry. And he's admitted to being selfish too. This is a revelation. Could it be that he really *has* had a wakeup call and changed? Maybe we do have a chance at making it work, because let's face it, everyone makes mistakes. It's whether they learn from them that counts.

'Oh... right... well... yes, you *were* selfish.' I nod my head reprovingly, while struggling to keep my composure. 'And it *was* cruel making up the trip to France, but... I do appreciate you making the effort to apologise.'

Dave seems pleased with my response, so I lighten the tone.

'What have you been up to, then?'

'Not much, really.' He shrugs. 'Was away for the weekend

with the guys there. Stag do. Been busy at work. That's about it. You?'

'Nothing major to report either. Nights out with the girls, that sort of thing.'

Having already exhausted the here and now, our conversation shifts to more familiar territory, chatting about old times, and very quickly, it's like we've been transported back to the early days of our relationship. Dave's blatantly flirting with me and I'm giving it back just as good. Pushing all anxieties regarding his motives out of my mind, I allow myself to relax and enjoy being with him again, because despite what I said about being better off without him, this moment feels so right.

'So, anyway...' I'm reluctant to break the spell between us, but as it's evident he wants us to get back together, I'm keen to hear what he has to say on the matter. 'Why are we here, Dave? There must be a reason.'

'I'll get to that.' He takes a slug from his beer, waving my question away. 'How's work going?'

I freeze, unsure how to answer. After rapidly weighing things up, I decide it won't do any harm to tell the truth on this one. I don't need to mention my win. People quit their jobs for all sorts of reasons.

'Erm... no idea. I quit.'

'*Really?*' He looks shocked, but I clock straight away that it's not genuine.

'You already know.' I give him an affectionate push.

'OK, I admit it. I know.'

'How? Did you bump into one of the girls?' I'm smiling, but there's something starting to gnaw at me. A slight suspicion. Brushing it away, I put it down to uneasiness with the whole situation. Giving him another chance − *if* I decided to − would be a controversial move. My parents certainly wouldn't approve, and Amber would kick off big style. But Dave's showing a new side – one that proves he can change, be a better person. They'll eventually see it too.

'Nope, haven't seen any of them,' he says.

'You talked to someone from my work?' I sip at my wine, while continuing to quiz him.

'Also, a negative.'

'Oh, come on. How did you know?'

'I bumped into your mum and dad's next-door neighbours in town the day before yesterday. They were down here for a day trip. Don't think they knew we'd split up.'

'*Oh.*' There's that uneasy feeling again.

'They're insufferable bores those two.' Dave acts out a fake yawn to illustrate his point. 'They have nothing going on in their own sad little lives, so they entertain themselves by gossiping about other people. Every time I was at your parents' house, their curtains were twitching...'

As he continues his character assassination of my parents' neighbours, which I have to admit is pretty spot on, my uneasiness grows and grows – until something dawns on me. There's no way my status-obsessed mother would have told the neighbours about me quitting my job without telling them about my lottery win. And Dave's quite right. Mum and Dad's neighbours are as gossipy as my mum, which means they must have brought it up. They'd be fishing for information. I suddenly feel sick to my stomach. This may not be the potential reunion I thought it was, and if I'm right, then I'm going to have to call him on it.

'What else did they say?' I encourage him to dig himself into a bigger hole, while keeping my tone even.

'Not much really.' He shrugs. 'That was about it. I tuned

out after a few minutes. They could have been talking about being kidnapped by aliens for all I know.'

'Really? They didn't say anything else?'

'No... no, I'm fairly sure that was it...' He makes a show of searching his memory, but I can see right through his fakery and it makes me angry. He really is a piece of work, trying to manipulate me like this.

'*What a crock of shit!*' I cry out, shocking even myself.

'Sorry?'

'I said... *what a crock of shit.*' The barman gives me a look and I lower my voice. 'You know about my win.'

Dave obviously realises he's been caught out and tries to cover it up. 'All right, you got me... I just wanted to give you the chance to tell me your exciting news yourself.'

'Really?' I desperately want to believe this, but I know it's not true. 'Do you want to know what I think? I think you heard about my money, decided you fancied a bit of it for yourself, and that's why you've turned up like this, all charm and wanting to get back together. I was warned about this happening.'

'What? No, Emma, you've got it all wrong—'

'*Don't you dare gaslight me, Dave!*' My fury spills over, hurt and humiliation overriding my instincts to shuffle away quietly and pathetically. 'How long were you going to keep up this charade? Until I'd spent a shedload of money on you? Or until we were married and then you could divorce me and take half? I knew you were selfish, but I never had you down as a full-on scumbag.'

I sit back in my chair, arms folded, waiting for the lies to continue. I'm shaking inside, almost faint from finding out I've been duped. But I'm determined not to lose this one.

'Are you quite finished?' he asks in his irritatingly superior way, clearly already over being caught out.

I nod, tight-lipped, eyes locked on his.

'Where did you get the idea that I want to get back together? That's the last thing I want. I finished with you for a reason, Emma, and that reason hasn't changed. Plus, do you really think I'd be the one who benefitted most financially if we got married and divorced?'

Nausea washes over me like a cloak of doom. He never wanted to get back together at all. I've made a complete fool of myself.

'You think I've come here with pound signs in my eyes?' he all but growls. 'Well, you're right. I came to ask, quite reasonably, for the two grand you stole when you took that vintage red from my wine cupboard to drown your sorrows. I noticed that one quickly, though sadly, not fast enough. Thought we could have had a laugh about it and settle things like adults, especially now you're flush, but clearly, I was wrong.'

In my mortification, I nearly miss the fact that I was right about everything else: just not about him wanting to rekindle our relationship under false pretences. When this registers, I'm so outraged that I spring back into action.

'So, you *were* after my win,' I shout, ignoring another look from the barman. 'All this apologising, reminiscing, being charming. It *was* about the money – about getting me to pay you back for the wine I... took.'

'Look, Emma, I just want what I'm owed, and I was being serious about—'

'*You manipulative bastard.*' I cut him off before he can spin me any more lies. 'You're still totally and utterly selfish. Everything is about *you*. You can more than afford to write off that wine... a small price to pay for treating me like shit. But your greed won't allow that, will it? I'm sorry I took your wine. It's not like I knew what it was worth. If I did, I would never have touched it. I was trying to cope with having my heart broken, but you're too self-obsessed to understand that. If it's that important to you, I'll happily buy you another bottle, but I'm *not* going to hand you two grand.'

Dave, who until now, has been the calmer of the two of us, starts to spit with rage. 'You little *cow*. Got a quid or two and now you think you're it? Well, let me bring you down a peg or two. You were a complete pain in the arse and I was relieved to see the back of you. I haven't missed you – *at all*. You want to know why I made up the trip to France? To shut you up while I could figure out how to get rid of you. You think you know me so well, but you didn't even see what was going on right under your nose...' He tails off, a nasty, satisfied glint in his eye.

'Wh... what do you mean?' I feel myself starting to shake.

'You asked me if there was anyone else... well, there was. For a year-and-a-half and still going strong. She's a much better laugh than you ever were.'

Although I'd already sensed what was coming, this blow winds me. So much so that I feel like I'm going to throw up.

'How... *could... you?*' I can barely get the words out. 'What did I do to deserve that? It was Melissa, wasn't it? I knew it.'

Dave stares at me defiantly, his eyes now cold and unforgiving. 'Nope, not Melissa.'

He's won and he knows it. He may not have his two grand, but he's completely undermined my attempt to stand up to him, as well as destroyed my trust in men, perhaps for good.

'So, who?'

'None of your god damn business.'

I'm devastated, humiliated and livid at the same time, tears flowing down my cheeks. Conversely, Dave's face is smug. He's actually enjoying ripping me to shreds. I need to get the hell out of here.

'Enjoy your night out,' he sneers.

This is the final straw for me. I scrape back my chair so hard that it topples to the floor with a loud clatter. Then, I run out of the bar sobbing, and don't stop until I've reached my room – my sultry come-to-bed look replaced by a pair of Halloween-style zombie eyes.

Chapter Twenty-Three

On waking the next morning, I'm flooded with shame. After my rendezvous-gone-wrong with Dave, I should have done the sensible thing and reached out to Cat for moral support, but I was too humiliated and broken by the experience to admit to anyone what had happened. Instead, I spent the evening in my suite, sobbing my heart out.

I wince at the fleeting memory of a hotel staff member knocking on my door to check I was OK. Between that, the unintended display in the bar and my endless caterwauling, every employee in this place must know who I am.

Too mortified to show my face at breakfast, I call room service and ask them if they'll bring some food to my room. Not that I have any appetite, but I know I should try to eat something. They are, of course, very obliging.

I even consider ditching my plans for the day, as I've had next to no sleep and I could probably quite successfully audition for a part in *The Walking Dead* (or a similar post-apocalyptic horror drama series). Last night's bombshell has really messed with me – to the point that I still can't bring myself to talk to Cat about it. *He'd been cheating on me for a year-and-a-half?* How did I not see that? Or not even suspect a thing? I was never comfortable with his friendship with Melissa, but my worries were that he would leave me to go back to her, not cheat on me. And if it's not Melissa, do I know her?

My breakfast arrives, and contrary to what I thought, I discover that I'm famished; probably due to last night's dinner consisting of hand cooked crisps and cashew nuts from the minibar. Though at least I didn't touch a drop of alcohol this time.

Hoping that I'll feel better after a long hot shower – which seemed to help yesterday – I let the water drench me, willing it to wash away the torment in my mind. However, the impact of Dave's revelation is the emotional equivalent of drawing all over my body with permanent marker. It will fade but it'll take more than one shower to scrub it away.

I had convinced myself that I was pretty much over him, but I'm obviously not, especially if I was considering taking him back after everything he's done. I shiver at the humiliation of thinking he wanted to get back together when it had never even crossed his mind. But at least I now know that. And while my brain may be as scrambled as the eggs on my breakfast plate, the stark light of day is grounding me enough to realise that I need to pick myself up and keep going – even though that's the last thing I feel like doing right now.

Forcing myself to get ready, I plod to the hairdresser. The hotel doesn't have an in-house salon, so Sammy from the Spa has kindly arranged a nine a.m. booking at a high-end place on George Street – the one the hotel recommends to all its guests. The plan being that if I'm creating a fresh image for myself, a new hair style is an important part of the package.

On opening the door to Hunter Philips, I'm hit by a gust of warm air and fragrance. I've been in nice salons before, but I can see from the real hardwood flooring, single centrepiece chandelier and enormous vases of freshly cut flowers, that this is in a different league. The stylish waiting area welcomes me with expensive-looking, grey-brown fabric sofas and a coffee table piled high with fashion magazines. And in the corner, a Nespresso machine sits regally, surrounded by its army of multi-coloured coffee pods.

Still feeling vulnerable from last night's events, I feel my 'designer' anxiety kicking in; the irrational feeling that I'm not worthy of being in such a high-end place. Dave really has done a masterful job of ruining this experience for me.

I give my name to the young receptionist, who, despite sporting bright blue hair, manages to look like she's walked off the cover of Vogue. If I tried that, I'd end up looking like I'd had an accident with the toilet cleaner. She invites me to take a seat and I scuttle over to one of the couches,

I'm absently flicking through a magazine (which I'm also using as a shield), while fantasising about Dave catching a nasty STD from the woman he'd been seeing behind my back, when my thoughts are interrupted.

'Well, hello there, lovely.'

Peering over the pages, I find myself looking at the person who must be my hair stylist for the morning. He's tall, gorgeous and very flamboyant. I love him the second I clap eyes on him, which instantly lifts my mood.

'Hi.' I smile nervously at him.

'Fabulous to meet you, Emma.' He gives what looks like a little bow and leads me to a chair where he gestures for me to take a seat in front of the mirror. 'I'm Cameron. I'm the Executive Stylist Director here, so you're in very safe hands. What do I have the pleasure of doing for you today?'

I self-consciously tug at my limp hair and frown. 'Hair transplant?'

Cameron gives a tinkling laugh. 'I'm afraid we don't do that here. I get the impression you're looking for a big change, though?'

'Yeah... I am. I want a totally different hairstyle. A new... well, me.'

'Don't you worry, lovely, I'll have you looking like a catwalk model by the time you leave.'

'That sounds like the next best thing to a hair transplant.' I give a resounding nod.

'OK, *fabulous*.' He makes a show of inspecting my hair section by section.

It's been a while since my last haircut, so I've got quite a bit of length he can play with. I imagine how I'll strut out of the door with a huge mane of beautifully styled, golden-blonde tresses, swishing them around in slow motion like those women in the shampoo adverts, while passers-by gape in envy. Yes, that would do nicely.

'Are you ready, Emma...' Cameron shocks me out of my daydream. 'I'm thinking... let's make the most of that beautiful bone structure in your face. Having so much length isn't doing you any favours and neither is that flat, straight style. You need a shorter, choppier, stylish cut.'

'Shorter?' I wince. 'I was hoping to keep it long.'

'No, definitely not, lovely... doesn't suit you. Now, I see you have a natural wave in your hair that you're trying to hide. We're going to make use of that... and I'm thinking fringe to add statement.'

My discomfort turns to disbelief. 'Wavy short hair... and... a fringe? Erm... Cameron... I'm not sure that's a good idea. The last time I had a look like that I was seven, and the boys chased me around the playground calling me a scarecrow.'

Still wrapped up in his creative visioning, Cameron doesn't appear to have heard a word I've said. 'Yes, that's perfect... and some colour to lift. We'll stick with your natural colour overall but add some lowlights to bring texture and dimension. Mmm... that's going to be quite stunning. So, are we good to go?'

I blink at him, speechless and terrified.

'Um... it's... an interesting option.' I try to be diplomatic. 'But I was thinking maybe long with layers and perhaps going blonde.'

Planting his hands on his hips, Cameron appraises me with a look I can only describe as withering and condescending. 'With the greatest respect, lovely, *who* is the professional here? With your pale complexion, blonde will wash you out. Layers would improve things slightly on your current style, but do you want to be average, or do you want to be a fricking masterpiece?'

Not one for diplomacy himself then.

'Erm... well, I guess I'll... be a masterpiece then.' It's clearly futile to argue with him, and I don't think I could muster the courage or motivation today anyway.

'Great choice.' He throws a gown over me and gets to work, while I start saying my prayers. I don't want to have to turn up at my regular salon tomorrow morning, grovelling, and begging her to fix it for me. I'd end up getting a long lecture on not being fooled by high price tags and pretentious decor.

Once he's applied the dye to my hair, Cameron wastes no time in adding yet another dimension of discomfort to my experience.

'Right, lovely, are you ready for the transformation of a lifetime?'

'I guess so.' I squirm in my seat.

'Fantastic. Now, I have a little ritual I do with all my new customers...'

I wonder if he's going to a spiritual hair dance of some sort.

'To make sure you get the full effect of your transformation– a sort of "before" and "after" effect – I'm going to do your hair away from the mirrors.'

Is he kidding me? I just want my hair cut and coloured. This isn't a makeover TV show.

'Erm... Cameron, I realise this is probably something you do regularly, but it's not for me. I like to be able to see—'

'Where's your sense of adventure, lovely? Good for the soul, this is. It teaches you to trust more and obsess less. Really, you're getting two for the price of one – therapy and a hair style. You're welcome. Now, I don't want you seeing a thing until it's done, so if nature calls, let me know. There's a small toilet through the back with no mirror that you can use.'

Well, I guess that's me told. Not wanting to make a scene, and because I really do want my hair done today, I reluctantly sit back and await my fate.

~

A couple of hours later, Cameron is 'oohing and ahhhing', making the final tweaks before the big reveal. I, on the other hand, have been taking myself through sporadic deep breathing cycles while sitting on my hands to stop me chewing the crap out of my newly done nails. I've had no choice but to sit back and let him do his job. And in the process, I've told him everything that has gone on in the last few weeks, with the exception of last night's disaster, which is still too raw. There's something about hairdressers that makes me more loose-lipped than my mother after a community coffee morning – and I have a sneaking suspicion that I'm not the only person who experiences this curious phenomenon. To say Cameron was interested was the understatement of the century. I've never heard the phrase '*shut up*' so many times in my life.

'Right, lovely, are you ready to see what a masterpiece looks like?' asks Cameron.

'OK...' I put an anxious hand to my stomach.

'Calm yourself. You're going to love this.'

He leads me across to a mirror, and on taking in the image before me, my mouth forms a perfect 'O'. Cameron, true to his word, has performed a near miracle. If it weren't for seeing my stunned face staring back at me, I'd swear it wasn't me. My mousey brown hair is now shoulder length, with hints of rich chestnut and mahogany. I have that sexy, tousled, just back from the beach look, and a stylish fringe that frames my face in a way I never knew I could look.

'*Wowsers!*'

'I know.' Cameron admires his handiwork.

'Cameron, you are nothing short of a genius.'

'*Right?*' He holds out his hand for a low five, and I obediently oblige.

'I mean... I've never looked even remotely as good as this.' I touch my hair with my fingers and a thought pops into my mind. 'Wait... what if I can't replicate this myself? What if I do end up looking like a scarecrow because I don't have the styling skills?'

To my surprise, Cameron looks mortally offended. 'Did you not just call me a genius?'

'Yes, but—'

'Emma, *did you not just call me a genius?*'

'Yes.' I realise I'd better shut up.

'And what does a genius like me do when he cuts your hair?'

'Erm... I don't know.' I feel like a child getting a scolding for forgetting the three-times table.

Cameron sighs theatrically. 'He does it through balancing creativity with making the most of what he's got. I told you I was going to make use of your natural wave, and that's what I've done. You'll have minimal styling time because you had it all already. I've simply brought out your natural beauty.' He then proceeds to tell me how to recreate the look.

'What, *really*? That's all I need to do?' I'm hugely impressed by this man's confidence, self-belief and ability. 'You're like the hair stylist equivalent of Van Gogh.'

'Oh, I like that.' He seems to bask in the compliment, while I swish my new hair in the mirror to see if I can still pull o the move I was imagining earlier.

While Cameron is seeing me across to the reception desk to pay my bill, I have an idea, which is quite ludicrous, but I decide to follow my instincts. 'Erm... as a thank you for making me sit on myself – quite literally – and giving me the best hair of my life, how would you like to join me and some friends for champagne tomorrow evening? Only if you've not already got something completely fabulous planned... which I expect you will have.'

He looks thoughtful. 'You're right, I do... but I'm sure I could swing by for a glass or two.'

'Great. I'll see you tomorrow, then.' I give him the details, pay my extortionate bill – ensuring there's a generous tip in there too – and head back to the hotel.

Chapter Twenty-Four

Back in my suite, without the distraction of Cameron and the hair salon, memories of Dave's heartless disclosure the previous evening return to haunt me. The hurt and humiliation slices through me like razors – to the point that I consider calling Cat or Lottie for some much-needed comforting, but I just can't face having to say the words out loud. The anxiety that I had brought under control in recent days is also rearing its head again, making me twitchy and insecure.

I decide that there's only one thing for it: I need to head straight back out again, before I sink back to the depths of the period following D-day. If I don't, I'll have let Dave win.

Grabbing my handbag, I'm on my way down in the lift when my phone buzzes with a notification, which turns out to be an email from James about our freebies.

Hello Emma,

I hope the preparations for your upcoming trip are going well.

Just a quick note to say that your travel kits have arrived. I can put them in the post for you and they should arrive in time for your departure, but obviously I can't guarantee this. I wanted to offer you the option of coming by to collect them in case you happen to be passing. Please let me know what is most convenient for you.

Best regards,

James

Rather than creating the positive reaction it probably should (I mean, who doesn't like a free gift?), this intrusion by James irritates me.

'Oh, who cares about the damn travel kits?' I mutter, stepping out of the lift. But I soon realise that, as much as I'm not a fan of the guy, James is only doing his job.

I'm about to reply and politely ask him to post them to Cat's address, when something dawns on me. If they don't arrive before we leave for our holiday, and Amber finds out that I had the option to collect them and didn't (which she will), I'll get it in the neck. I may not care about our freebies – thanks to my current status of being able to buy pretty much whatever I want – but she and Cat are not in the same fortuitous position. Amber was also quite proud of her success in securing this extra perk.

As I'll be going in that direction (more or less) on my way to my shopping spree, it does makes sense for me to make a pit stop at the travel agency – I'm assuming the items won't be big and bulky if they're for travel – but the problem is... I really don't want to. The last thing I need right now, when I'm bogged down and feeling like crap, is to be one-upped by smart arse James – yet again. And let's face it, that seems to be the only type of interaction I have with the guy.

Or... maybe I could ask Amber or Cat to pop by for them?

Nope, that won't work either. There's no way Amber will let me off the hook about this, and she'll see through any excuse about not being able to do it myself. Plus, she and Cat have been working all week. It would be pretty selfish of me to try to palm this task off on them.

'*Fine*, you win again, James.' I give a heavy sigh and ping back a response to say I'll be passing in about fifteen minutes.

Rather than battling my way through the crowds on Princes Street, I walk along Rose Street, where I pass a welcoming looking café with cakes in the window. Deciding that a pick-me-up is what I need to get through the day, I drop in to buy a takeaway coffee, and after only a few sips, I can already feel the benefit of the caffeine and the sugar.

By the time I reach Archer & Crombie, I'm thankfully feeling slightly sharper and more able to deal with whatever comes my way with this encounter. Pushing open the door, I can see James and one of his colleagues, who's talking into a headset, sitting at the desks at the back of the shop.

'Emma, hi. It's good to see you.' He gets up and approaches me with his usual sparkling-slash-smarmy grin. 'That was handy that you were passing.'

Was that a hint of sarcasm in his voice? As if I shot along here the minute I got his email, just so I could see him again? The presumptuous sod.

'A lucky coincidence.' I give him a thin-lipped smile while doing my best to avoid direct eye contact.

Unfortunately, while I've been mentally dressing him down (not to be mistaken for mentally undressing him), my senses have tuned into James's citrusy aftershave, which unfortunately happens to be *so* god damn sexy. This break from the ranks is not just unwelcome, it creates havoc in my brain. *Come on, Emma, don't fall for that. Anyone can smell good – it doesn't make them a decent person.*

'Take a seat and I'll grab the kits,' James pats the top of the sofa. 'I would have offered you a drink, but I see you already have a coffee.'

'Yup, I'm on the go.'

I reluctantly park myself as invited, while he heads to the back of the shop and through a door.

He reappears about thirty seconds later with the travel kits, which I'm pleased to note seem high quality and filled with scrumptious designer goodies.

'Will you manage OK without a bag to put them in?' he asks, after handing them to me.

This again. Why does he have to check on me all the time, as if I'm incapable of looking after myself?

'I'll manage just fine, thanks.'

'Are you sure? They're light enough, but carrying three of them plus a drink might be a bit much. You're welcome to finish your coffee here if you like?'

'Er... no, thanks,' I say a bit too quickly. 'Got a lot on today, so best I keep moving.'

'Sure, no probs.' He seems mildly disappointed that I'm leaving so soon, but it's not like we can have our 'forced' date right here in the shop. *That bloody date that I don't even want to go on.*

Slinging my handbag back over my shoulder, I get to my feet, clutching my coffee while cradling the travel kits with my other arm. I'm already wishing I *did* have a bag to carry them in. I can't go shopping like this, but there's no way I'm giving him the satisfaction of knowing that.

'Thanks very much for these, James. I'm sure the girls will enjoy them.'

'But you won't?' He cocks his head, appearing to cringe as he eyes my precarious load.

'No, erm... I'm sure I will too.'

'Let me at least get the door for you,' he says, and I'm about to object, when I realise that I have no free hands to open it with.

'Uh... OK, thanks.'

I carefully manoeuvre round the coffee table, and as I do, one of the travel kits slips. In my attempt to avoid dropping it, I inadvertently squeeze my coffee cup and the lid pops off, propelling the contents down the front of my white top.

My face blazes with mortification while I survey the huge soggy brown stain in despair. James's hand goes to his mouth, and I swear the bastard is stifling the urge to laugh.

'Are you all right?' His expression quickly morphs into one of concern. 'You've not scalded yourself, have you?' He picks up the lid and places it back on my cup.

'I... I'm...' I do a quick self-check, because being physically injured was not my first concern. 'No, it wasn't that hot anymore. But I'll need to go back and change.' I feel close to tears as I try to gather myself together, still struggling with how to carry everything.

'Want me to get rid of that for you?' He nods towards my cup and I allow him to take it from me. 'Emma... please don't be—'

'Look, I need to go. Sorry if I got any on the carpet.' I give him a fleeting apologetic look, unbearably making eye contact for a split second, then use my now free hand to haul open the door and bolt from the shop as fast as I can.

While hurrying along Rose Street back in the direction of the hotel, my eyes overflow with humiliated tears, soon accompanied by a runny nose I can't blow because I don't have any tissues.

Why did that have to happen? Why could I not have made it through one encounter with the guy without having my dignity stripped away? And why do I end up feeling so inferior around men like that? My tortured mind floats back to last night and my horrible encounter with Dave – adding to my pain. How I let myself get sucked in like that when he had zero regrets about ending things is almost too much to bear. That was the one thing I had to hold onto. The misguided belief that he has somehow lost out. But he hasn't, because he's been with someone else the whole time.

I'm still crying, agonising at new depths, when I walk straight into someone.

'*What the...?* Hey, watch where you're going.'

'Sorry,' I mumble, head down, any instinct to stand up for myself overridden by my misery. But, at the same time, something nags at me. That voice. It has sent a familiar shock wave through me, an unpleasant feeling I've felt once too often. Slowly, I look up.

'So, you damn well... *oh. It's you.*'

For the second time in as many days, I find myself in an unexpected and wholly unwelcome interaction with Karla. She looks positively gleeful at the sight of my tearful, no doubt mascara-streaked face and the super-sized coffee stain down my front.

'So, this is the great change you were talking about, is it, Emma? Wandering round the city in a right state. You look like you've been begging on the street.' She smirks, looking me up and down in disgust.

Unfortunately, putting her in her place at the restaurant

doesn't seem to have had the desired e ect of scarring her for life.

I stand frozen to the spot, just as I did when I met her in the restaurant toilets last week, all sense of power and self-confidence having deserted me. And this time there's no champagne or adrenaline rush to give me a boost. I'm lost in a torrent of anxiety and insecurity, which feels so unjust. I was ahead. I'd taken her on. Have I not suffered enough at the hands of this woman?

The silence is unbearable. She stands there, blocking my path, revelling in my discomfort – and I'm letting her do it. I proved nothing before. I'm still weak and she knows it.

Then something stirs within me. I may look and feel like shit, but I'm not the one in the wrong here. Am I really going to let her bully me and negate everything I achieved?

No.

There's no way I'm letting her pull the same nonsense Dave did last night and leave me feeling even worse than I already do. I'm absolutely *sick* of people thinking they can trample all over me.

Taking a deep shaky breath, I pull myself up to my full height and look her straight in the eye. 'No, Karla, I haven't been begging on the street. And I don't think homelessness is something to joke about.'

'Oops, my mistake. It seems you've joined a convent... *Saint Emma*.' She laughs, enjoying her own joke.

'Ha ha, that might actually be funny if it made sense.'

She ignores this and continues to berate me. 'I always knew you were the type to go nowhere. I mean, look at you. You're like something the cat dragged in.'

That's it, I can't take any more. The only thing she's going to respond to is being shown up – or rather, shut up. I'd never dream of doing what I'm about to do anyone else, but for the nasty cow that is Karla, I'll make an exception.

'You know what's funny? That you have no idea how wrong you are.' I attempt to stare her out while fighting the urge to break the excruciating eye contact.

She snorts, obviously thinking I've lost it, but she says nothing.

'It's true. And it's also true that looks can be deceiving. Sure, I'm having a bad day.' I shrug. 'So what? Bigger picture... Karma came through for me. For having to endure everything you threw at me, I got my reward. One lottery ticket was all it took and now I'm over three quarters of a million pounds richer. In fact, I'm enjoying a bit of a shopping spree this week. Already bought myself a nice new car.'

From the expression on her face, you would think I'd told her I'm immortal. 'How sad are you that you have to make up a fairy story to stop you looking like a loser?'

She doesn't believe me, and as much as I dislike her, I'm not surprised.

'That's fine, Karla. I expected this reaction. But it's true.'

'So, prove it.' She crosses her arms, surveying me woefully.

I waver. *Shit.* It was a valiant attempt at rescuing my pride, but I can't give her the evidence she's demanding. I'm not letting her near my banking app like I did with my parents, which means I've lost this one. Unless... I suddenly remember about the telephone banking account the bank set up for me after my visit to the financial adviser last week. I hadn't been bothered about it because I do everything online, but they suggested I have the number stored on my phone in case of any issues with significant purchases going through.

'Excuse me a moment.' I pull out my phone, connect to my bank and punch in my security details. When prompted, I then switch to speaker phone, select the option to hear my savings account balance and the automated voice comes through loud and clear.

'The balance of your instant savings account is seven-hundred and twenty thousand pounds. Would you like to hear your balance again?'

'Would you, Karla?' I ask. 'Or is once enough?'

My ex-boss looks like she's been punched in the face.

Ending the call, I know I could leave it there, but I'm still fizzing from the way she's treated me. I had her down as a nasty boss, but I never realised she was just plain spiteful. I decide to make for the home run.

'I wish I could say it's been lovely to see you, Karla. But it hasn't. Now, if you'll excuse me, I'm heading back to my hotel suite to change, and then I'm going to hit the shops.'

And with that, I walk off, leaving my ex-boss speechless for the second Thursday in a row.

Chapter Twenty-Five

Back at the hotel, I do a quick change and then I'm on my way out again – this time with a smile on my face.

Coming out on top after my brief encounter with Karla – booze-free – has lifted me out of my misery and elevated my mood. She and Dave are as bad as each other. In fact, Karla's probably just the type he'd cheat on me with. If only I'd managed to walk away from him with my head held high too. Nonetheless, what I need to do is focus on my triumph, put them both out of my mind (easier said than done, but I can give it a damn good try) and make the most of my shopping spree.

On walking through the doors of the vast department store just off the east side of Princes Street, my eyes soak up the sea of beautiful clothes in different colours, styles and materials. Every single piece perfect in its own way. A bubble of excitement forms in my stomach, quickly followed by the realisation that I have no idea where to start, so I begin browsing from where I'm standing.

Twenty minutes later, my arm already laden and straining under the weight, I head for the changing rooms, where a sullen looking shop assistant takes the clothes from me to count them.

'Erm... this might be a silly question,' I say to her. 'But I don't suppose you have shopping trollies here?'

She looks at me like I've grown a unicorn horn. 'No, madam.'

'OK, no problem.' I feel stupid for asking.

I'm about to head into a cubicle when another staff member with a petite frame and bouncy long blonde hair approaches me.

'Excuse me, madam? I couldn't help overhearing your question. Are you looking to buy a number of items today?' She's wearing a pristine tailored suit jacket and trousers, so she must be a manager or something.

'Yes, a whole new wardrobe actually, which is why I was asking. I'm not sure how I'm going to carry everything round with me, never mind get it all home at the end.'

'Well, you're in luck.' She gives me a bright smile. 'I'm Jana, one of the store's personal shoppers, so if you're interested, I'd like to offer you our free service today. I can help pick out items that will best enhance your shape and colouring, and the items you choose can be kept in our personal shopping area until you've finished. We also have a free home delivery service. How does that sound?'

'Like you're my guardian angel.' I'm so relieved that someone else is going to co-ordinate this exercise for me. Having never done anything like this, I hadn't thought it through.

She laughs. 'OK, great. Let's go have a chat about what you're looking for and go from there.'

She takes the clothes from the moody shop assistant and ushers me to the personal shopping space, which is similar to the changing rooms, only bigger, with a seating area and only a couple of roomy cubicles.

'So...' She invites me to take a seat on a duck egg blue sofa. 'I've been a personal shopper here for... ooh, seven years now, which means you can rest easy that I know this place inside out. May I ask your name?'

'I'm Emma.'

'It's lovely to meet you, Emma. Now straight off, I want to put your mind at rest. My role is to help meet your needs, not to pressure you into buying anything you don't want. I'm not on commission. I work solely for the purpose of giving you a great shopping experience.'

'That's helpful to know.' I try to sound knowledgeable and reassured, when in reality none of that had crossed my mind.

'Let's start with your shopping goals for today. What outcome are you hoping for?' Jana asks. 'And if you don't mind me asking, why are you seeking "a whole new wardrobe" as you put it? Often my clients have a story behind their desire for a new look. It can be helpful background information.'

'Um... I can tell you why I want to do this, but being honest, I don't really know what outcome I'm looking for.' I cringe, feeling out of my depth.

'OK, let's start with that then. Tell me why you're here.'

'My story... right... You'd maybe better get comfortable.'

Same as with Cameron from the salon, I find myself telling my story to another complete stranger. Jana appears gripped by my tale, getting outraged at the right moments and saluting my bravery at others. And when I tell her about my win, her squeal of excitement is so high-pitched that I worry for the crystal on the homeware floor. She's so genuine and friendly – even sharing some of her own experiences in a gesture of solidarity – that by the time we get around to the shopping part, I feel like we should be taking an oath of eternal friendship.

Jana's great at her job too. She helps me work out a plan of attack to build a new wardrobe perfectly suited to me. One that will stand the test of time, both from a quality and style perspective. None of this 'fast fashion malarky', as she put it. This is music to my ears because today is a one off – for warmer weather clothes anyway. I will, of course, need to top things up when it's approaching winter. She also arranges an appointment for me with the beauty department so that I can choose new makeup.

When we get up from the sofa to start our mission, I suddenly remember something. 'Oh, there's one more thing I need your help with.'

'What's that?' asks Jana, and I fill her in on my request.

'Not a problem at all, Emma. We'll definitely be able to see to that.'

God, this is totally amazing. Why have I never done this before? It certainly beats buying stuff online, finding it's nothing like I imagined and doing endless laps to the post office as I fruitlessly try to top up my wardrobe.

∼

It turns out to be the most amazing shopping experience of my life. First, we take a walk around the store so that Jana can get an idea of the styles I'd normally wear. She also asks me to trust her judgement where she chooses pieces or colours that I wouldn't ordinarily pick out myself. Then she sets me up in a changing room, where she critiques each and every item I try on.

I'm in heaven, unable to contain my excitement, as my

cubicle fills with outfit after outfit, piece after piece. My fingers roam over pink chiffon, black lace, silk, cotton and linen. My eyes drink in greens, blues, greys, a dash of dark red and purple, a kaleidoscope of colours.

I try everything: long, floaty skirts, clingy dresses, more revealing but still classy pieces, various cuts of trousers and jeans. I pose in a range of smart jackets and elegant coats. And I try on tops I would never have looked at, let alone actually put on. My manicured feet are treated to everything from pretty ballerina pumps to boots, trainers and sky-scraper heels. It feels like I'm doing the Clothes Show Live in fast-forward, and it's exhausting, but at the same time super inspiring and empowering.

Before I know it, I have a whole new wardrobe of stylishly sophisticated and flattering outfits, matched with the perfect accessories. Jana has hand selected pieces so I can mix and match, and dress my look up or down and still look a million dollars. She's the style equivalent of what Cameron is to hairdressing.

After we've done the clothes and accessories, Jana takes me down to the beauty department where she introduces me to a raven haired, beautifully made-up and high energy young woman called Trudy.

Following another whirlwind of questions, excited chatter and activity – which includes telling my whole story once again – Trudy unveils my new look by holding up a mirror in front of me.

'*Ta da*. What do you think?'

I gawp at myself, absolutely speechless. My eyes roam over my now flawless skin, glittering eyes, cheekbones I never knew existed and plumped-up, moisture-drenched lips. It's a bit over the top for this time of day, but it's a killer look for a night out.

It's as if Trudy's read my mind. 'Now, Emma, I've made you up in your new evening look. For daytime, you can pare it back with a tinted moisturiser and brown-black volumising mascara, as well as the nude lip gloss and neutral eyeshadow we tried on you earlier.'

'It's... unbelievable,' I finally manage to say.

'Unbelievable good or unbelievable bad?' She asks. 'If it's too much I can tone down your eyes.'

'Oh no, sorry, I *love* it,' I continue to admire my face in the mirror. 'I'm just gobsmacked. I've literally never looked this good in my life. Can I take you home with me? I'll never be able to recreate this, especially the eyes.'

Jana, having nipped away for a bit, suddenly reappears and clasps her hand over her heart. 'Emma, look at you. That ex-man of yours is a fool.'

'All true.' Trudy gives Jana a wink, while I beam like a five-year-old who's been told she's the prettiest princess in the world. 'Though I just did the art, you brought the canvas. You have lovely features, Emma. It's about learning to make the most of them. And don't worry, I'll give you an instruction leaflet to take away with you. You'll be a pro in no time.'

'Thank you *so* much, Trudy.' I feel completely humbled. 'And you too, Jana. You've both made my day. And as you know, it started *very* badly.'

They both grin, obviously pleased to have made a customer so happy.

With nothing left to do but settle my bill, I find myself facing the same urge I had with Cameron at the salon. Once again, it may be completely ludicrous, but I feel like I've really connected with Jana and Trudy and I find myself wanting to thank them for treating me so well.

'Erm... this might sound a bit strange,' I say to them. 'But

I'm having a champagne celebration with a few friends tomorrow to mark the end of this amazing week. I wondered... if you maybe fancied popping along for a glass or two? Just if you're free...'

'*Oh man!* I'll be at my parents' house because my aunt is visiting from abroad,' Trudy says, pouting in disappointment. 'I always miss out on stuff like this. Thanks for the invite though, Emma. That's really nice of you.'

'I'm free,' says Jana. 'I'd love to come. Only if you're sure, though?'

'Of course, I'm sure. You have no idea how grateful I am to you both for today.'

'*But it's our job,*' they cry in unison, not for the first time today.

'I know that.' I chuckle. 'But I also know that not everyone would have gone out of their way to make it such a nice experience for me.'

Jana gives a sympathetic nod, probably aware that I'm referring to the first shop assistant I spoke to.

'Oh, come here, you,' she says suddenly, and the three of us end up having a group hug in the middle of the department store, much to the amusement of the other staff and customers.

Chapter Twenty-Six

Back in my suite after my shopping escapade, I decide that I can't risk a repeat of the previous evening. My sanity and self-esteem must be my priority, and despite having had a positive day in the end, I know I'm vulnerable now that I'm on my own. I also finally feel the need to open up to someone about everything that's happened in the last twenty-four hours, so I message Cat to ask if she'll join me for dinner in the hotel restaurant. Thankfully, she jumps at the chance to celebrate the start of her annual leave – she's taken Friday off as well as the time we're away.

To preserve my professionally applied makeup, I message Lottie with a quick summary of my day and let her know that I'll call her in the morning. I have a much better chance of holding it together during an enjoyable evening out with Cat, than I would baring my soul on FaceTime. Lottie messages back soon after, telling me to focus on enjoying myself – she has a neighbour coming round for a sherry anyway – and that she's looking forward to hearing my news tomorrow.

Lottie's socialising with someone other than me? This

must be a first in the whole time I've known her, and something I'm mighty pleased to hear.

I take advantage of the time before Cat arrives with a quick (face-up) cat nap in the giant bed before finishing off my look with one of my new outfits I brought back to the hotel with me— an understated, figure-hugging, olive-green dress, with cute strappy sandals, a fitted cropped cardigan and a liquid silver necklace.

I'm doing a slow twirl in front of the mirror, admiring my new look, when there's a knock at my suite door. Flinging it open, I launch myself on Cat before she has a chance to enter the room.

'Hey, honey. Everything OK?'

'Yeah, fine.' I bury my face in her shoulder to hide the fact that I'm already welling up.

'How was your day at the spa?' She gently prises me off her. 'And your shopping trip? Oh my goodness, look at your hair... and your makeup... and that outfit. You're *stunning.*'

'Thanks. I've had an amazing time.' I quickly perk up again. 'I'm actually pretty pleased with how I look.'

'You should be. Honestly, you look incredible. I feel like you're living in a parallel universe to me right now – one where I'm stuck in Humdrum Land while you're rubbing shoulders with the rich and famous in the swanky bar downstairs. Tell me, what did you do last night? Spend the evening drinking martinis with James Bond?'

'Erm... not quite.' I usher her back out the door. 'I'll tell you all about it over dinner.'

～

'You did *what?'*

We're seated in Adair's, the hotel's classier than classy restaurant, and I've broken the news about meeting Dave.

'I know, I know.' I cover my face with my hands. 'Don't worry, I've learned my lesson. It didn't turn out well.'

'I can't believe you would meet with him after everything he did,' says Cat. 'He doesn't deserve a thing from you. What happened?'

I fill her in on the disaster of the previous evening and her reaction is stronger than I even expected. She's probably the angriest I've ever seen her, and I find myself quite shocked by this.

'*What an absolute creep.* That bastard really couldn't sink much lower. You deserve so much better, Emma... although...'

'Although what?'

'Well, I suppose it means that you can move on once and for all.' She searches my face, obviously trying to gauge my reaction.

'You're right.' I nod, after a short pause. 'Though I still feel really raw and humiliated. I'm not sure I'm ever going to be able to trust a man again, Cat.'

'You will, honey, but it may take time. They're not all like Dave.' She sips from her water glass, looking thoughtful. 'I guess now's not the best time to ask if you've been in touch with that guy, James, after he gave you his number?'

'I have, but only because he emailed about our freebies, and I went to collect them from the shop.'

'Oh. And how did that go?'

I rearrange my cutlery distractedly. 'Um... the freebies are great, but I managed to humiliate myself by spilling half a takeaway coffee down my front and rushing out of the shop.'

Cat's hand goes to her mouth in much the same way as

James's did.

'It's fine, you can laugh.' I give a resigned shrug. 'I'm sure someday I'll be able to as well.'

'I'm not laughing, honestly. I feel for you.' She reaches across and clutches my hand. 'You didn't hurt yourself, did you?'

'No. Only my pride took a beating – again.'

'Aww, Emma. I'm sorry. You know you don't have to see James again if he's having such a negative impact on you. Amber will obviously have something to say if you don't keep to your bet and go on a date with him, but I'll have your back, I promise.'

'It's OK, I'll do it, just to shut her up. That is, if he hasn't changed his mind after my dramatic exit today. Really what I need is a bit of time to get past what happened with Dave. The holiday will give me that. Oh, and please don't share any of this with Amber. I will tell her, but I'm not ready for the tough love yet.'

'Of course. I won't say a word.' She looks at me with a concerned expression. 'Honey, why didn't you call me? You shouldn't have been on your own in such a state.'

'I know.' My shame comes flooding back. 'I was beside myself and my anxiety had kicked in again, so I wasn't thinking straight.'

I pause briefly as the waiter delivers the wine we ordered. We thank him and clink glasses.

'You know, winning this money, it was like everything changed overnight. I thought all my problems were solved. It put Dave to the back of my mind, though only temporarily, I now realise. I could quit my job and leave my bullying boss behind – who, by the way, I only went and bumped into again today.'

'*You didn't.*' Cat seems horrified.

'I did.' I shake my head, still struggling to believe it myself. 'But it's all fine, don't worry, I managed to walk away with my dignity intact. I'll tell you about that later. It's been a whirlwind twenty-four hours.'

'I'll say.'

'So, yeah, I thought my life was suddenly perfect, but I'm starting to wonder if anything's actually that much better. Sure, I have lots of new *stuff*, but that's about it. I'm clearly not over Dave. I just feel stupid and humiliated, and I'm starting to dread the idea of a new job as well. What if I end up with someone even worse than Karla for a boss?'

'I don't think anyone has the perfect life, no matter how much money they have,' she says. 'But you've not just got *stuff*, you've got opportunities you didn't have before – and to be honest, I don't think you could find a boss much worse than Karla.'

'I hope you're right,' I take a freshly baked bread roll from the basket on the table and tear it with a sigh. 'The thing is, Cat, I just can't help going over it all in my head, how I didn't so much as *suspect* Dave was seeing someone else. I mean, *who is it?* What if I know them? What if it's Melissa?'

'Does it matter who it is? Whoever they are, they won't be a patch on you.'

'Thanks.' I give her an appreciative smile. 'I can always rely on you to help me feel better. Anyway, I promised myself I wouldn't spend another evening moping, so let's talk about you. Has your mystery man been in touch? Are you still meeting him at the weekend?'

Right on cue, Cat's cheeks turn pink. 'Yes, I've had loads of messages and we're still going out on Saturday.'

'Oh, Cat. That's fab. You'll be planning your wedding in no time.'

'Please, don't jinx it, Emma.'

'Sorry. I couldn't help myself.' I give her a guilty grin.

With my confessions out of the way, and feeling lighter from having shared my woes, we're able to kick back and enjoy our meal. We giggle while throwing back our oysters, unable to do so with even the slightest hint of elegance. I treat Cat to a blow-by-blow account of my shopping experience while we moan with satisfaction over our mains of roasted cod and confit duck. Then we fantasise about our upcoming holiday over scrumptious salted caramel parfait and decaf cappuccinos.

After dinner, we head up to my suite to chill out before Cat heads home. We've agreed that, as much as it would be nice to go to the bar, it'll only remind me of last night. Anyhow, given I've paid a small fortune for the suite, we should really make use of it.

On entering the small living area, we gasp in surprise. Sitting on the coffee table is a bottle of sparkling wine in an ice bucket, accompanied by two champagne flutes and a plate of mouth-watering French macarons in a rainbow of colours.

'Hey, what's this?' I dive across to inspect the wine and find a card propped up against the ice bucket. Picking it up, I read the message and clamp a hand over my mouth.

'What's up?' Cat asks. 'It's not from Dave, is it? If it is, we're sending it back.'

'Ha, like Dave would send me this after how things went down. It's from the hotel. Listen to this: "Dear Ms Blake, we aim to make every guest's stay a perfect one, and we heard that you need some cheering up. Please accept this gift with our compliments. We would also like to offer you a complimentary late checkout tomorrow. We hope to see you again soon, Guest services."'

Cat bursts out laughing. '*Oh, my goodness!* You were right when you said the whole hotel must know what happened.'

'Tell me about it.' I groan, feeling really lame. 'I'm surprised they've taken the sympathetic stance, given I was involved in a noisy argument in the bar.'

'Well, you *are* paying them a lot of money to be here. And perhaps the barman and other staff members took your side in the end.'

'Maybe.' I eye up the chilled bottle of fizz. 'Shall we crack this open?'

Cat whoops as I pop the cork and pour us a couple of glasses. We make ourselves comfortable, sipping away at our wine in between chatting and polishing off the whole plate of macarons.

'I think we need some music,' I announce, once the bubbles have got to work.

Retrieving my phone, I pair it to the Bluetooth speaker by the TV, select an upbeat playlist from my Spotify app and turn the volume up.

It doesn't take long for us to get in the mood. After coaching Cat through her usual self-conscious stage, we end up dancing and singing the evening away, moving from room to room like a couple of excited kids, shaking it on the bed, even in the bathroom – something I could only do with my very best friend.

Eventually, we're all played out, and as my bed is big enough to host a small family, Cat ends up staying over. It reminds me of simpler, more innocent times – the sleepovers we used to have when we were young. As I'm drifting off to sleep, my last thought is whether any hotel staff have passed my suite this evening while undertaking their duties. If they have, they'll hopefully be pleased to hear that their gift very much did the trick.

Chapter Twenty-Seven

C at leaves the next morning, having kindly offered to receive my delivery from the department store, so that I can take advantage of my late check out. But not before the two of us make the most of the hotel's top notch breakfast service and eat so much that we're fit to burst.

I make the most of my last few hours in the hotel by indulging in some 'me time' in the swanky leisure club (I more or less have the pool, sauna and rooftop jacuzzi to myself, which is sheer bliss), then I chill out watching a movie in my suite, before tucking into a delicious pasta dish from the room service menu.

Shortly after finishing my lunch, my phone lights up with the incoming FaceTime call I've been waiting for. I hit the 'answer' button and Lottie's anxious face appears on the screen.

'Dear girl, what have you been up to – *again?*'

'A simple "hi" would have done.' I grin at her. 'It's arrived then?'

'Yes, it's arrived. *They* have arrived. They're absolutely

beautiful, Emma, but I simply cannot accept them. This is too much.'

'It's nothing less than you deserve. Anyway, you need some new clothes now you're socialising again. How was your sherry with your neighbour? Was it a man?' I raise my eyebrows suggestively

'No, it wasn't a man.' Lottie tuts at me affectionately. 'It was the lady who lives over the road. We got chatting the other day when I was out tending to my pansies, and I don't know what came over me, I just invited her over.'

'Good for you. I'm so pleased that you did that. I've always worried about you spending so much time alone.'

'It was nice having her company, I must admit. Although, I am fine by myself.'

I frown. 'I know you're "fine", but "fine" isn't good enough, Lottie. You need more from life. Loneliness is an epidemic in our country. I hate to think that you're part of that statistic.'

'I'm not though, am I? You've made sure of that.' She smiles at me.

'So, back to your new clothes... Are you going to try them on and show me?'

'What, now?' Lottie seems perplexed. 'You won't be able to see them on this little screen.'

'Uh-uh, don't you be making excuses.' I waggle my finger at her. 'Prop your iPad up somewhere, like on the table in your hallway, and then you can stand at a distance. I'll get enough of an idea.'

'Oh, Emma. I can see that you're not going to accept no for an answer. Though it may take a while. I'm not flexible like you young things.'

'I have time.'

I watch the random flitting images of Lottie's hallway on

the screen, as she attempts to position the iPad so that I can see a full-length view of her.

'That's perfect,' I say after several tries. 'Now off you go. I'll be here waiting.'

Over the next hour, Lottie tries on the three outfits I picked out for her. They're elegant, but also practical and casual enough for daytime wear, and they fit beautifully. I squeal with excitement each time she appears in front of the screen, which she seems to find entertaining.

'Thank you ever so much, my love.' Her face appears close-up again, after trying on the final piece. 'They are quite divine. You really should not have done that, but as it's clear that I have no say in the matter, I must accept them graciously.'

'Yes, you must. I'm glad you're finally getting it.' I beam at her angelically, noticing for the first time that she's looking tired and a bit pale, just like at the spa. 'Lottie, are you OK? You don't look so good.'

'I'm fine.' She dismisses my concerns, but her voice has weakened. 'It's nothing a sit down and a cup of tea won't fix.'

'OK... as long as you're sure. Get some rest and call me if you need anything.'

'Enough of the fussing, my love. Go and prepare for your big night out. I'm looking forward to hearing how it goes immensely.'

I reluctantly accept her direction and end the call. Then I realise that, in the flurry of excitement, I haven't told her about what happened with Dave. That's probably not such a bad thing – especially when I need to move past it.

Ensuring I've made the absolute most of my stay, I check out of the hotel and head back to Cat's, where I'm astonished to be met by a mountain of shopping bags. I wasn't aware that I'd bought quite so much.

'Hi.' Cat waves from the other side.

'Er... hi. *Jeez,* sorry about this Cat. I'll move everything into my room.'

'I can't wait to see what you've got.'

A while later, after showing a delighted Cat almost every single item, and modelling a few of them at her insistence, we decamp to the kitchen for a cup of tea. I talk to her a bit about my concern for Lottie, before lightening the tone.

'So, are you looking forward to your first taste of Amber beyond native soil?' I ask.

She pauses thoughtfully. 'I think it's going to be... a learning experience.'

'Very diplomatic, as ever.' I chuckle. 'You do know that when she and Rich go away, they're like a couple of kids – zero fear and incapable of relaxing. A right pair of adrenaline junkies.'

'Well, yes, I have heard about her adventures. Her comments at the travel agent did unnerve me slightly too. If Amber wants to seek out extreme sports while we're enjoying the best sun loungers, then that's fine. But there's no way I'm joining her.'

'Don't worry, she's pretty independent, so I'm sure she'll be happy on her own. It's her potential for mischief I'm more concerned about.'

We look at each other with wide (semi-jovial) eyes and start to laugh.

'Well...' says Cat. 'If there's one thing that's guaranteed, it's that it won't be a boring trip.'

~

Shortly after seven p.m., Cat knocks on my bedroom door.

'Come on in,' I call to her, and gasp in amazement as she enters the room. '*Cat! Wowsers!*'

Instead of wearing one of her usual nice-but-plain outfits to help her blend into the background, she's in a statement black and white print dress that ends halfway up her thighs. She has also tonged her hair into soft waves and is wearing more make up than usual – and she's completely pulled it off.

She hangs awkwardly in the doorway. 'Is it... OK?'

'*Are you kidding?*' I'm incredulous she can't see the impact of her transformation. 'You look like you've walked off a catwalk.'

'Nah, no way. Not with these legs. And this tummy. But I'm glad you like it.'

'Enough of that,' I scold her. 'I'm being deadly serious. What's brought about this change?'

She looks ever so slightly bashful. 'Actually, my inspiration for this is... well, you.'

'Me?'

'Yes, you. Your new image has made me feel really dowdy. So, I nipped to the shops after your delivery arrived, and got this dress and some new makeup. And I suppose... it's maybe a tiny bit because I'm keen to hold onto this one if I can...' She trails off self-consciously.

She is, of course, talking about her new man.

'Aww, hon. I'm glad I've inspired you, but when it comes to a bloke, you shouldn't feel you have to change who you are.'

'I don't. Not really. It's just that he always looks really smart and sexy, so I don't want to risk putting him off by not making an effort.'

I sit down on the bed while she looks at the floor, saying nothing. 'Cat, I would have done anything to get Dave to love me... to put me first and see me as the yin to his yang. I tried for four years, but it was a waste of time and energy – he was simply shallow and self-obsessed. I learned that the hard way. I don't want to see it happen to you.'

'Me neither,' she mumbles. 'But I also don't want to be single anymore. I really like this guy.'

'Look, you're the most kind, caring, loyal, fun-to-be-with person I know. And you're pretty with and without the makeup. If he's worth it, he'll like you for you – not what you look like. And if not, well... his loss, not yours.'

Cat stands quietly for a few moments longer. I really feel for her, having had such a tough time when it comes to men.

'You know, you're right.' Her spirits visibly lift and she sits down beside me. 'I'm not good at it, but I'll try to remember that.'

'Good.' I give her a little wink, happy to see her more positive.

'You look incredible too.' She takes in my chic, long-sleeved black mini dress and bling heels. 'Another fabulous outfit. And I just love your eye makeup. Those girls in the department store did their job well. Is the personal shopper one still coming tonight?'

'As far as I know. I don't have her number, I just gave her mine, so we'll have to wait and see.'

Twenty minutes later, we pile into our booked taxi, and as it tears along the city streets, I'm a jumble of nerves and excitement. With everything that's happened this week, I haven't given any thought to my 'champagne for everyone' announcement, and now I'm wondering if I should have rehearsed a little speech. I also have an uneasy feeling building in my stomach, because I've never been one for public speaking, and there's a reason for that.

'You OK?' Cat peers at my face.

'Yup... totally.' I'm keen to keep this looming issue locked away in my denial closet for now.

'Are you sure? You look a bit green all of a sudden.'

'Oh... well, I am feeling ever-so-slightly car sick.' This isn't actually a lie. Despite wearing seatbelts, we're being thrown around like ragdolls by the driver's overenthusiastic driving style.

Our taxi pulls up outside Liberté Nouveau, a cosy but popular hang-out just o George Street. We're the first to arrive, so we go straight to the bar to order a bottle of the house champagne, and while it's being poured, Amber appears.

'Cheers, you guys.' I hold out my glass and clink Cat and Amber's.

'*Cheers.*' They grin back at me.

I savour the cool, crisp and slightly fruity explosion of bubbles. It whips up that same giddy feeling of excitement I felt in the restaurant just over a week ago, and from what I can tell, it's having the same e ect on my friends.

'Has anyone heard from Sara?' I ask, as we make our way to the booth I reserved for this evening. 'I messaged her earlier, but she hasn't replied.'

'I bumped into to her last night on my way home,' says Amber. 'She's working late again — something about a day of back-to-back meetings, but I reckon it's back-to-back sex with the boss. I wonder if they actually pencil in—'

'Please stop.' I halt her in her tracks. 'Will you do me a favour and leave out that chat tonight? *Please*? We have new people joining us, and I'd rather Sara isn't introduced to them in that way. I also don't want you scaring them off.'

'What are you, like the fun police or something?' Amber surveys me disdainfully. 'I hope you're going to chill out once you have some booze in you. Here, have some more champagne.'

She tops up my still two-thirds full glass, while I attempt a convincing 'I'm serious' face.

'I feel bad for Sara,' says Cat. 'I know she enjoys her job and gets overtime, but this is bordering on slave labour.'

'Is it?' asks Amber, a cheeky glint in her eye. 'Or maybe she's a slave of a different—'

'*Amber.*' I stop her short again.

'*Oh. Come. On.*' She throws her hands up in the air. 'Cat handed me that one on a plate.'

'All I'm saying is that Sara works really hard,' says Cat. 'And if she really is having a relationship—'

'Affair.' Amber corrects her.

'OK, if she is having an affair with her boss – remember we don't actually have any proof of that – then I'm sure she's not... having it off with him all day, every day.'

Amber hoots with laughter.

'Right, *enough,* Amber.' I come to Cat's rescue. 'Stop winding her up.'

'Aww... *muuumm,*' she mocks me.

'And don't even think about starting on me... oh, hi.'

We're interrupted by the arrival of Cameron, who's immediately followed by Jana and Trudy.

'Hi, *all of you.*' I clap my hands with excitement. 'Thanks so much for coming. Trudy, I thought you couldn't make it.'

'Change of plan.' She punches the air with a triumphant fist.

'I'm so glad,' I say and quickly introduce everyone. 'So, how are you two ladies?' I ask her and Jana.

'Exhausted,' says Jana.

'Ditto.' Trudy agrees. 'But ready for some fun.'

They both look fresh-faced and perky to me.

'Busy day?' I ask.

'Like you wouldn't believe.' Jana sighs theatrically. 'It felt like every tourist in the city spent the day in our store today. And we're both working tomorrow, but that won't stop us, will it, Trudy?'

'No way.'

'How about you, Cameron?' I ask. 'How was your Friday?'

'Oh, fabulous as ever, lovely.' He reaches out and touches my hair as if it's a piece of fine art. 'Another day of performing miracles. It's what I live for.'

'And the world thanks you for it.' I give him a little salute.

I leave my friends – old and new – to chat while I head to the bar. Based on my limited knowledge of Cameron, I'm fully expect that he and Amber will be competing to be the centre of attention in no time. I only hope she reels it in a bit and doesn't end up o ending him.

While I'm waiting for the barman to prepare the two bottles of champagne I've ordered, a male voice comes from my right.

'Champagne, eh? Celebrating something?'

I turn and find myself looking at a man around my age. He's tall, with a slim-but-muscular physique, dirty blond hair and striking blue eyes. Not what I'd call my type, but still nice to look at.

'Erm... yes... sort of.' I desperately try to think up a fake reason for our festivities, because I know what the next question's going to be.

'What's the occasion?'

'Well... it's kind of... personal.' I hope my vagueness will put him o .

'*Aha*... it's your engagement party.'

'Nope. I'm happily unattached.' I'm flattered that he's

interested enough to be fishing, but disappointed he's not letting it go. 'I'm... celebrating new doors being opened.'

'Well, aren't you cryptic.' He eyes me, and I feel myself blush, more from his scrutiny than any sense of enjoying his attention.

Thankfully, the barman interrupts our little 'to and fro', indicating to me that he'll bring the champagne over.

'Well, I'd better get back to my friends,' I say. 'See you later.'

'I certainly hope so...'

I realise that he's waiting for my name. 'Emma.'

'Good to meet you, Emma. I'm Simon.'

I turn and walk away, feeling his eyes on me. While it's a nice compliment to be chatted up, he was a little full on, and anyway, I'm giving men a wide berth for the foreseeable future. Tonight is about me and my friends – and that's it.

Back at our booth, I'm delighted to see that everyone's getting on brilliantly, and that Sara's arrived. She's standing next to our booth chatting to Jana.

'*Sara!*' I call over the rabble of music and voices. 'I'm so glad you're here.'

She excuses herself from her conversation and struts across to me, planting air kisses either side of my face. 'Great atmosphere! Well done, girlfriend.'

'Thanks. How are you?' I ask. 'I've been concerned about you working all these hours. They're asking too much of you, Sara.'

'Sweetie, it's fine.' She snakes an affectionate arm around my shoulders. 'Honestly. The project is an interesting change for me and the extra money's great for topping up my wardrobe. We can't all be nearly-millionaires, you know.'

I look away, embarrassed by her words. I hope she

doesn't think I've already forgotten what it's like to be tied to a job or to have to budget tightly.

'I didn't mean—' I go to apologise, but she's laughing.

'*Relax*. I was kidding. I'm happy, so there's nothing for you to worry about.'

'I guess I'm still disappointed that you can't come with us next week.'

'Sure, I am too. But it's no biggie. Your new additions are super nice, by the way. You're a good judge of character.'

'With friends maybe. Perhaps not so much with men.' I fill her in on my altercation with Dave and running out on James at the travel agency.

'Hey, don't beat yourself up.' Sara lifts my chin with her finger. 'Dave wasn't right for you and maybe this James isn't either. But don't give up on men altogether. You need to shop around, figure out what kind of guy meets your needs. Have a few on the go at a time.'

'That's an apt choice of metaphor, coming from you, Ms Shopaholic. It's not really my thing, though. I struggled enough to keep *one* man in my life.'

'Actually...' She arches an eyebrow. 'More than one man means less pressure, because you're less invested. If one doesn't work out then you have other options so there's less chance you'll get hurt. You don't have to sleep with them all. Enjoy their company, lap up the attention. It'll help mend that bruised ego of yours.'

'You certainly seem to know what you're talking about. Have you had to do the same in the past?'

'Not really...' Sara purses her lips. 'Not for that reason anyway. I've always been the one who does the dumping.'

'*Well now I feel better,*' I wail.

'Oh, sweetie, no.' Sara yanks me in and strokes my hair, making me feel like her pet pooch. 'Let's just say I see the world a little differently to you. It comes from... never mind. I'm not looking to settle down. I live for me, for enjoying myself – and for my Jimmy Choos, of course. But I know that you want something different, and I believe that, if you broaden your options and focus on having a good time, you'll find a smoking hot guy who can't get enough of you.'

'Thanks, Sara. I'll think it over.' I give her a grateful hug, and we rejoin the others.

Chapter Twenty-Eight

With an excitable Friday night feeling in the air, it's not long before things get lively. As I predicted, Amber and Cameron are locking horns, but to my relief, it's all good natured. Having had an arm-wrestling contest – which Amber won despite being half his size – they're now engaged in a bizarre drinking game, which involves launching wasabi peas at each other's champagne flutes and swigging at their fizz each time one lands in their drink which, unsurprisingly, isn't often . The rest of us are chatting and enjoying watching this theatre unfold.

I've still to make my 'champagne for everyone' announcement, but as I feel distinctly queasy every time the thought of it pops into my head, I'm now leaning towards conveniently forgetting about it – if I can get away with that. This evening with my friends – old and new – is perfect as it is, so hopefully Cat, Amber and Sara are having such a great time that they'll forget about it too.

While sat in the booth chatting to Trudy about what led to her family plans being cancelled, I sense someone hovering near me. Expecting it to be one of my friends, I turn with a smile and I'm surprised to see that it's Simon from the bar.

'Oh, hi there,' I greet him.

'Hello... Emma.' There's a hint of a slur in his voice, but he seems in good enough form. 'Mind if I join you?'

I hesitate, not really wanting to say yes, but having been put on the spot, I don't feel like I have a choice. 'Erm... sure, take a seat.' I shift over to let him squeeze into the booth beside me.

Looking around the table self-consciously, I note that Amber has clocked our new arrival and is wearing a devious expression. *Oh god, please don't start.*

'Who's your *friend*, Emma?' she calls across to me and everyone looks at me expectantly.

'Eh... this is Simon.'

'*Hi, Simon,*' they chorus to my embarrassment.

'Hi.' He gives them a wave, then turns to me. 'Do these friends of yours have names too?'

'Sorry... yes.' I work my way round the group. 'This is Sara, Jana, Cat, Cameron, Amber and Trudy. I only met Jana, Cameron and Trudy this week, but they feel like lifelong friends already.' I beam at the three of them.

'I'll toast to that!' Cameron cheers at the exact moment the music cuts out, making everyone laugh.

'So, how come you just met this week?' Simon asks.

He really is an inquisitive one.

'Well, there's a question...' I laugh, stalling for time, while shooting a blatant under-no-circumstances-do-you-divulge-the-truth warning look to my friends.

They seem to get the message loud and clear, but that doesn't stop Amber having some fun.

'They're her hair stylist, her makeup artist and her

personal shopper,' She grins wickedly, before recommencing her drinking game with Cameron.

'*Really?*' Simon is wide-eyed. 'It must have been quite a week, Emma. May I ask what kind of "doors" have opened for you?'

Thanks for that, Amber. Now what do I tell him? I glance around the table again, this time seeking a bail out, but my friends have returned to their own conversations, no doubt to give me some privacy (that I don't actually want). I try to think of something plausible to answer Simon's question, but being rattled and a bit irritated by his persistence, I come up with nothing.

'Look, would you mind if I didn't say?' I try to communicate this politely, but my annoyance unfortunately sneaks through. 'As I said, it's kind of personal, and... we've only just met.'

A flicker of what seems like resentment passes across Simon's face, making me uneasy.

'Sure. Everyone's entitled to a private life.' His smile appears forced as he slowly gets up, once again attracting the attention of my friends. 'I'll leave you to enjoy your night. It was nice to meet you, Emma. See you later, everyone' He gives another wave to my friends who wave back, seemingly confused by this turn of events.

Watching him walk away, a wave of guilt sweeps over me. He was a nice enough guy, if a bit full on, and I completely snubbed him. The moment he's out of earshot, Cat starts quizzing me.

'What happened, honey? Are you OK?'

I fill her and the others in, and to my relief, they unanimously agree that I have absolutely no obligation to divulge my personal life to anyone who asks.

'Thanks, guys. You're the best. Now let's get back to

what this is really all about.' I raise my glass, inviting them to join me and they reciprocate, flutes clinking, while Amber and Cameron throw in some encouraging whoops.

The lively ambience quickly returns, and it's not long before my mishap with Simon is forgotten.

'*Hey, Emma,*' Amber shouts across the table, way louder than necessary. 'When are you doing your big announcement?'

'Oh yeah, I nearly forgot about that,' says Cat. 'Better not put it o too long or you'll miss your opportunity.'

Damn. So much for them forgetting about it.
Instead of being diluted by the reassuring hug of a few glasses of champagne, my nerviness at the idea of standing up in this bar full of people has intensified. I now *really* don't want to do it – and especially not after what happened with Simon.

'What announcement, Emma?' Jana asks. 'You haven't told us about it.'

'Nor me,' says Cameron. 'C'mon, lovely. Spill.'

'It's nothing really. Just a daft idea I had.' I'm hot with embarrassment at the thought of telling them my plan – but with all eyes on me, it seems I have no choice. 'I... um... I wanted to do that thing that you see in films... you know, where someone shouts "champagne for everyone". Totally ridiculous, I know.'

'It is *not,*' Cameron states. 'It's fricking awesome. What are you waiting for?'

'I'm... I mean...' There's no point in even finishing my sentence. With Cameron being as fearless as Amber, it's clear that he'll never understand my concerns.

'What is it, Emma?' Cat seems to have tuned into my discomfort.

'Nothing... I'm just having such a good night with you guys, I don't want to ruin it by—'

'*Poor excuse!*' Amber gives me a thumbs down.

'Anyway...' I turn desperately back to Cat, my only possible escape route now being the bare truth. 'I'm also a bit... um... OK, I'm terrified.'

'Aww, honey,' she says. 'You don't have to do anything you don't want to.'

Trudy and Jana both nod sympathetically.

'Thanks for understanding.' I smile gratefully at them. 'I know it's a cop out but—'

'I think you should do it,' Sara says suddenly.

I turn and look at her hopelessly.

'Come on, sweetie.' She reaches across the table and takes my hands in hers. 'You've been handed a brand-new start and you said you want your life to be different. Now's the time to face your fears. It won't be nearly as bad as you think.'

My frantic eyes land on Cat once more, but she simply shrugs, clearly feeling my pain but also seeing Sara's logic.

'I suppose...' I fan my face in an attempt to stem my rising panic. 'But it's so loud in here. I'll never get everyone's attention.'

'Leave that to us.' Amber gives me a sly wink.

Before I know what's happening, she and Cameron have scrambled into a standing position on the seats, dinging their champagne flutes with cutlery snaffled from another table and hollering at the punters in the bar to be quiet. Gradually the voices die down, and a sea of curious faces turn in our direction. Cameron signals to one of the bar staff to turn down the music, and to my surprise, he obliges.

'Emma, you're up.' Amber gives me a nod.

With my heart in my throat, I climb shakily onto my

seat, where, seeing so many people staring back at me, I'm paralysed by stage fright. Thankfully, Cameron's impatience quickly resurfaces to give me the kick up the backside I need.

'Emma, lovely, you've about five seconds before you lose them. Or they turn on you. *JFDI*.'

He's right. There's already a murmur welling up across the bar. I have to do this *now*.

Taking a deep calming breath, I start to speak. 'Erm... hi... everyone.' I sound like a balloon with a leak. 'You've... all made a good... no... a *great* choice, in coming here... to this bar tonight...'

I trail off and glance down at my friends, who are all giving me encouraging looks and gestures. My eyes meet Cat's and she mouths, 'You've got this.' It's exactly what I need to keep going.

'So, the thing is... I'm celebrating something... special... with my amazing friends... and I'd like you all to be part of it...'

'*Get to the point!*' a voice from the crowd yells.

'Sorry... OK... so, what I mean is... I'd like to buy champagne... *for everyone!*'

Despite my faltering, cringeworthy speech, the bar suddenly erupts with cheering and clapping, and there's a surge towards the bar. I'm still shaking uncontrollably, and I won't be winning any awards for public speaker of the year, but I've done it and that's what matters.

While I'm recovering, someone taps me on the shoulder. I turn, half expecting it to be Simon again, but it's the barman who served me earlier.

'Hi there.' Perhaps he's come to thank me for giving them so much extra business.

'Might I have a word?'

Shit. He doesn't look, or sound, particularly grateful. 'Of course, what's up?'

'I'm sure you meant well with that little speech there, but the problem is, we don't have enough champagne in stock. You've already almost cleaned us out.'

My stomach sinks as I tune out of the barman's words and into the noise in the background. The punters at the bar have started chanting, 'champagne, champagne!' and look like they're minutes away from turning rowdy.

'Oh... my god. I'm so sorry.'

'I'm sure you are.' He raises his eyebrows at me. 'And, as you got us into this mess, you're going to have to get us out of it.'

'Of course, anything.' I push up my sleeves like I going into battle. 'What do you need me to do?'

Chapter Twenty-Nine

The barman gives me my orders, which include making a second announcement and a payment up front for the drinks.

'Consider it done.' I give a resolute nod, then draft in Amber's help and climb to my feet again, this time with no chance even to think about what I'm doing. The chanting is getting louder and louder, and a couple of 'missiles' have already been thrown at the bar, which means I need to fix this – *fast*.

The barman takes off to deal with the rest of the fallout from my idiocy, while Amber and Cameron get everyone's attention again, though it takes a lot longer this time.

'Erm, hi... again,' I address the sea of impatient faces once they've settled down enough for me to speak. 'It turns out there's not enough champagne to give to you all. Silly me...'

'*Loser!*' someone shouts, and I do my best to ignore them.

'So, anyway...' My pulse is racing, my awkwardness shining through like a beacon. 'I still want to buy you all drinks... I've agreed with the bar staff that you can have any drink of your choice, except champagne or shots — for the next hour. Oh, and... one drink at a time. No double measures. Anyone taking the piss, or giving the bar staff hassle, won't be served again... and... neither will that guy who called me a loser.' That gets a bit of a laugh, making me feel less like I'm going to have a heart attack. 'So, I guess all that's left to say is... *enjoy your night!*'

There's another roaring cheer. I even get a smattering of applause, before everyone turns back towards the bar, order seemingly restored.

After dashing across to make the agreed upfront payment, I flop down on my seat, take a swig from my champagne and sigh heavily.

'Well done, Emma!' Trudy gives me a double thumbs up. 'You totally nailed it — second time round.' She giggles, and I return the gesture with a grimace.

'Nice save, girlfriend.' Sara high fives me. 'You did good.'

'Emma, I'm so proud of you.' Cat pulls me into a squeezy hug. 'That was really brave getting up there... and twice.'

'It's not like I had much choice.' I eye Amber and Cameron, who feign innocence.

For the next hour, the atmosphere in the bar is electric. My friends are in top form and keep playing back my botched announcement, which has been the source of much hilarity. Other punters in the bar approach me to thank me and quickly get involved in the fun, causing our group to expand significantly. Thankfully, no one presses me to share my situation like Simon did. All they seem to care about is my apparent generosity. I'm so ecstatic at how it's turned out that I can't suppress the ridiculous grin that's plastered across my face. It's exactly how I imagined it, though perhaps without the stuttering and naïve oversight on my part.

Excusing myself from a conversation with Jana, I sneak off to the ladies to touch up my makeup, and as I'm heading back through the short corridor towards the main bar, Simon emerges from the men's loos.

'Hello, again.' I decide I'll be a little less guarded this time.

'There she is, the woman of the moment.' He waves his arms in mock praise. 'Nice touch, buying everyone drinks.'

'Thanks.' I make a point of laughing at his joke, noting that the slur in his voice has become more evident. 'You look like you've been taking full advantage of it.'

'I have.' He sways slightly before me. 'So... am I allowed to show my appreciation to the woman of the moment?'

'Erm... yes, I... guess so.' Bit of a weird question. Does he want to buy me a drink in return?

'Nice one.' He stumbles towards me, and I instinctively move back.

'*Hey, what's wrong?*' He seems offended. 'I was going to give you a thank you kiss.'

Oh hell. This is not good.

He approaches me once more, and unsure of what else to do, I put up a hand to stop him.

'All right, you.' I try to keep my tone light and jovial to avoid things escalating. 'I don't need a kiss. What would people think if I went around kissing everyone I bought drinks for? Maybe... you could buy me a drink as a thank you instead?'

Just like earlier, Simon's mood seems to switch in an instant. 'Think you're too good for the likes of me, Emma?'

My irritation with him returns. '*What?* No. That's not it. I... need to get back to my friends.'

'You're a bit stuck up, aren't you?'

'Look, Simon—'

'Bit of a princess, eh?' He's now so close that I can smell the alcohol on his breath. 'I bet Mummy and Daddy bought you a pony and a castle, and now you've decided to pity the commoners by throwing scraps to them...'

I can't believe what I'm hearing. How dare he judge me like this! My irritation shifts up a gear.

'It's not my fault you can't take rejection,' I throw back without thinking. 'If I'm so up myself, then why won't you leave me alone?'

At first, Simon regards me with derision, then his demeanour becomes darker and more threatening.

'Shut it, you little *slut*...' His voice drips with contempt. I take yet another step back and make contact with the wall. 'You're nothing but a basic bitch who throws her money around to make herself look good.'

He's not actually touching me, but his broad frame towering over me is as menacing as his words. The anxiety I've been wrestling to keep under control this last couple of weeks bubbles up, and I start to panic. I want to scream at him that he's got me all wrong and to leave me alone, but I can't get the words out. And there's no one around to help me. Frightened tears spill down my cheeks.

'And here come the waterworks, right on cue,' Simon continues to berate me. 'You're all the same, you rich bitches. All money and show, and no *fucking substance*. Nothing but a *sad little tease*.'

'*Get away from her,*' a male voice suddenly thunders out of nowhere.

'This is none of your business, mate,' Simon growls back at the man. 'This is between me and my girl.'

'You've just made it my business, *mate*.' The man's tone is harsh and commanding. 'I don't care if she *is* your girl. Get away the fuck away from her, before I make you.'

I can't see the man behind Simon, but it's clear he's not going to let this go.

Simon holds his position for a few seconds longer, then obviously decides that this isn't a fight worth having. Shooting me one last filthy look, he stumbles down the corridor towards the bar, while I slide down the wall, head in my hands, gasping for breath.

'Are you OK?' The man approaches me. 'I know it's none of my business, but that looked pretty bad. He has no right to treat you like that.'

With the threat of the situation having passed, I'm finally able to process my surroundings, and I release that I know that voice. Lifting my head, I find myself looking at James.

'*Emma?* What the... I didn't recognise you there. Are you OK?' He bends down, gently cupping my face with his hands.

My tortured eyes meet his and as he holds my gaze, a feeling of deep humiliation takes over me. I know how this must have looked: like Simon and I were together, and quite possibly like I was being an almighty tease. I look away quickly, my senses locked in overdrive, self-preservation being the overriding instinct. This fuels a sense of illogical defensiveness, ultimately propelling me to bat his hands away from my face.

'*What is it about you, James?* You seem to turn up everywhere, playing the god damn hero.'

'Huh? No, Emma, I was just—'

'What? Concerned? Worried about me? *Why?*' I swipe at my eyes with my sleeve, as if to erase my vulnerability. 'I don't even know you. Is this what you do with women? Pull shit like this so you can get them into bed?'

'Emma, that's not it at all.' James rubs his jaw, brows

tightly knitted. 'You've had a shock and you're misreading this. Let me...'

'I don't need to *let you* do anything,' I bite back. 'Can you not get the message? It's weird, you suddenly turning up like this. *Please, leave me alone.*'

I defiantly get to my feet. James studies me for a moment, hurt seeming to cloud his face, but I'm so done. Right now, no man deserves even an ounce of my trust.

'This isn't what you think, Emma. But I hear you, and I'm gone.' Turning away, he strides back down the corridor and disappears through the door to the bar.

Moments later, Cat, Sara and Amber burst through it, take one look at my wobbly bottom lip, and bundle me into the toilets.

I fill them in what happened with Simon and how James intervened, but I leave out the fact that I snapped at him because I know I'll get a hard time for that – and it's not something I can cope with right now. Once I've had a good cry and deterred Amber from going after Simon, they clean me up and I reapply my eye makeup. We head back into the bar to join the others, and try to keep the fun of the evening alive, but it's not the same. Eventually, Cat senses that I've had enough and we take a taxi home, my head resting miserably on her shoulder. It's the worst possible end to what had been a phenomenal evening-slash-grand finale to my big week.

Chapter Thirty

I wake up on Saturday morning with a pounding thick head. At first, I'm disorientated, then as I gingerly lift my head o the pillow, the events of the previous night come flooding back.

Why did it have to go so wrong? It had been a fantastic evening. Even my faux pas with the 'champagne for everyone' announcement, though it didn't amuse the bar staff, was actually quite funny. It added to the experience. Gave us something to remember, to laugh and joke about at our table – creating the type of fond memories Lottie wanted me to have. Had things continued that way, it would have been the best night out I've ever had.

My mind keeps transporting me back to that moment in the corridor when Simon cornered me. I shiver, remembering how intimidated I felt, how cruel his words were. Then James turning up, trying to be the rescuer yet again, and me laying it on him. What was he even doing there? Should I be concerned – or suspicious – that he just happened to turn up the moment I was in trouble?

After checking my phone, which is displaying messages

from Amber, Sara, Cameron, Jana and Trudy, all asking how I'm doing, I hear Cat open my door a crack, no doubt to check on me.

'*I'm awake,*' I call to her. 'Come in.'

'How are you feeling this morning?' She enters the room, climbing onto the other side of the bed and reaching over to give me a hug.

'Hungover. And a bit miserable.'

'I'm not surprised.' She peers at me with a concerned face.

'Cat, why did it have to end up like that?'

'Oh, honey, I don't know. That Simon bloke clearly has issues.'

'I guess.' I shrug. 'Though he made out that *I* was the one showing off... and that I led him on.'

'Don't you go blaming yourself.' She takes my hand and clasps it tight. '*He* chose to pursue you. And *he* chose to intimidate you.'

'He was drunk. *Really* drunk. I obviously offended him when he came to speak to us—'

'Emma, please don't do this to yourself. He didn't have to get hammered. Did you see anyone else that drunk? I bet not. You are *not* responsible for the actions of a grown man.'

'You're right, I'm not,' I say, feeling more convinced.

'I'm just so glad that James found you when he did,' says Cat. 'He really was brave standing up to Simon.'

I smart a little at the mention of James, and Cat seeing him for something that he's not. But I bite my tongue, not wanting to seem ungrateful.

'It *was* intimidating.' I rearrange the covers around me. 'I can't deny that. But in hindsight, because of where it happened, someone was bound to pass through and intervene.'

'I suppose so. I'm just so glad you're OK.' She leans back against the headboard, stretching her legs out in front of her. 'So, not to labour the point, but... as James *was* the hero, you must see now that he's a good guy?'

Not this again. This is the last thing I want to discuss right now.

'Surely anyone would have done what he did.' I'm careful to keep my tone casual.

'Perhaps. But maybe not. He certainly seemed very concerned for you when he told us what had happened.'

'He spoke to you? Ah, so that's why you knew to come through and get me.'

'Yeah, honey.' Cat's expression suggests that she thinks this was obvious.

'Well, perhaps on some level I owe him a thank you, but it doesn't change the fact that he's arrogant. He seems to love it, playing the rescuer. That must be his thing.'

'Whatever.' Cat smiles and shakes her head at me.

'I mean, what was he doing there anyway?' I frown. 'I seem to keep running into him. It's too weird. Why is it always the people you don't want to see that turn up everywhere?'

'Eh... actually...' She looks shifty all of a sudden.

'What did you do?'

'Me? Nothing. But... Amber might have sneaked a peek at his business card in your purse and messaged him.'

'*She didn't.*'

'She did. But to be fair, she didn't know about you seeing him yesterday and how badly that went. It also sounds as if James was in two minds as to whether he should pop along – he was out with friends not far from us – but you know Amber, she's very persuasive. The poor guy had only just arrived when he nipped to the loo and... well, you know what happened next.'

'What the *fuuuck?*' I groan, rubbing my forehead in exasperation. 'I could kill Amber sometimes... *oh... no...*'

A sick feeling washes through me as I piece everything together. That James didn't *happen* to turn up. He was invited – by my friend. And I more or less accused him of being up to something when he did exactly what any person should do when they witness someone being harassed. Plus, he didn't even know it was me at first. In amongst all the drama and the unbearable stress of the situation, I forgot about that.

Like the flick of a switch, I finally see James for who he really is – kind, caring, the opposite of Dave. Not to mention utterly gorgeous – now I finally allow myself to admit it. The kind of guy any woman with half a brain would want in their life. And now he's seen the worst side of me. Not who I really am, but who I became in the moment. A moment of confusion and panic, where my threat response was in overload and I wasn't in control. *Oh god, I've really messed up.*

'What is it, Emma?' Cat asks. 'What's wrong?'

'I... um... can we maybe talk about something else?'

'Sure, whatever you need.' She rubs my shoulder supportively while I try to ignore the gut-wrenching churning in my stomach.

'Oh, Cat, tonight's the night of your big date,' I say, finally tuning into the present. 'How are you feeling about it?'

She plays with the ring on her right hand. 'It's been rearranged.'

'What? Why?' I cross my fingers that she's not about to be blown off again.

'Something came up.'

'What "something"? What could be more important than taking you out? It had better be a good excuse – like a death in the family or something.'

Cat raises her eyebrows at me and I wince.

'Argh, you know what I mean. It had better be a genuine, unavoidable reason, because I won't stand by and see my best friend get hurt by some—'

'Emma, please shut up. It was me who asked to postpone, not him.'

I blink at her. 'But why?'

'Because it didn't... feel right.'

'What do you mean it didn't "feel right"? You've been on top of the world all week looking forward to this. It's been oozing out of you.'

She looks out the window and a thought passes through my mind. 'Wait a minute... you've postponed because you don't want to leave me on my own tonight.'

'No, it wasn't like... I mean, I didn't...' She trails off looking distinctly guilty.

'*What the hell, Cat?* I'm fine. I don't need a babysitter. Sure, I got a bit of a fright last night. Maybe I'll be a bit more cautious when I talk to men in bars. But I'm not going to turn this into something it's not.'

'Hey, calm down.' She pats my leg. 'I know that. I thought you might want some company, that's all. You were really shaken, so you can't blame me for wanting to look after you.'

This is true. I can't.

'OK, OK. Cat, thank you. I really don't know what I'd do without you. But seriously, you need to contact that man and change your date back to tonight before he makes other plans – or worse, thinks you're not interested.' I climb out of bed and give a big stretch to prove that I really am fine.

'He won't think that. He was understanding and said that I was right to look out for you.'

'Which means he sounds like a keeper, so get yourself moving and back on the path to true love.'

'Right.' She snickers at the adamant look on my face. 'I can tell I won't be welcome here this evening.'

'That is correct. You are not. *Chop chop.*'

~

In the evening, with Cat out on her date and having exhausted my capacity for binge watching TV shows, I become increasingly restless. I genuinely thought I was fine, but as it turns out, the cumulative impact of recent events has eroded my resilience to the fragility of a crumbling cliff edge. Though I make a valiant attempt at keeping myself positive and upbeat, the negative, burdensome thoughts that have been lurking finally break through and start to plague me.

The way I treated James weighs on me heavily. I could never have known that Amber had invited him to join us, and I *was* in shock, but I still should have shown a bit of gratitude. I've read his sense of humour, confidence and concern as him wanting to be the 'big man'. He has so many similar characteristics to Dave that it was almost impossible not to draw comparisons, but there's one defining difference between them, I now realise: he's not a self-absorbed dickhead. I feel physically sick at the thought of James now hating me and thinking that I'm the 'basic bitch' Simon made me out to be.

My troubled mind flits to another memory: the smell of alcohol on Simon's breath, how vicious he was and how vulnerable and panicked I felt in that moment. Then thoughts of Dave's infidelity flood my consciousness. Why was he unfaithful? And why do I care so much? I should be glad to be rid of him, but not knowing who he cheated with is gnawing at me. No matter how much I distract myself with fun, friends and bank funds, that unanswered question seems to undermine everything.

Unable to shake myself back into a more positive frame of mind, I realise that a change of scenery is badly needed, so I go for a walk to clear my head.

It turns out to be the best possible distraction. I wander right along Fountainbridge and down Lothian Road, entertained by the Saturday night revellers behaving in ways they would never dare to in the stark (and sober) light of day. I pass a man declaring his undying love for a woman, who by the look on her face, has no idea who he is. A group of women try to ignore the fact that their friend is throwing up in a bin, while three young-looking guys (probably students) fight over a single doner kebab.

Despite being on my own, I feel quite comfortable. There are enough people around and there's almost a sense of community that doesn't exist during the day. People who would normally avoid eye contact at all costs, transported into a world where everyone's a potential friend or date. It's such a mood lifter that I keep walking for some time, enjoying the distraction of the action around me.

After a while, I realise that I've inadvertently gravitated towards Stockbridge where Cat's on her date, and an idea creeps into my mind. I could sneak a look at her new man. Would that be so bad? She wouldn't even need to know I'd been there. And surely, the worst I could be accused of is being nosey.

Now just a couple of blocks from the bar, I know I'm fighting a losing battle with myself. I don't have the willpower to respect Cat's privacy, because I'm too intrigued. The longer she keeps this man a secret, the more I want to know who he is.

The exterior of the bar is traditional and welcoming, with whitewashed walls, imitation candles framing the entrance and Georgian-style sash windows that are the perfect height to take a peek through without being spotted. The cloak of darkness around me also acts as a helpful camouflage, allowing me to see in better than anyone can see out. I peer inside, taking in the traditional wooden floorboards and the tasteful minimalist furniture, all occupied by happy looking couples and small groups. It's so inviting that, for a second, I feel a bit lonely standing outside on my own. Pushing that feeling away, I focus on the excitement of the task at hand. Let's get a look at this secret man Cat's been squirreling away.

I scan the space and my eyes eventually land on Cat. *Bingo.* She's just emerged from the door to the toilets, and is making her way across the room. She joins a man standing by the bar, and although I can't see his face, I can tell from his body language that he's enjoying her presence. He slips his arm round her waist affectionately, and she laughs, whispering something in his ear. The intimacy between them is evident: comfortable, flirty, like they've known each other a while.

Frustrated that I can only see the back of him, I move to another window to get a better view. I can't see Cat's face anymore, but I can almost make out her new man's profile. Then, by a stroke of luck, another man approaches the bar. Cat's companion acknowledges him and shifts over to make space, allowing me to finally get a proper look at him.

What the fuck? My stomach lurches and I stare in disbelief and panic, unable to comprehend the scene before me.

Rather than clapping my eyes on a handsome stranger as I expected, the man cosying up to my best friend is Dave.

Backing away from the window, I desperately try to catch my breath and shake off the unbearable nausea that consumes me. A passing couple watch me, and I shy away from them, unable to stomach any concerned looks or offers of help. I need to get out of here. With my most primal instincts in charge, I take off down the road, running as fast as I can manage, and hail the first taxi that I see.

Chapter Thirty-One

Arriving back at Cat's flat, I'm shaking to the point that I can barely get my key in the lock and my legs are threatening to give way. After a few failed attempts, I throw open the door, tear down the hallway and launch myself onto the bed in her spare room, sobbing my heart out. The scene of Cat and Dave getting up close and personal seems to have been programmed on repeat in my mind.

How could this be? My best friend and my ex. Right under my nose.

Unable to comprehend what I've witnessed, it's like I'm suffocating, tears streaming down my face for the second time this weekend. I go over and over what I saw, trying to find the part where I got things wrong and the man she was with wasn't actually Dave – but much as I wish that my eyes have deceived me, there's no mistake. I saw them plain as day. They were intimate, familiar, touchy-feely. I just can't believe that she'd do that. We've been inseparable since we were kids, and she's never done anything remotely bad or wicked in her life – especially not to me. We tell each other things we'd never tell anyone else. As far as I know, she doesn't have a single secret I don't know about.

But she does, a little voice in my head reminds me. She's been keeping this man hidden away, making out that her budding relationship is too new and shiny and vulnerable to share. What if that wasn't the full truth?

It still doesn't make sense, though. The Cat I know would never *dream* of betraying me.

Come on, Emma, don't be naïve. These things do happen. 'My best friend slept with my boyfriend'. It's a well-worn headline from women's magazines.

But why would Cat go near Dave when she knew how he treated me?

Sadly, I already know the answer to that one. Dave was absolutely charming for the first couple of years. He knew how to play the ultimate boyfriend – while it was in his interests to do so. Then things shifted, so subtly and slowly that I didn't notice until it was too late. I made so many excuses for him.

No doubt Dave has persuaded Cat that he wasn't being so awful to me; that we just weren't right for each other and that I'd realise it was for the best. She's been so desperate to have a successful relationship that she's probably fooled herself into thinking he's genuine. And she'll know it's wrong, but perhaps can't stop herself. The need to feel wanted, desirable, even just for a few minutes, stronger than any attack of conscience. Then, with that line crossed, it has been be easier to justify doing it again and again. Because the damage has already been done.

I get up and pace around the room, searching my memory for any other signs that I've missed. At first, I come up empty handed, but then little snippets begin to surface.

So fleeting, I almost can't catch them as they whizz through my mind. Those strange, troubled looks I saw on Cat's face. She was the one who rescued me from the park on D-day. I never questioned for a second why Dave had her number. The strength of her reaction when I told her I had met up with him this week – was it jealousy, perhaps? And, of course, keeping her new man (who might not be so new after all) a secret when she always shared everything with me. I thought I understood. Her explanations made sense, but it must have been an attempt to conceal what was really going on. Cat also talked about how her bloke had been away with his friends, while Dave had mentioned being away too – at the same time. I can't deny that it all adds up.

Realising there are so many signs that I've missed, it's clear that I've not just been blind, I've been a complete fool. I didn't have a clue.

What am I going to do? I can't stay here at Cat's and pretend everything's OK. I have to confront her about this, which means I'm about to find myself homeless for the second time in just a few weeks. I have the money to get my own place, but that's not going to happen overnight and there's no way I'm going to stay with my parents. There's only one solution: I'll need to check back into a hotel.

Wrestling with the urge to have it out with Cat the moment she gets home, I'm lucid enough to realise that I'd be better to sleep on it, get things straight in my head, and move my stuff out in the morning when it's light. I'm also too devastated to have that kind of showdown tonight.

Before going to bed, I pack as much as I can into a couple of suitcases, quickly realising that there's too much. My new wardrobe has doubled the number of belongings I have, so I'll have to come back for them at a later date. Then,

I lie in bed in the dark, rehearsing the conversation with Cat. My tortured mind creates multiple versions of what I'll say and how she'll respond: running through scenario after scenario until I hear her key in the lock at around two a.m.. She tip-toes past my door to her bedroom, where she'll no doubt dream about her not-so-new-after-all man while I'm left lying awake, in an endless cycle of torment.

~

Waking after a fretful sleep, which only engulfed me when the sun was coming up, I'm groggy and exhausted for the second morning in a row. I can hear Cat clattering around in the kitchen, no doubt cooking up a tasty Sunday brunch. I had hoped my devastation would develop into anger overnight, fuelling my courage for the most difficult interaction of my life. Instead, my only overwhelming emotions this morning are sadness and a sense of loss. My stomach pools with dread, while I automatically search for excuses to put the conversation off, perhaps even altogether. But it has to be done and there's no easy way about it. I'm just going to have to get it over with.

Realising I'll need to be ready to leave as soon as this is over, I take a quick shower, and throw on some clothes, which helps me feel fresher and stronger. However, as I'm about to enter the kitchen, that strength deserts me and I almost flee back to the safety of my room. But I know I can't. Any woman with an ounce of self-respect wouldn't let this go.

Steadying myself against the doorframe, I take a faltering breath and enter the kitchen.

'Morning, sleepy head.' Cat doesn't look round. 'I

thought I would be the last one up today. You must have been really done in after Friday night.'

She's so busy coordinating the cooking of the food, getting the plates, cutlery, tea and toast ready, she doesn't notice that I haven't said a word.

'By the way, where's your favourite mug?' she asks. 'I've looked everywhere but I can't see it.'

I remain silent, causing her to turn and look at me properly for the first time.

'Emma... are you OK?'

Tears are welling in my eyes. I'm terrified. After it's out, there's no going back. I heave a loaded sigh.

'Um... no. Actually, I'm not OK.'

'What's up?' Her face brims with concern. 'Oh, honey, I knew I should have stayed home with you last night. You've had such a challenging time recently. It's all become too much, hasn't it?'

'Cat... *stop*.' I can't take this facade any longer. 'My mug is packed in a suitcase in the bedroom.'

She appears perplexed, but says nothing.

'You're right, things have become too much for me. But it's not really about Friday or the last couple of weeks. It's about... *argh*, I don't know how to say this...'

'Emma, you're scaring me. What's going on?'

'I... I know, Cat. About you. And Dave. Your... little secret.' I can't bring myself to spell it out, but I know that she's understood because the colour has drained from her face. She switches off the gas under the food she's cooking.

'You... you know?' she stammers as my worst fears are confirmed.

I still had a flicker of hope that maybe it wasn't Dave she was with and my overtaxed brain was causing me to hallucinate, but I didn't get it wrong. It was him, and it's clear from Cat's reaction that there's no mix up.

'Yes, I know, Cat. And quite frankly, I feel shocked and betrayed beyond belief. I thought we were friends... *best friends*... who tell each other everything. Not to mention trust each other completely.'

Cat looks like she's about to burst into tears, tugging on my natural instinct to comfort and protect her, as I've always done. I can't do that now. Not when the reason she's upset is because she's been caught out deceiving me.

'Emma, I never meant to hurt you...' She looks at the ground. 'Sorry, that's such a predictable response, but it's true, I really—'

'How would I *not* be hurt by this, Cat?' I cut across her.

'I know, and I'm so sorry, but it was a shock to me as well. It put me in a terrible position, and the longer I left it, the more I realised that I couldn't tell you. The guilt was eating me up, but you were getting on with your life and doing so well. I thought it would do more harm than good.'

This is completely absurd. I can't believe I'm having this conversation with Cat. And what the hell does she think she's doing? It's like she's looking for sympathy from me when she's the one in the wrong. The anger that was so noticeably absent, finally starts to simmer.

'More like you didn't want to admit it,' I throw back. 'And risk destroying our friendship.'

'Well, obviously. We've been friends forever.' Tears are now trickling down her cheeks. 'We've never fallen out in all the time we've known each other.'

I stare at her, unable to fathom her response. 'So, you chickened out? That's convenient. I should have guessed something was up when you started being secretive.'

Cat's gaping at me now, stunned into silence. She looks like she might faint, but I'm all out of sympathy.

'Want to know how I found out? I took a walk last night because I was restless and I found myself near the bar you were in. I thought I'd be a bit naughty and take a sneak peek at your new man, and boy did I get a shock. What I can't understand is, why Dave? Why *my* man? Ex-man, obviously, thanks to you. All this time you've pretended to be so supportive... the best friend in the world. What was it really, Cat? Guilt? Or just a way to keep me from suspecting anything?' I come to an abrupt and defiant halt, while on the inside I'm on the verge of meltdown. This confrontation is one of the worst moments of my entire life.

'Emma, I can't believe what you... It's not like that at all.' Cat's demeanour has shifted from one of entrapment and guilt to hurt, which winds me up even more. I can't believe she has the nerve to act like an injured party in this.

'*Oh, come on*, Cat. How can anything you say make this better?' I continue to glare at her.

She seems like she's about to speak again, but instead goes to the hob, switches the heat back on and restarts cooking the food.

'I hope he's worth it.' I find myself talking to the back of her again. 'Because I can't help thinking he'll screw you over the same way he did me.'

She stays silent, the only sound her sniffing as she continues to cry.

'All right, I guess I'm out of here then.' I rub my face wearily, unable to comprehend that this is happening. 'I'll ask Amber or Sara to come and collect the rest of my stuff.'

Leaving the kitchen, I head to the door with my things and call a taxi, aware that I have far too much to fit in the boot of my (totally impractical, I now realise) new car.

'Where to, love?' The taxi driver asks, as he helps me with my luggage and I climb forlornly into the back seat.

'Don't know. Nearest hotel, I guess. Make it a cheap one.'

'Right you are.' He glances at me in his mirror as he manoeuvres his way back onto the road. 'Bad day?'

I wipe a rogue tear from my cheek. 'You have no idea.'

Chapter Thirty-Two

The taxi drops me off outside what appears to be a budget hotel-slash-hostel near Haymarket Station. It looks pretty grim, but I know it wouldn't be wise to fritter away my winnings by checking into a nice one indefinitely – and especially not with Edinburgh hotel prices being what they are. It could take weeks to find a decent place to live.

On opening the door to my tiny, drab room, I survey the stained bedclothes and the ancient furniture, tired and dull from years of wear and tear. It's clearly been some time since this place had a refurb. There's also a musty smell of damp lingering in the air. I dump my stuff and sit on the bed in a daze, barely able to process what's happened.

After a while, my phone buzzes with an incoming call and I can see that it's Amber, but I ignore it. Seconds later, she tries again, and I briefly consider answering, but I can't face the reality of this – nor her tough love – so I let it go to voicemail. However, if Amber is one thing, she's persistent and she almost immediately calls again, causing me to throw my phone on the floor in frustration.

It buzzes once more with a message alert, and this time curiosity takes over. I lean down and pick it up.

Where are you? You're an idiot. Cat hasn't been sleeping with Dave. What the hell are you playing at??

Stunned by Amber's words, I'm at a loss as to what to do. What does she know? I'm the one that saw them together. And Cat admitted it. I haven't got this wrong.

I pace around my room for a bit, before coming to a decision: I need to see the truth for myself. I take a taxi back to Cat's, pick up my car and drive to Simpson Loan, where I park in a free space near the main door to Dave's plush apartment block. After quickly buying a ticket from the nearby machine, while keeping my face hidden as best I can, I settle back in the driver's seat and wait.

As the minutes pass, it dawns on me that, without a plan or knowing what Dave's doing today, I could be in for a long wait. Or he might not leave his apartment at all. But if Cat *is* seeing him, then it's likely that she'll have gone to him for comfort. I also consider going to get a coffee to keep me alert but then think better of it. Not only could I miss something while I've nipped away, the only thing worse than an inordinate wait, is an inordinate wait while desperate for the loo.

I sit for two hours and nothing happens. Then, as my motivation finally erodes into boredom, stiff legs and an aching bum, my patience is rewarded. The underground garage door slowly opens and out drives Dave in his obscenely expensive poser car (way more so than mine, I must add). I can't see much from where I'm parked but I can tell there's someone with him – and I'd put money on it that it's a woman. Now I should find out for sure, either way.

Pulling out of the space, I tail them, keeping my distance so they don't spot me. Dave has no idea I have a new car, but Cat does and I want to keep this particular mission firmly covert.

After following them through the city centre, Dave eventually parks near a stylish looking restaurant just off the bottom of Dundas Street, so I do the same a bit further away and wait. Moments later, Dave gets out of the car, and to my amazement, walks round and opens the door for his companion. *Where the hell was that chivalrous behaviour when he was with me?* I watch as he bends over and engages them in conversation. Then, a pair of long, slim, tanned legs emerge, followed by a killer body and blonde hair. I can only see the woman from behind, but one thing is immediately clear: it's not Cat. Cat has dark hair and definitely doesn't have legs like that. It must be Melissa after all. *Just friends, my backside.*

I blanch on realising the impact of this. Was Amber right? If so, what was Cat doing with Dave last night? Why was she acting so guiltily and what was she admitting to if it wasn't her seeing Dave behind my back? Or... is Dave seeing Cat and this blonde woman at the same time – and Cat doesn't know?

I wrench my focus back to the woman still standing with her back to me, and I don't have to wait long for my answer. She turns her head and for the second time in twenty-four hours, I'm stunned beyond belief. Dave's companion is Sara. And I definitely haven't got the wrong end of the stick this time.

Sick to my stomach, I watch them lock together in a passionate embrace. But instead of the panic, devastation and crushing hurt that washed over me when I saw Cat with Dave, I'm overcome by white-hot anger. Adrenaline pumps through my body so fiercely that I can feel my pulse between my ears. I *have* been betrayed, and by someone who's not only supposed to be my friend, she could have any guy she wants. And there's no way Dave's seeing her *and* Cat.

I'm livid as the realisation of all this slams down on me like a ton of bricks. Whatever the story is with Cat and Dave, it must be more innocent than I thought – which means I may well have destroyed my friendship with Cat over nothing (or certainly nothing that constituted a red line being crossed). It's actually my so-called friend Sara, who I took under my wing when she was new to the city, who's been messing around with Dave behind my back.

Suddenly remembering the infidelity debate she and Amber were having over dinner the week before, I shake my head at my own naivety. In stark contrast to Amber, Sara had a pretty relaxed attitude to cheating. She's relaxed about life full stop, so why would I expect her to have a strong moral compass when it comes to friendship?

With this turn of events and still reeling from my fight with Cat, there's only one-way things can go now. I have to have it out with Dave and Sara – right here, right now.

I get out of the car and march towards them. They're so wrapped up in each other that they're completely oblivious to my approach, but the moment Dave sees me, he pulls away from Sara, knocking her off balance.

'Hey, what's up, tiger?' She pulls at his collar, trying to coax him into kissing her.

With her back to me, Sara still hasn't clocked my presence, but I note with some satisfaction that Dave's face is ashen. At least he has the grace to look guilty. He backs further away from Sara and pretends to check something on his phone.

NINA KAYE

'Don't let me interrupt you,' I say when I'm about six feet away, and on hearing my voice, Sara goes rigid.

'Emma, sweetie. This is... a surprise.' She turns, trying to sound bright and innocent, but the absence of her signature air kisses further betrays her guilt.

I stare at her in disbelief. *Are you kidding me?*

'What, this...' She waves a dismissive hand. 'I just bumped into Dave now.'

She really hasn't a clue. She obviously thinks I've walked out the door of the restaurant and seen none of what came before. Dave, on the other hand, stays silent, staring at his phone, probably praying for this to pass quickly and painlessly.

No chance.

'Do you really think I'm that stupid, Sara?' My eyes narrow in fury, and I detect an uncomfortable shift in her stance. 'I followed you and lover boy here from his apartment, so you can drop the act.'

'You followed me?' Dave finally finds his voice. 'What are you? Some kind of sick stalker?'

'Oh, shut up and get over yourself, Dave,' I spit. 'You're nothing but a self-obsessed prick who likes the sound of his own voice too much.'

I brace myself for the same nasty retaliation I experienced when I met him for a drink, but it doesn't come. Holding my nerve, I fix my furious eyes on his and keep going.

'You hide behind your money and your powerful job, but strip it all back and there's nothing there. You're just a sad little man with not a lot going on. And you don't fool me anymore. You actually did me a favour by ending it, so, thank you.'

To my amazement, Dave's still not fighting back, proving

me right. I've shown him for what he is, and in doing so, I've confirmed that he's nothing more than a bully – just like Karla. All mouth and power until you call them for what they really are.

Having won that one quicker than I expected, I return my focus to Sara, whose demeanour has shifted. Infuriatingly, she's now inspecting her perfectly manicured nails with a bored expression. I also note that she's not made any attempt to come to Dave's rescue. I glare at her silently until she has no choice but to look at me, the awkwardness of her disinterest almost robbing me of my courage, but I stand firm. This is, or rather *was*, one of my best friends. Someone I looked out for, made part of my group, trusted with my deepest secrets.

'*How could you?*'

She doesn't even flinch.

'How could you?' I repeat in a lower tone, as she stands there looking like an insolent teenager getting a lecture from an annoying parent. I'm shaking inside, but it's more from rage than nerves. 'Amber thought it was your boss you were seeing. All those late nights—'

'What, that old codger?' She smirks. 'I thought that was daft banter. What does she take me for?'

'She was on the right track, though, wasn't she? And as she said, the expensive jewellery had to come from somewhere. It was convenient for you to play up to her suspicions so you could cop off with *him* without raising any suspicion.' I throw a disgusted look in Dave's direction.

'That's not entirely true.' Sara looks away. 'I have been working late... a lot.'

I throw back my head with a sardonic laugh and a thought comes to me. 'That's why you said no to the holiday too, wasn't it? You'd have nearly two weeks of freedom, knowing you'd never bump into us.'

'It wasn't that,' she complains. 'I knew it wouldn't be right to let you spend so much money on me when I hadn't told you yet. I was going to speak to you about it eventually.'

'No, you weren't. You've had plenty of opportunity to do that. So, how about you tell me now? Why, of all the men you could have had, you had to have mine?'

'You really want to know why?'

'Yes.' I fold my arms expectantly. 'Tell me why our friendship meant so little to you.'

'*Oh, please.*' She raises her eyes to the sky, as if I'm being overly dramatic.

Adrenaline continues to course through me like molten lava. I'm so incensed by her nonchalant response that I want to lash out at her; to make her feel something that resembles how hurt and disrespected I feel right now. But I know I need to control myself to retain my dignity.

'Go on then,' I prompt her.

Sara lets out an exasperated sigh. 'Look, it's not rocket science, sweetie. Do you remember our chat the other night at the bar? About how you and I are different?'

'*No shit.*'

'Look, do you want me to explain or not? I get that this has been a shock for you, Emma, but it needn't be such a big deal.' She stops and turns to Dave. 'Perhaps it's better if I talk to Emma alone. You head inside and I'll join you shortly.'

Dave doesn't need to be asked twice. He slopes off, avoiding eye contact with me while I wait as patiently as I can for Sara to continue. The idea that she's about to try and justify her actions – as well as continue with her original dining arrangement with my ex-partner – almost sends me into orbit.

Sara returns her attention to me. 'Where was I? Oh, yeah... To me, things like this aren't such a big deal. Lots of people aren't monogamous in their relationships. That's a fact of life. There's probably a higher chance you will be cheated on than you won't, so—'

'I don't know where you get your stats from,' I silence her. 'But I'm afraid I don't agree. Yes, cheating happens, but it's not the default option. If you want to have an open relationship, that's up to you. I have no issue with that. It's *who* you decided to have it with.'

'Emma...' Sara addresses me as if I'm two years old. 'You're a romantic. I get that. You want the happy ever after, but life isn't like it is in the movies. Relationships are... complicated.'

'And you're a pro, are you? You haven't been in a proper relationship since I met you.'

'I'm not saying I'm a pro, though I am realistic. I get that men are not physiologically programmed to have one life partner, so I don't have false expectations. I make the most out of the situation. I use them as much as they use me.'

I let out an Amber-style snort, unable to comprehend the nonsense coming out of Sara's mouth.

'Wouldn't you rather know that the man you're with is sleeping with other people?' she says. 'And at least have the option to do the same yourself? I know I would. I don't expect total commitment from any man, and I ask them not to expect the same from me. Dave and I have... an understanding.'

I'm floored by this statement. 'Sara, you may not expect that from a man, but *I* do. And as I do, you should have respected that and stayed the hell away from Dave. How long has this been going on anyway? Is it *you* he's been seeing for the last eighteen months?'

'Actually... no.' She furrows her brow, like this gets her off the hook somehow.

My mind races. *There was more than one? Was I really such a crap girlfriend?*

'Well how long then?' I demand. 'And who has he been seeing the rest of the time? It was Melissa, wasn't it? I knew he was making it up about her dad taking ill.'

'It's only been four or five months. And I have no idea who else he's been seeing. Why would I? We don't talk about that stuff. Maybe he exaggerated to make you feel worse.'

'Well... did you talk about me? Did you even acknowledge that what you were doing was wrong?'

'OK, I get it.' She winds her hair around her finger, a characteristic I previously found endearing, but in this moment, is completely irritating. 'I probably shouldn't have gone there, not when you were still together, anyway. But your relationship was over. You just couldn't see it. You know it was for the best, you two splitting up, so what does it matter?'

I throw my hands up in frustration. 'It matters because I want honest friends who won't deceive me, and a man I can trust. I don't think that's too much to ask.'

'Sure, whatever.' Sara's attitude is now one of indifference. She's clearly trying to disengage from the conversation, but there's no way I'm letting her think that she's a more evolved human being than I am.

'Because of you I destroyed my friendship with Cat this morning. I thought it was her seeing Dave—'

Sara interrupts me with a scoff. 'You thought Cat could do that? She's way too timid. Quite like you actually... Though saying that, I can see you're coming along nicely since your win.' She seems to ponder this as if it's an insightful piece of information to be analysed.

For me it's the final straw. She will not ridicule Cat, or me, or the mess our friendship is in.

'I don't know what the hell went wrong when you were born,' I explode. 'But you've clearly not been brought up to be a decent person like the rest of us. I was a friend to you when you didn't have anyone else. Cat and Amber welcomed you into our group. We all went out of our way to help you settle in and make a home here, and this is how you repay us? I got you *so* wrong. You care about nothing but yourself. Everything else is simply a possession to be played with, or discarded like rubbish, just like your shoes and handbags. Even men and friends. It's all the same to you.'

I eyeball her, hoping my tirade has had the desired effect, but instead of looking small and ashamed, Sara's regarding me with a piteous look.

'Emma, you need to relax. You get so worked up over everything. You and Dave are finished, and you've got another man chasing after you already, so what's the big deal?'

'If it's not a "big deal", then why did you hide it?'

'Because I knew you'd blow it out of proportion.' She shrugs as if this is obvious. 'And in my defence, it wasn't planned. We were both on nights out and our paths crossed. Dave told me that night that he was going to end it with you, but he was such a bloody coward that he bottled it.'

On digesting this information, I decide I can't stomach any more of this. Sara's not the person I thought she was, and I'm certainly not going to get a grovelling apology from her. She clearly has a set of morals that are alien *and* unacceptable to me. I also realise that I actually know very little about her. It's always been me sharing my life issues and dilemmas and seeking her opinion – and to give her her due, she's had my back in that sense. But other than that, all our conversations have been fairly superficial – about material things like clothes, makeup, TV shows and celebrities. Or about work gossip. I can't recollect a single time that she's shared anything really personal.

I almost feel sorry for her. She's probably never going to have the kind of friendships I've had all my life. But my overwhelming emotions are anger and betrayal. I'm so let down, yet I have no fight left in me. All I know is that I need to go out with my head held high, like I did with Karla.

'You know what?' I say with finality. 'You're right. Dave's a coward, but so are you. You can try and justify it all you want, but it will never make what you've done OK. You're both selfish and self-interested, which means you're a perfect match.' I turn and start walking away.

'Emma, sweetie, there's no need to be like that.' Sara gives a little laugh. 'OK, so it's a bit awkward and I get that you're upset, but I've said I'm sorry. This doesn't need to end our friendship. When you've calmed down, you'll realise that you've overreacted.'

I stop, tempted to launch something back at her to hammer the message home. But I've said all I need to say. Instead, I carry on walking, leaving Sara waiting for an answer that will never come.

Chapter Thirty-Three

I get into my car and drive. I don't know where I'm going – all I know is that I need to get the hell away from Sara and Dave. After a while, I pull over near the entrance to a park, switch off the ignition and sit in silence. I can't even bear to think about the mess I'm in. It's too painful.

My phone buzzes with an incoming call, and on pulling it out of my handbag, I see that it's Amber. I consider letting it go to voicemail again because the last thing I need – having hit rock bottom and even fallen through that – is one of her painfully honest appraisals of the situation. Then I remember that we're meant to be leaving for our trip tomorrow morning. A holiday and all the excitement that goes with it may be the last thing on my mind, but if I leave Amber hanging, I risk losing the last of my three closest friends.

Dejectedly, I hit the answer button. 'Hi, Amber.'

'*Where are you?*' she demands.

'I'm... actually, I don't know where I am. I assume you spoke to Cat then.'

'Well, I didn't get my information from anyone else.'

I start to cry.

'What were you thinking accusing her like that?' Amber's frustration with me is evident. 'From what I hear, you didn't even give her a chance to explain.'

'I... I don't know,' I say in a small voice. 'It seemed pretty cut and dried... until it didn't. Do you know the real story? Because Cat *has* been hiding something and Dave's at the centre of it. If it was Sara who was seeing him behind my back all this time, then what could it be?'

'What are you on about?' She's understandably confused. 'Why are you talking about Sara now? Emma, you need to get a grip.'

'*No, listen.*' I run a frustrated hand through my hair. 'It was Sara all along. When I got your text, I had to find out what was going on, so I went to Dave's apartment and sat outside...' I fill her in on the rest in between sobs.

'*The little cow,*' Amber growls once I'm done. 'Though, I'm not totally surprised.'

'What do you mean? Why would—'

'Look, forget about that. We can talk about it later. Right now, you've got some serious damage limitation to do. Cat's in a right state, so I suggest you get round there fast, before you lose her forever – if you haven't already.'

'OK, but can you tell me what happened with her and Dave, so I can at least go in prepared?'

'No, Emma.' Her tone is firm. 'Cat deserves the opportunity to explain that herself. Move your arse and call me when you're done, yeah?' She hangs up without saying goodbye.

Stuffing my phone back in my bag, I rub my red, puffy eyes, willing myself to keep it together long enough to get to Cat's and try and fix things.

I use my phone to figure out where I am and race across

the city, reining in my frustration at being caught at every set of traffic lights on the way. When I eventually screech to a halt outside Cat's apartment block, I abandon my poorly parked car and rush to the main door where I buzz her flat.

'*Come on...*' I dance around with impatience, but there's no reply.

She must be in. I buzz again, but there's still no answer. Then I remember that I still have a key. In all the drama this morning, I never returned it. Hastily letting myself into the building, I take the lift to Cat's floor, gently unlock the door and slip inside. The flat is silent and I wonder if she's gone out, but when I reach her room, I see her curled up in the foetal position on her bed, cuddling a pillow while staring out the window. My heart sinks. *I've* done this to her.

'Cat...' My voice is almost a whisper. 'You didn't answer, so I let myself in. Can we talk?'

She doesn't reply.

'Cat?' I try again from the doorway. 'Is it OK if I come in and speak to you?'

Still nothing. But she hasn't told me to get lost, so I'll try my luck. I'm jittering with nerves, acutely aware that if I botch this, I'll have lost the best friend I've ever had.

'Cat, I need to apologise to you. I've been... an idiot. These last few weeks... well, they've been a complete rollercoaster, and... I think it's all overwhelmed me. It's like I've been living on adrenaline, which has warped my sense of reality and I've lost perspective. I'm so ashamed of myself, and I'm ready... I mean... I want to hear your side of things. Will you tell me what happened with Dave?'

Cat maintains her silence, and I feel a slight flicker of hurt that she won't even acknowledge my presence. But knowing that I've gotten things so wrong, I can hardly hold it against her.

'Um... OK. I guess I'll go then.' I turn away, the weight of Cat's silence too much to bear.

I make my way back through the hallway towards the apartment door, resignedly placing the spare key on the hall table as I pass.

'I did do something wrong.' Cat's voice, weak and hoarse from crying, comes from the bedroom. 'I admit that, but it's nothing like what you thought.'

I waver slightly in my stance, but I stay quiet, not wanting to discourage her from continuing.

'I wasn't *with* Dave in the bar last night, though I did speak to him,' she continues. 'I was telling him exactly what I thought of him, which is not something that comes easily to me, but I was furious with him for the position he put me in.'

'What... what position?' I appear at her bedroom door once again and see that she's now sitting up. 'Cat, none of this makes sense. You were smiling and laughing, and he slid his arm around your waist. You... whispered in his ear. It looked intimate, like...' Clocking the look on her face, I realise that I need to stop or she'll shut down again. 'Sorry, sorry... I'll be quiet. You go on.'

She exhales heavily, her face etched with raw emotion. 'From the outside looking in... with no context... I accept that's how it looked. I was hardly going to make a scene in front of my date, so, when I spotted Dave on the way back from the toilets, I made it look like I was saying hello to an old friend, when I was actually telling him in no uncertain terms what I thought of him. He made it easy for me, trying to be all pally when he saw me.'

I'm utterly gobsmacked and bewildered. 'But what were you hiding from me then? It was clearly something.'

'Yes, it was. A couple of months ago, I bumped into Dave

at a hotel in Dundee, when I was on a spa day with friends from my uni days.'

'I remember that. With Becky and Prisha.'

'That's right.' Cat nods, her gaze fixed on the floor. 'He was acting shifty, so I kept an eye out and spotted him with a woman as I was leaving.'

I gasp at this revelation, even though I now know that woman was Sara.

'I didn't see her face. Only that she was blonde. I didn't want to be the one to hit the "destruct" button on your relationship. I've seen how that can play out and how friendships can be ruined – the messenger always gets shot, as they say. So, when I was over at your apartment a few days later, I got Dave on his own and told him if he didn't tell you, I would. He said he'd do it, but he kept putting it off, and it got to the point where I couldn't tell you either, because I'd left it so long.' She pauses, evidently pained by her actions and subsequent inaction. 'Then, when he finished with you... You were so broken... I couldn't bear to add to your pain, especially when you started to perk up again and had your win. It seemed cruel to even *think* about telling you. What would it have gained? I just wish I'd done the right thing and told you as soon as it happened.'

'Oh, Cat. I wish you had too,' I grimace. 'Though I can't pretend I don't understand your fear. Who knows how I might have reacted? I wasn't wise to Dave's arsehole-ness in the way that I am now. I was always defending him. There's still something that doesn't make sense to me, though. Why did you wait 'til last night to tell him what you thought of him? He called you on D-day night. You clearly both had each other's numbers.'

'When he called that night, finding you and making sure you were all right was my priority, not making myself feel better. I wasn't *planning* to confront him, but when I saw him last night, I just saw red. And... Dave had my number from when you and I went on holiday together a few years back, remember? You gave him it as a backup.'

'Oh... of course, I remember now.' I feel even more ashamed, as this realisation dawns.

'I'm sorry, Emma, I really am.' Cat looks at me properly for the first time. 'I know I did the wrong thing, and I should have told you, but I wasn't seeing him behind your back. I can't believe you would even think that.'

Cat's words slice through me like tiny razors, making my legs weak. I enter her room and perch on her bed. I haven't had time to properly process her admission, but I *can* see that she was thinking about me and trying to protect me. My actions, on the other hand, are not as easily justifiable.

'I can't tell you how sorry I am, Cat.' I hang my head and shudder. 'I should never have doubted you.'

'Thank you,' she says simply.

We sit in silence for a good minute.

'So, can we put this whole misunderstanding behind us?' I say eventually, offering her a weak smile. But to my surprise, the response I expected doesn't come.

'I don't know, Emma.' She looks distressed and I wait anxiously for her to continue. 'I know I didn't help the situation. And this may sound a bit hypocritical, but... you've shown that you don't trust me. The Emma I thought I knew would never have suspected something like that.'

'I... I know.' I wring my hands pathetically. 'I didn't want to believe it, Cat. I really didn't. There were just so many things I reflected on, and they all seemed to make sense when I put them together—'

'But it's *me*, Emma. Other than finding myself in that impossible situation Dave put me in, have I ever done anything to hurt you? I don't think so. You've been my best friend for as long as I can remember. It feels *so* awful... so *crushing*... to think you could even *consider* I would do something like that. It makes me wonder whether we have the kind of friendship I thought we had after all.'

We're both crying now.

'I really am so sorry.' I wipe the tears from my eyes. 'I've been a stupid, paranoid idiot. Of course I trust you. It's been a weird time lately. It's messed with my head.'

'I know it has, but even still, I thought you and I were rock solid. I'm so desperately disappointed to find out that we're not.'

I can feel my heart breaking for the second time in as many weeks.

'I'll make this up to you... please let me, Cat.' I'm desperate not to lose her too. 'We're meant to be leaving for our holiday tomorrow. I'll be the best friend in the world and I'll never doubt you again. *I promise*. If I could trade all the money I won to get things back to how they were − so I'd never done that to you − I'd do it in a heartbeat. That's how much you mean to me.'

Cat looks at me through sad, glassy eyes. 'I'm sorry, Emma. I just won't feel comfortable coming on the holiday now. I was already uneasy with the idea of you spending so much on me and this has tipped things over the edge. It's probably best to have some space from each other for a bit.'

I stare at her, silently begging her to change her mind, but she looks away.

'OK, well I'll leave you in peace then,' I murmur.

Heading to the door of the apartment once more, I'm about to close it behind me when I realise something. Cat doesn't know the full story.

'By the way, it was Sara you saw with Dave,' I call to her.

'I caught them earlier with their tongues down each other's throats.'

There's no reply from the bedroom, so I shut the door and head downstairs to my car. As I'm driving off, I look up at Cat's flat, and see her face at the window for a brief moment – then she's gone and my broken heart is mashed by a steamroller.

Chapter Thirty-Four

Losing Dave was awful. It was painful beyond belief. But once I'd worked through the initial shock and devastation (helped by him showing his true colours), I realised it was for the best. While my battered and bruised ego might still ache for him to see what a mistake he's made, I've been able to reflect and finally see that things had been wrong for some time.

This is so much worse. My closest friendship, twenty-five plus years of laughter and sharing, all in tatters.

Cat did withhold a truth, but she did it for reasons that I understand. The whole thing has been a huge misunderstanding, and it's not like I came to the conclusion I did without some pretty damning evidence (or so it seemed at the time), but no matter how I spin it, I can't deny the reality of what I've done. I basically insinuated that my kind and selfless best friend was capable of lies, deceit and selfishness. Why didn't I give her the benefit of the doubt, tell her what I saw – so fleetingly and out of context – and offer her the chance to explain before jumping to conclusions? Hindsight, of course, is a wonderful thing.

Hunched miserably in the doorway of my dingy hotel room, my eyes roam across its discoloured, shabby looking contents, moth-eaten curtains and grubby carpet. It matches my mood: how I feel I deserve to exist right now, so in a way I get a distorted, cold sense of comfort from it.

Here in my makeshift prison cell, I'm past the crying stage, feeling lost and numb. Every now and again, the rational part of my brain surfaces, telling me to get it together. I have enough money, my health, Lottie, a solid friend in Amber (I think) and parents who love me, despite being suffocatingly overprotective. Others have nothing at all. But in this moment, it's no comfort. Knowing I have no best friend, no loving partner, nowhere I can call home...

Eventually, I can't bear it anymore. I need to speak to Lottie. I've been putting off calling her out of shame, but I know that she won't judge me. She never has. It's not in her nature.

Grabbing my keys, I head to my car and drive to her cottage in Ratho, and as I ring the doorbell, I almost can't bear to be alone for another moment. However, she doesn't answer. I try the bell again. Nothing.

I walk round to the back garden, thinking she's maybe gardening and hasn't heard the door, but there's no sign of her. *Where is she?* She hardly goes out, even having her shopping delivered. Distracted by these concerns, I jump with fright when someone appears around side of the house, striding towards me. It's a man around my dad's age.

'Hello.' He seems pre-occupied. 'I saw you arrive. Are you looking for Charlotte?'

'Yes, that's right.' An uneasy feeling creeps over me. 'I'm her friend, Emma. Do you know where she is?'

'Ah, you're Emma. I'm Archie. I live a couple of houses

along, on the other side. We were going to try to find a way to contact you when we knew more.'

'Knew more about what? Has something happened? Where's Lottie?'

'Why don't you come across the road for a cup of tea?' he suggests gently. 'And I can fill you in.'

'Uh... that's really kind of you, but please can you just tell me where Lottie is?' I clasp my hands together as if in prayer.

'Of course.' Archie gives a solemn smile. 'I'm sorry to have to give you this news, Emma. Lottie's been rushed to hospital in an ambulance.'

'Wh... *what?*' My legs buckle and the man catches my arm to steady me. 'What do you mean? Is she OK? What's happened?'

'Charlotte appears to have had a bad fall. My wife, Eva, popped by to give her a few bits and pieces she'd picked up for her at the farmer's market in Edinburgh. When she didn't get a reply, she became concerned, because Charlotte was expecting her. Eva looked through the letterbox and saw Charlotte lying unconscious on the floor at the bottom of the stairs. She called for an ambulance straight away and we were able to get access to the house through an open window.'

I slowly sit down on Lottie's back step to digest this information.

'How bad is it?' I look up at Archie, terrified to hear the answer.

'They don't know yet. I drove Eva to the hospital – we only have one car, you see, and she wanted to be there for Charlotte – and then I came back here to make sure Charlotte's house was locked up properly. Eva's going to call as soon as she has any news. The paramedics were concerned about a possible head or spinal injury. I'm so sorry to have to tell you this, Emma.'

'No... thanks, I'm glad you did.' I shake my head, trying to clear the disorientated feeling suddenly consuming me. 'I... can't believe this has happened. After all the nice stuff we did together... and... oh no... *oh no*, this is all my fault.'

'Emma, this is no one's fault,' Archie attempts to soothe me. 'Accidents happen. You couldn't have done anything to prevent this.'

'You don't understand.' I clamp my hands on the top of my head. 'The other day, I saw that she wasn't looking so good. She dismissed it, said she was fine, but she obviously wasn't. All I wanted was for her to have some enjoyment, some nice memories for herself. She has so few of those. I pushed her too hard and it was too much for her.'

'I'm sure that's not the case. Why don't you come across the road and have a cup of tea? I know this is a shock.'

'No. Thank you for the kind offer, but I have to get to the hospital.' I jump to my feet. 'I need to be with her.'

'Emma, I'm not sure you should be driving right now.' Archie frowns, giving me a concerned look. 'You'll be no use to Charlotte if you have an accident yourself.'

'I'll be fine, honestly. I'll drive carefully. Which hospital is Lottie at?'

'The Royal Infirmary.'

Dashing to my car, I pull out of the driveway, giving a defeated-looking Archie a grateful wave as I go. I tear along the Edinburgh bypass to the hospital, where I park my car and rush into the Accident and Emergency reception area, all thoughts of my own situation now banished from my mind.

'Can I help you?' the receptionist asks as I approach her, panting slightly.

'Yes, someone I know has been brought in. Her name is Charlotte Maybury.'

'Are you a relative?'

'Yes... well... no, not officially. But she's pretty much family.'

'I'm afraid I can't give you any information if you're not a relative or next of kin,' she says.

'Right, so how do I find out how she is?'

'Excuse me?' A voice comes from behind me. 'Are you Emma?'

'Yes, that's right.' I turn to face a woman who appears to be in her late fifties.

'I'm Eva. I gather you met my husband, Archie, at Charlotte's house. He called and asked me to look out for you.'

'Oh, yes.' I'm so relieved to see her. 'How is Lottie? Do you have any news?'

'Not yet, I'm afraid.' She shakes her head. 'And they won't tell me much either. But they said if she comes round, they'll tell her I'm here.'

'*If* she comes round... that doesn't sound good.' With the adrenaline having depleted, all I'm left with is a feeling of hopelessness. Tears well in my eyes.

'I think they meant if she comes round while I'm still here. At least, that's what I'm hoping. Come and have a seat.' She puts a soothing arm around me. 'There's no sense in jumping to conclusions. Let's have a cup of tea and wait it out together.'

Eva guides me across to the waiting area, where I take a seat while she buys two cups of tea from the vending machine. She hands me one, then sits down next to me.

'It's nice to meet you, Emma. Though, obviously, I'd rather it was under different circumstances. Charlotte talks about you very fondly. She's a lucky lady having you in her life.'

'Is she?' I assume a pained expression. 'If it weren't for me, she probably wouldn't even be here.'

Despite having just met me, she seeks out my hand and gives it a reassuring squeeze. 'Archie mentioned that you're feeling some responsibility over this. Emma, you must not blame yourself. You don't know the facts, and I'm afraid this is just something that happens when people get older.'

'I know, but I pushed her too hard this past week. She said she didn't want to join me, and I didn't listen.'

'I'm sorry, I'm not sure what you mean. But from what I've heard, you're quite the young woman, looking after Charlotte the way you do.'

On hearing these words, I start to sob. Nothing could be further from the truth right now. All I seem to have done is hurt those I love the most.

'Hey... *sshhh*.' Eva puts her arm around me and pulls me close. 'You have a good cry. I'm right here and not going anywhere.'

I allow her to stroke my hair and do exactly what she says. I cry and cry, until there's nothing left, then, once I've composed myself enough to have a conversation, we chat a bit. She's so easy to talk to and before long, I've told her way more that I would ever have planned to – about my break-up, my win and the events surrounding it and how things have gone so wrong.

'Emma, you're only human,' Eva gives me a kind smile. 'We all make mistakes and misjudge things. With the confusing time you've had recently, I'm not surprised you've lost your way a little. It will all blow over, I'm sure, and one thing is very clear to me – you are not responsible for

Charlotte being here. What you did for her was very thoughtful.'

I appreciate her attempts to help me feel better, but I'm not at all convinced. And I'll never forgive myself if Lottie doesn't wake up.

'Excuse me, ladies?' A nurse approaches us. 'I've been given permission to share an update on Charlotte.'

Chapter Thirty-Five

Eva and I sit up expectantly. My heart is in my throat, my chest heavy with anticipation.

The nurse sits down beside us. 'Charlotte is awake. She has a moderate concussion, two fractured ribs and a badly bruised hip. We're going to keep a close eye on her for the next couple of days, but I expect she's going to be fine. She's been very lucky.'

'*Oh, thank god!*' I blurt out. 'Can we see her?'

'Yes, you can. She's asking for you both. Come with me.'

'Why don't you go in first, Emma?' Eva suggests to me. 'I think you have something you need to talk to her about.'

'Erm... OK, if you're sure. Thanks, Eva.' I give her a grateful nod and follow the nurse to a receiving unit beyond the Accident and Emergency reception.

On entering the room, I can see Lottie lying propped up on a trolley in a cubicle with the curtain part drawn around her. I rush across to her and kiss her gently on the cheek.

'I'm so glad you're OK. Are you in pain?'

'It's not too bad.' She gives a weak smile. 'They've given me some paracetamol to take the edge off.'

'Lottie, I'm so sorry.' I take her hands in mine and bow my head. 'I should have listened to you when you said you didn't want to be involved in my plans for the week. I only wanted you to have some fun and happy memories of your own, but it was wrong pushing you like that. And now this has happened. I'm so, *so* sorry.'

'Dear girl, what are you talking about?' Lottie appears utterly baffled by my outpouring. 'I thought I was the one with the head injury.'

'Your fall. It must have happened because you overdid things during the week. I saw you looking tired and pale. If I'd respected your wishes in the first place, you wouldn't be here.'

'Well, that's nonsense.' She chuckles and then winces in pain. 'You didn't cause this. I slipped on a piece of paper I must have dropped on the stairs. I remember it clearly.'

'You did?' I cock my head in surprise.

'Yes, I did.'

'You're not just saying that to make me feel better?'

Lottie gingerly shakes her head. 'I'm not. This past week was the most alive I've felt in years. And I have you to thank for that. I might have been a bit more tired, but that didn't do me any harm. It actually meant I slept better. I'm thinking I'll need to work on my stamina if I'm now going to have one of these things you youngsters call a social life.'

I'm flooded with relief, giggling momentarily until I realise that, although Lottie is going to be OK, my friendship with Cat is still in bits.

'What's wrong, my love?' She has clearly picked up on my change of mood.

'Oh, um... nothing. Nothing at all.'

Much as I want to talk to her about things, it doesn't feel appropriate to bring them up right now.

'Emma, I know you well enough to know there's something else going on. Something that's upset you. And as I'm stuck here with little else to do, you may as well tell me.'

'OK.' It doesn't take much to persuade me.

I sit in the plastic seat next to her trolley and fill her in what's happened since I last saw her (all between fresh tears and nose blows), finishing with my fight with Cat and the fallout from that. She listens intently until I'm finished, then regards me thoughtfully for a moment.

'You've got yourself in a bit of a pickle, haven't you?'

'That's an understatement.' I suck in a tremulous breath.

'I understand that, right now, it probably feels like the end of the world, but I think Cat will come around from this. She needs some time to work through her feelings, and if I can offer some guidance – which you can accept or ignore – it would probably be wise to give her that.'

'I don't think I have a choice anyway.'

Lottie tries to readjust her pillow and I jump up to help her.

'This will work itself out, my love,' she says once she's comfortable again. 'Have some faith. You've done all you can for now, so go and enjoy your holiday with Amber, and you can try to mend things with Cat when you get home.'

'*What?*' I blink at her in amazement. 'I'm not going on holiday now. Cat not coming was bad enough, but you being like this? No way. The holiday is off. I can come and stay with you while you recover. I don't have anywhere to live anyway, and—'

'No, Emma.' She interrupts me, something she almost never does. 'You must not cancel that trip. I'm a bit battered and bruised, that's all, and I'll be stuck here for the next few days at least, so there's nothing for you to do.'

'Then I'll come and visit every day. You'll need help once you're out. We can set up the downstairs bedroom for you.'

'Is Eva still here?' Lottie suddenly asks.

'Oh, yes, she is.' I'd forgotten about Eva. 'I should give her a shout.'

'If you want to be helpful, why don't you tell her she can come in, and then maybe you could pop along to the shop and get me a magazine?'

'Of course, sure, anything.'

I trot off to fetch Eva and then head to the hospital shop. When I return, armed with three magazines and some chocolate biscuits, Eva and Lottie are chatting pleasantly. I'm so pleased to see them getting along, especially as Eva seems to be as kind and caring as Lottie.

'Here you are.' I dump the stuff on Lottie's bedside cabinet and pull up a second chair. 'So... what's the chat?'

'Eva and I have been talking,' says Lottie. 'And we've solved your little dilemma.'

'What dilemma?' I look from one to the other.

'About the holiday.' Lottie glances at Eva with a look I can't decipher. 'It turns out that Eva and Archie would like to support me with my recovery. They're going to collect me from the hospital when I'm discharged and help me out until I'm back on my feet. Isn't that kind?'

'What? But, there's no need for that. I can do it. It's no trouble. I'm not even working at the moment.'

'Archie and I are both retired, Emma,' says Eva. 'It's not a problem for us either. And I used to be a nurse, so Charlotte will be in good hands.'

They both smile at me with innocent faces and it dawns on me that I've been had.

'You did this on purpose.' I eyeball Lottie accusingly. 'To

stop me from cancelling my holiday. I can't go, Lottie, not when you're like this.'

'Of course, you can.' She chuckles lightly. 'You haven't fully followed through on my request yet. I asked you to have some fun and create fond memories and the holiday is part of that. Now, I must insist – yes, this time I *am* telling you what to do – that you go and enjoy your time with Amber. No arguments.'

I look helplessly from Lottie to Eva. It's obviously futile to argue with them. 'OK... if you're going to gang up on me, then I guess I have no choice.'

They both laugh and share conspiratorial winks.

'My love, please do this for me,' says Lottie.

'You know I can't say no to you.' I lift my hands in surrender. 'So, I suppose I'm going. And I'm going to have fun.'

'Good.' She seems satisfied with my response.

I stay for a little longer, then leave Lottie with Eva so I can go and get organised for my trip tomorrow. I also need to call Amber before she thinks I've gone AWOL – again.

While hurrying to my car, I glance across the car park and do a double take. James is walking towards the main entrance of the hospital, but he doesn't see me. My stomach flutters and I feel a pang of longing as I take in his gorgeous features and confident stride. I even briefly consider going after him to apologise and thank him for looking out for me on Friday night, but then think better of it. There's no way he's going to want me anywhere near him after I told him to leave me alone – and who knows what delicate situation he's here to deal with.

Unlocking my car, I slip into the driver's seat, pluck my phone out of my handbag and gulp on seeing that I have eight missed calls: three from my mum, no doubt calling for our usual Sunday chat, and the rest from Amber. Feeling immensely guilty, I call her back.

'*Where the fuck are you?*' Amber bellows before I can even say hello. 'You were meant to call me back.'

'Sorry, it's been a hell of a day.'

'Did you speak to Cat?'

'Yes. It didn't go well.' I close my eyes and try to breathe through the moment. Without the distraction of Lottie and Eva, reality has come back to bite me. 'She's not coming on the holiday and I honestly don't know if she's ever going to forgive me. I've really messed up, Amber. I wish I'd never won that money. It's changed me. Before it, I would never have dreamed of accusing Cat of something like that.'

I hear what sounds like a rabid gurgle from the other end of the phone.

'Amber? Are you still there?'

'I'm still here. But seriously, Emma, *are you freaking kidding me?* The money is useful, but not in the way you thought it would be. You had unrealistic expectations, thinking your pot of gold would reinvent your life and make everything perfect. It hasn't. And it can't.'

'I know that. I'd already reached that conclusion myself.'

'Well, good. Because quitting your job, and sticking two fingers up to your boss in the process is easy to do with a bulging bank balance. But money doesn't fix the difficult stuff.'

My chin wobbles and I swallow down the bubble of emotion that's threatening to take over. 'I know... I know all this. I guess I was just so relieved to get away from Karla and have some financial security after Dave kicked me out. Believe me, I've had one hell of a reality check.'

'OK, then.' Amber's tone surprisingly softens. 'Lucky for you, you still have me. I'll knock you into shape.'

'Thanks, Amber.' I manage a feeble laugh. 'You have no idea how much that means to me right now.' I tell her about my conversation with Cat and about Lottie's fall.

'You've had a shitter of a day,' she says once she's up to date. 'Go get your stuff and get out of that hell hole you've checked into. You're staying at mine tonight.' She hangs up before I have a chance to protest or even respond.

Once again, with my boot being too small for all my stuff, and not knowing what else to do with my car while I'm away (I don't have a permit to park it on the street outside Amber's place), I drop it off in one of the visitors' spaces outside Cat's apartment block. Then I make my way to the hotel on foot, feeling grateful that – for me, absolute rock bottom appears to have been a very temporary state.

Chapter Thirty-Six

It's mid-evening by the time I get to Amber's place in Newington. Rich puts my stuff in their spare room while she makes me a bowl of pasta carbonara, then she sits with me on the sofa as I pick at it. I know that I need to eat but my appetite seems to have gone on strike.

I brace myself for more of her tough love, but it doesn't come. Instead, Amber asks me to tell her everything that happened with Sara. I'm expecting her to threaten to go and beat the living daylights out of her and Dave, but she simply listens patiently until I'm finished.

'Can you believe it?' I'm hugging one of her cushions, which is currently playing the role of comfort blanket. 'I thought she was a friend, one of my close friends. And yours too.'

'Actually, I wasn't so keen on her.'

'What? What do you mean?' I search Amber's face for an explanation. 'We were all friends. We did everything together.'

'Yeah, we did.' She nods. 'And I liked her to begin with. I

just started to wonder whether she could be trusted, and I was proven right.'

'You picked up on it? Why didn't you say anything?'

'It was nothing more than an instinct at first. She was closed off, never really shared anything. Then there was the alleged affair with her boss. Something was off. I tried to give her the benefit of the doubt because you put a lot of faith in your relationships—'

'You mean I'm naive.'

'Emma, I'm trying to be diplomatic here. You know that's not my forte.'

'Well, don't then. Why are you tiptoeing around me now? Say it how it is. That's what you do best.'

She hesitates, evidently at odds with herself. 'OK, sod it, but remember, you asked for this. Sara's a manipulative little cow who'd steal your man quicker than you can swat a fly. She tried the same with Rich last year. Well, not the same exactly, but she made it clear it was on the table if he wanted it.'

'*No way.*' My mouth drops open in disbelief.

'He only told me what happened a few months ago. It was nothing concrete – only some flirting and inappropriate remarks. I told him to get over himself and I don't think he took that so well.'

'I bet.' I laugh, despite myself, and Amber gives a wry smile.

'I thought he was feeding his ego, but then I started to notice the way she behaved around other men who were unavailable. It was like she saw them as a challenge, couldn't bear them wanting someone else over her. Sure, she has the laid-back act down to a tee, but I reckon she's insecure. She hides behind all that glitz and glam, and she's nice to look at, but ultimately there's not much more to her.'

I consider what Amber's said. 'Sara says she's different from us, that she doesn't want or expect monogamy.'

'Huh-uh, I don't buy it for a second.' She shakes her head. 'I reckon there's something in her past that's affected how she views life, men and relationships. Anyway, good luck to her. I'm sure she'll find her eternal happiness through sleeping with hundreds of "unavailable" men – *not*. Hey, do you remember how I had that conversation with her at dinner the other week, about infidelity? That was me testing her, and as far as I'm concerned, she gave herself away loud and clear.'

'I thought that was just chat. You two were always winding each other up. Oh, why am I such an idiot?'

'You're *not* an idiot. Not this time, anyway.' Amber nudges me playfully. 'She's a piece of work. Don't beat yourself up about it. Best thing to do is forget about both of them and move on. Speaking of which, have you messaged that hot man yet?'

'No.' I look at the floor.

'Why not, you loser? James is potentially the best thing that could happen to you – ever. Maybe I'm wrong, maybe you *are* stupid after all.'

'Amber, I'm not ready for anything else yet, and the last thing James needs is to be dragged into my crap-heap of a life. Let me get myself sorted out first, then I'll think about dating again when I'm ready.'

I can't bear to vocalise that I've already cocked things up with James as well. Plus, I'm not lying. Having reacted to him the way I did in the travel agency and the bar, my statement about not being ready is evidently true.

'Look, you're having a shit time, but you'll get past it quicker than you think. Especially with me cracking the whip.' Her eyes glint wickedly.

I throw the cushion I'm holding at her, and we laugh together until I remember that everything is not fine. The lighter tone that has emerged drops like a stone.

'What about Cat? It's eating me up, Amber. I'm terrified that she won't speak to me again. I couldn't bear it.'

She shrugs. 'There's nothing you can do. We'll go on this holiday tomorrow, just the two of us. A bit of distance will give her time to cool off. Then, when we get back, you can try and smooth things over.'

'That's what Lottie said. I don't actually want to go anymore, but she's made me promise to do it for her. It'll feel like I'm rubbing dirt in Cat's face, though. And I hate the idea of leaving Lottie when she's in hospital.' I rub my weary face, plagued by these burdening thoughts.

'I get where you're coming from but knowing Cat, she'd be well upset to find out you'd cancelled the trip because of her. And Lottie will be fine. You said the neighbour's a retired nurse. That trumps anything you could do for her and it'll do her good to spend time with other people. You can FaceTime her from the resort.'

'I know you're right, but I can't help feeling like I don't deserve this holiday. I'm not going to be able to enjoy it at all, knowing Cat's not there and I'm the reason.'

'Then I guess I'll have to make you enjoy it.' Amber gives me a devilish grin. 'Go and pack. You have your holiday clothes with you, right?'

'Yeah, everything's in my cases. I also need to give my mum and dad a call before they send out a search party.'

'Sure thing. Say hi from me.' She heads to the kitchen with my empty bowl while I make myself comfortable in her spare room, then take a moment to mentally prepare myself before dialling my parents' number.

'Hello?'

'Hi, Mum, it's me.'

'Emma, oh thank goodness. I've been trying to call you all day.'

I sigh. 'I know, Mum. I've been... busy.'

'Busy with what exactly? You're unemployed. In fact, speaking of your current job status, I was talking to your dad earlier, and we've had some thoughts about some new career options you should look into...'

Exhausted from my day of emotional turmoil, I lie back on the bed and let her go. She's like a wind-up toy when it comes to our Sunday chats, so all I need to do is make the right noises every now and again, and I'm home and dry. There's no way I'm taking her on tonight.

~

When my alarm sounds at six a.m. the next morning, the drowsiness engulfing me from the deepest sleep I've had in days makes me momentarily forget where I am. However, on peeling open my heavy eyelids, I'm quickly reminded, including why I'm there. The gaping hole in my heart for Cat that temporarily closed overnight, reopens immediately. A vast chasm of emptiness and loss that makes me want to hide under the covers forever. There's also something nagging at me. What if Amber and Lottie are wrong and me continuing with this trip seals the end of my friendship with Cat?

The reality is that I can't know for sure, which means I have to go ahead with the holiday, because I can't let Amber down and I've made a promise to Lottie. It would also be a massive waste of money if we didn't go – 'I fell out with my best friend' is hardly a plausible reason for claiming on my travel insurance.

Dragging myself out of bed, I take a shower and get ready. The whirlwind of last-minute preparations proves a welcome distraction, and I even find myself starting to look forward to the trip. Then, before we know it, the taxi has arrived.

'I still can't understand why you booked our ride to the airport so ridiculously early,' Amber complains as we fly past each other in the hallway, grabbing the last of our things.

'And I can't believe you let me.'

'Guess I must be feeling sorry for you,' she calls from her bedroom. 'Otherwise, there's no way I'd have entertained your paranoid delusions of a multi-vehicle pile-up, a freak storm and all taxi drivers declaring a strike at once.'

'Thanks.' I grin at her when we finally meet by the front door, packed and ready to go.

Amber ushers me outside, a contemplative look on her face, as if she's plotting something – which, to be fair, she usually is. I greet and pass my case to the driver, who puts it in the boot, then reaches for Amber's.

'Actually... it's just the one,' she says.

'*What?*' I freeze as I'm about to climb into the passenger seat of the private hire car. 'You're not bailing on me too, are you?'

'Obviously not, but I've had an idea. I'll catch you up.'

I look at her helplessly.

'Emma, if Cat's going to have any doubts about not joining us, it'll be this morning. So, if I show up out of the blue, I might be able to talk her round. We can get her packed in no time, and she's so organised, I bet she'll be more or less ready to go anyway.'

'But what about the flight? You'll miss it.' I'm torn by this sudden turn of events. Having one last try at getting Cat to come sounds worthwhile, but the idea of Amber heading off somewhere else when we're meant to be on our way to the airport – no matter how early we are – fills me with sheer panic.

'Calm it, would you?' She eyes my forehead, which I can tell has developed a stress-induced sweaty glow about it. 'We were going to be three and a half hours early. That's bananas.'

'No, it makes sense to—'

'Emma, it's bananas. The bag drop closes one hour before the flight. I'll be there well before that – with or without Cat. Now come on, get in the car, you're wasting valuable time. I'll grab an Uber to her place.'

'OK, fine.' I give in and get into the car. Amber's not going to change her mind, so I have no choice but to go ahead and hope for the best. 'Good luck. Keep in touch, though, so I don't have to sit there worrying my backside off.'

'*Attagirl.*' She gives me a wink, slams the taxi door shut and gets straight on her phone to order her ride.

Chapter Thirty-Seven

An hour and a bit later, I'm on my second cappuccino in one of Edinburgh airport's numerous cafes, continually checking my phone for messages. There hasn't been a peep from Amber and it's starting to make me very nervous. Although the rational part of me knows there's still plenty of time, I'm finding it difficult to keep calm – particularly as I have zero control over this situation.

'Come *on*,' I mutter at my phone, earning myself some strange looks from fellow customers. Unsurprisingly, it doesn't oblige.

I finish my drink and head to WHSmith where I impatiently flick through some magazines until I finally receive a message from Amber.

Couldn't convince Cat. On my way but caught in some traffic. Go ahead through security and I'll catch you up.

Great. Just great. I knew something like this would happen. All I can do now is hope that she'll make it in time.

Grabbing my things, I see off my case at the bag drop

and join the queue for security, where it only then dawns on me that I've missed the key point in Amber's message – Cat's not coming. My heart sinks. I'm so disappointed by what this means that it takes everything I have to hold back the tears. Men can be replaced – well, they definitely can if you shouldn't have been with them in the first place – but a true, lifelong best friend can't.

Unable to bear the thought that it might upset Cat even more that I'm going on this holiday as if nothing ever happened, I tap out a message to her.

I know I've hurt you more than I can even imagine. I can't put into words how sorry I am. This holiday is only going ahead because Lottie's asked me go and I don't want to disappoint Amber, but I won't enjoy a minute of it. My heart is irreparably broken without you as my best friend. xxx

I hit 'send', knowing there will be no response, and as I dwell on this, all the other disasters of the last few weeks elbow their way into my consciousness: Lottie's accident; my break up with Dave and him cheating on me; Sara not being the friend I thought she was; my unfortunate encounter with Simon from the bar; and of course, James. Lovely James, who I pushed away.

After security, I spend some time browsing the shops in the departure lounge as a way of distracting myself, but it's futile. Negative thoughts devour me like midges in a Highland forest. I need Amber with me to help me maintain perspective – or preferably to give me a good kick up the arse. As much as her tough love approach can be difficult to stomach, I'm genuinely understanding the need for it right now.

With only ten minutes left until the bag drop closes, I

can't stand it anymore. I call Amber, but it goes straight to voicemail, and, as I'm cursing her once more for this final heroic, yet crazy endeavour, my phone buzzes in my hand. Checking it, I see to my dismay that it's not a message from her, it's my phone signalling that it's out of battery and shutting itself down. I've forgotten to charge it overnight.

'*Nooo...*' I groan, attracting yet more unwanted attention from those around me.

Leaving the shop I'm in, I rake through my hand luggage looking for my charger in the hope that I can plug my phone in somewhere, but it's not there. I must have packed it in my hold luggage by mistake, and as I don't know Amber's number off by heart, I now have no way of contacting her or knowing when she's going to get here. *If* she's even going to get here. All I can do is wait.

I look up at the departures board and see that our flight now indicates 'Go to gate', so I trudge along to it, and I'm still alone when boarding is announced soon after. I've now resigned myself to the fact that Amber's not going to make it. My worry about her going off on her own, which I admit seemed irrational at the time, has been confirmed. I watch dejectedly as the passengers around me queue up and board the plane one by one, until I'm the only person left at the gate other than the airline staff. For a moment, I consider going on my own, but I can't think of anything worse than having only myself for company for the next ten days. With the flight now on final call, I have no choice but to approach the staff member by the gate door and explain what's happened.

'So sorry to hear that, madam,' she says to me. 'I'm afraid we can't wait any longer, though. I'll arrange to have your hold bag removed from the aircraft. You can collect it from the desk near the luggage carousels.'

'Thanks.' I return glumly to my seat and watch miserably as our flight status changes to 'departed' and eventually disappears off the screen.

I sit for what feels like ages (but is probably only ten or so minutes), unable to muster the energy or motivation to leave the airport. I may have been reluctant to go on the holiday, but I've now realised it was far more preferable to the alternative. Passengers for another flight eventually gather around me, a welcome temporary distraction, but it's not long until I inevitably find myself isolated with my thoughts once again.

'*There she is!*' a familiar voice suddenly cries out of nowhere.

My head jerks up and I'm surprised to see Amber hurrying towards me. What's even more of a shock is that, not far behind her, is – Cat.

Chapter Thirty-Eight

'**I** *'ve been trying to call you!*' An exasperated Amber finally reaches me.

'My phone battery died.' I pull myself up from my slouched position on my seat. 'And being so tired last night, I must have stupidly packed my charger in my case – or I've forgotten it.'

'And? You could have bought a new one here and found somewhere to charge it.'

'Oh... so I could have.' I mentally kick myself for not thinking of that – a clear sign I'm still not in top form. 'Anyway, that wouldn't have changed anything. The flight went ages ago. How did you even get in here with an expired boarding pass? And Cat... you're... here?' I add tentatively, as if one false move will cause her to spontaneously combust.

'Yes, I'm here. I got your message.'

'That's good.' My gaze drops to the floor. 'I... I know I've already said it but I'll say it again. I'm so sorry, Cat. I really don't know what came over me.'

'Well, actually, you do.'

I look up at her, taken aback by the gentleness of her tone.

'You explained it all to me yesterday,' she says. 'I just wasn't in a place to listen. It was only when I read that lovely message you sent that I finally snapped out of it. You really have had an unsettling and confusing few weeks, so it's quite understandable that you lost perspective. You knew what you'd done, albeit a little late, and you had the guts to admit it and apologise. That had to count in your favour. As well as the fact that this is the first time we've ever fallen out.' She pauses briefly. 'Also, if I'd been straight with you in the first place, things might not have happened in the same way.'

'No, Cat, you have no responsibility in this. It was—'

'Hey, enough.' She puts a finger to my lips. 'You've already apologised many times over. You made a mistake, but I made one too. I also didn't put myself in your situation, where it's easy to act first and think later. With the rollercoaster you've been on, you probably don't know whether you're coming or going.'

'You're right, I don't. It's been... a lot.'

'I know. So, it would be ridiculous to throw away our friendship, especially when it turned out that one of your close friends *was* doing exactly what you thought. It just wasn't me. You may have acted out, but I can understand what drove you to that.'

'Oh, Cat, thank you.' I'm welling up again. 'I'll never, *ever* hurt you again. I promise.'

She smiles at me. 'I know you won't. You've learned your lesson and I've learned mine too. I should have told you about seeing Dave with Sara, although I obviously didn't know it was her. And I shouldn't have been so secretive about Mike.'

'Mike?' It takes me a few seconds to twig. 'Oh, right. Mike. That's his name. Is it still going well?'

'It is. We're now officially exclusive.'

'That's amazing, Cat. I'm so pleased for you.'

'Me too.' Her cheeks turn crimson and we hug it out, me clinging on as tight as possible, fearful that she might change her mind at any moment.

'All right, you two, break it up,' Amber complains. 'You're making everyone uncomfortable.'

We look around the gate and see that there's no one there.

'OK, you're making *me* uncomfortable.' She gives an unapologetic shrug.

Laughing, we dive on her, pulling her into a group hug she'll loathe being part of.

'I'll introduce you to Mike when we get back from our trip,' Cat promises, as we separate and get up from our seats.

'That would be great. Wait... what trip?' I'm perplexed. 'We've missed our flight. There's no holiday to go on now.'

'I'll let Amber tell you the rest.'

'Yeah. The story of how *I* saved the day.' Amber puffs out her chest, looking immensely pleased with herself.

'Right, well, this I'm dying to hear,' I say to her. 'Though can I go buy a charger and find somewhere to hook my phone up while we chat? I feel lost without it.'

'I've got a portable one you can use.' She digs in her carry-on luggage and hands it to me.

'Thanks.' I connect the power supply to my phone while she and Cat take a seat next to me. 'So? Do share.'

'OK...' Amber makes it clear she's going to enjoy every second of this. 'As you know, my taxi got stuck in traffic. It turned out there had been an accident on the road—'

'*I knew it.*' I look triumphantly from Amber to Cat.

'Things like that *do* happen. That's why I go to the airport so early. It's completely—'

'No. It's not,' Amber cuts me off before I can finish. 'And that's not why I didn't make it in time. The taxi driver took a detour via Kings Knowe to avoid the worst of the traffic jam, but then the taxi had a tyre blow out on the bypass. Quite scary, even by my standards.'

'*No way.*' My hand goes to my mouth.

'Yeah-huh. We were stuck at the side of the road, traffic racing past, waiting for a recovery vehicle. The driver tried to get me another taxi but they wouldn't pick me up from there. Said they weren't covered on their liability insurance or some nonsense like that.'

'Then what happened?'

'Well, luckily Cat called me and admitted she'd been an idiot. She wished she'd come with me, but knew there was no way she'd make it on time. She'd tried to call you but got your voicemail, so I told her to get packed and come and get me.'

'*What?* Why? If you knew you weren't going to make it.' I'm utterly riveted by this story.

'That's the good bit.' Amber continues her peacocking. 'While I was waiting for Cat, I called your sexy friend, James, at the travel agency, and for a small fee he managed to switch us onto another flight.'

'*You. Are. Kidding.*'

'I'm not. You need to go to the airline's customer service desk to pick up a physical boarding pass – something to do with the change. And we'll have a slightly longer journey through a different connecting airport, but it means we'll still have our holiday.'

'*Wow.*' I'm absolutely blown away. 'You're both amazing.'

'That's right.' Amber's grinning from ear to ear.

'She did a fabulous job,' says Cat. 'It was all Amber really.'

'Well, no, you also decided to come,' I say. 'That's massive. *Oh, I'm so happy right now!* You know, when the flight was about to close, I did actually consider going on my own.'

Amber snorts. 'I don't believe for a second you would have got on that plane alone. You'd have lost it completely. Also, with a dead phone, how would they have scanned your boarding pass?'

'Oh, yeah.' I face palm. 'So, how much do I owe you for the flight change?'

'Forget that,' says Amber. 'It wasn't a lot and it's sorted.'

I try to protest but she shuts me down, so I let it go – for now.

'I honestly can't thank you enough.' I beam at my two best friends. 'I have to tell Lottie you're coming, Cat.'

'Of course, how's she doing?' she asks. 'I'm so sorry to hear about her accident.'

I bob my head. 'She's OK, thankfully. A few injuries that should heal in time, and all being well, she'll be home in a couple of days.'

'That's a relief. Amber said you've been feeling guilty about leaving her. I get why, but you shouldn't. She wants you to go, and it sounds like she's being well looked after.'

'Yeah, Lottie's neighbours are great. Really lovely. I'm much more comfortable knowing that they're keeping an eye on her. Eva was going to get her iPad so I can keep in touch with her, so I'll try her now.'

I switch on my charging phone and dial Lottie through FaceTime.

'*Hi!*' I squeal excitedly as her face appears on the screen. 'How are you?'

'Hello, my love.' She smiles at me, and I'm pleased that

she looks a lot better than yesterday. 'I'm doing fine. Being well looked after. Is that you at the airport?'

'Yup, and guess who's here?' I aim the camera at Cat and Amber, who wave and call hello.

'You're all going together. That's wonderful news. I hope you have a fantastic time.'

'We will. We're doing it for you, so we're going to do it properly. Ten days of nothing but relaxation, fun and new experiences,' I say, as Amber points to the time on her own phone to hurry me along. 'Anyway, it was just a quick call, we need to go. I'll be in touch.'

'I look forward to it,' says Lottie. 'Safe journey, all of you.'

'Bye.' I blow her kisses until the image freezes and the call disconnects.

Chapter Thirty-Nine

Amber shares the instructions for me to go and pick up my new boarding pass, and I make my way out of the busy departure lounge, collecting my case on the way. On approaching the airline's customer service desk, which is near the bag drop, I'm relieved to see that there's only one person in the queue ahead of me.

At first, I wait patiently, but the man in front of me doesn't seem to be being served by anyone. He's also leaning on the counter poring over some paperwork and there's no one behind the desk, which means he's probably a staff member, not a customer. As he seems to be in the middle of something, I wait patiently for him to finish and attend to me, but after another minute or so, it's apparent that he doesn't even realise I'm here.

'*Excuse me?*' I call to him. 'Are you from the airline? I was told to come here to collect a boarding pass?'

'I'll be with you in a moment, madam,' he replies, without looking round.

I frown, unsure what to do. Isn't the whole point of a customer service desk to provide a service? Which he is not.

I wait a bit longer, trying to refrain from tapping my foot with impatience, because I can't help thinking this guy is making me stand here unnecessarily. What could be so important that it requires him to ignore a living breathing customer who's got a flight to catch?

'Um... excuse me, sir?' I call across to him again. 'I realise you're in the middle of something, but I'd really appreciate your help. I've already missed my first flight today and my friends will kill me if we miss the next one.' I don't actually know the departure time of our new flight – Amber didn't tell me – but she *was* hurrying me along before. And I just need this to work out.

'*Relax.* Your flight isn't for a while yet,' he replies to my utter bafflement.

'OK, but...' I stop dead. 'Hang on... how do you know when my flight is? You haven't even asked my...' I tail off, an uneasy feeling settling over me.

I scrutinise the back of the man's head. It couldn't be, could it? No, he has a different voice. I'm losing the plot. My brain is now making stuff up.

While I'm giving myself a mental shake, the man finally turns towards me and I discover that my brain is, in fact, functioning just fine.

'Hello, again,' says a smiling James, this time in his own voice.

'Oh my god... *you*... what are you... *why would you even do that?*' I'm half-mortified, half-relieved and (if I can be allowed to go over quota just this once) half-delighted to see his gorgeous face. This is clearly another set-up of sorts, orchestrated by Amber. And undoubtedly the reason why she was rushing me to get down here.

'I *knew* you liked me.' His grin is as sharp as a crescent moon.

303

'Eh… what? I never said that.'

'Are you really going to keep playing that game, Emma?'

'I'm not playing a game…' I raise my eyes to the ceiling and let out a monumental sigh. 'Amber told you. Of course, she did, even though those words never came out my mouth. Fine. I'm too exhausted for this. Yes, I like you… as it transpires. And I'm sorry for the way I've acted pretty much every time we've crossed paths during the last few weeks.'

'Apology accepted.' He chuckles. 'Especially as you had no idea why I was in the bar on Friday. I get why it looked weird.'

'You do?'

'Sure. And maybe there was an element of truth in what you said. Maybe I overstepped a bit when I ran into you the first couple of times. I have a habit of trying to solve other people's problems for them.'

'Right. *Gosh.*' My eyes widen at this admission. 'So maybe we can start again?'

'I think that's a great idea.'

'Me too.' I bite my bottom lip while drinking him in properly for the first time. He's taller than me, but he's more of an average height, with broad shoulders and a natural-looking, muscular physique. My eyes roam over his thick, dark hair, his days' old stubble and deep, chestnut-brown eyes that feel like they could bore a hole through my soul. He's even more attractive than I remember and apparently a decent guy. Who'd have thought it?

'So…' James moves closer to me, giving me a waft of the alluring, citrusy scent I smelled on him in the travel agency, causing my legs to turn to mush. 'As you have some time to kill, how about we have that date now? I'll make sure you're on your way in plenty of time.'

My anxiety over potentially missing another flight is

already kicking back in at this suggestion, when I remember that I'm here at the airport – and there's no way he would let me miss it. What could possibly go wrong now? Unless the queue for security gets really long or

'I'll make sure you get through security if there's a delay.' He interjects my thoughts, seemingly reading them. 'I have contacts here. And Amber's checked you all in for your new flight, so your new boarding pass will already be on the app in your phone – that was just a ploy to get you down here.'

I fold my arms and laugh. 'Why is that not a surprise? Well, as you've left me with little excuse to say no – one drink, OK?'

'Of course.' His chestnut eyes glint, leaving me in no doubt that there will be a second round.

He leads me to a pub slash bar opposite the café I was camped out in earlier, where a waiter immediately appears at our table to take our order.

'Two glasses of champagne, please,' says James after quickly consulting the drinks menu – but not me.

'Hey, that's too much,' I protest. 'A glass of house wine would have been fine.'

'I don't like "fine".' He winks at me, displaying a row of near perfect white teeth. 'Anyway, I know after Friday that you have a taste for the finer things in life.'

'That was a...' I stop before I say too much. He doesn't know my situation, and as much as I've admitted that I do like him, I'm not ready to share it yet.

James must sense that something has made me uncomfortable because he diverts the conversation to more neutral territory. We chat lightly about holiday destinations we've visited until the waiter reappears with our champagne.

'Cheers.' His gaze locks on mine as he clinks my glass and a shiver of desire runs through me.

'Cheers. So... eh... you must get discounts on holidays working for a travel agency then?'

'I sure do. One of the perks of the job. As is getting to serve a beautiful woman like you.' He raises a flirtatious eyebrow, sending my core temperature through the roof.

'Right, well... that's good,' I say, flustered. 'It's... um... a good job then?'

'It pays the bills.' He appears amused by my faltering conversation. 'It's part-time and temporary until I finish the uni course I'm doing.'

'Oh? You're a student?'

Please don't tell me I'm on a date with a man who's almost a decade younger than me. I will *never* hear the end of this – even despite Amber being the one who set it up.

'I'm what's classed as a mature student. I worked in the corporate world for several years after my first degree, but it wasn't for me, so I went back to do a full time Masters in Astrophysics.'

'You're going to be a scientist instead?' I'm both intrigued and impressed by this.

'That's the plan. It's also why I know the solar system more intimately than you.' He grins cheekily, reminding me of my faux pas at the travel agency.

'Perhaps not my finest moment.' I sip at my champagne to hide my embarrassment.

'Hey, I thought it was cute.' He touches my arm gently. It's like a bolt of sexy lightning rushing through me. I look at him and this time he smiles a warm, affectionate smile, making my insides melt. I want so badly for him to kiss me. Or to reach over and kiss him. But I'm not brave enough to initiate either scenario, nor am I able to maintain the intensity of the eye contact, so instead I examine my gel nails.

'Oh, by the way...' James rests his champagne flute on the table. 'I forgot to say – my parents say hi.'

'Huh?' I look at him quizzically. 'Do I know your parents?'

'It turns out you do. Eva and Archie. They live in —'

'The same street as Lottie.' My jaw drops in astonishment.

'That's right.' He nods. 'When my mum told me about this young woman called Emma who was so upset about their neighbour's accident, I knew the chances of it being you were slim. But I had an instinct, so I found you on Facebook and showed her a photo. She confirmed it was you.'

'*What are the chances?*'

'It's nuts, isn't it? But good news for you.'

'How so?'

'Means you've already met the parents.'

'That's a bit presumptuous.' I raise my eyebrows at him, while still trying to get my head around this information.

That must be why James was in the car park when I was leaving the hospital the day before. He must have been picking Eva up. Then I realise something else. I told Eva – his *mum*, as it turns out – everything that's happened in the last few weeks. Including all the drama with James. *Oh my god, what's she going to think of me?* What if she's told him?'

James laughs, evidently reading the emerging horror on my face. 'Don't worry, my mum's discreet. She won't tell me anything. I don't know what you said to her, but she thinks you're lovely.'

'Thank goodness for that.' I rub my jaw with relief. 'I like her just as much by the way.'

'Most people do. She'll take good care of Charlotte while you're away. And I'm going to help out too, until I go on my own holiday, that is.'

'Well, it's certainly reassuring to know that Lottie's in such good hands. So, thank you – to both you and your mum. And your dad.'

We clink glasses again and finish our drinks, then, as expected, James orders us two more. With the ice now well and truly broken, we laugh and flirt our way through our second glass of champagne, leaning in further towards each other and snatching any opportunity for the slightest physical contact. The chemistry between us is unmistakable.

By the time we've left the bar and are about to say our goodbyes by the entrance to airport security, I'm already disappointed about not seeing James again for another couple of weeks.

'That you all sorted, then?' he asks. 'Got your boarding pass ready on your phone?'

'Yup.' I wave it in front of him. 'I still can't believe you lot, scheming like that to get me on a date with you.'

'It was all Amber really. I was just part of the supporting cast – as well as her lift to the airport.'

'It was *you* who picked her up from the side of the road? She said it was Cat.'

He raises his hands. 'Guilty as charged. It was on the way here that she came up with the whole surprise date plan and roped me into it. And before you say anything, I went and got her because I would never leave a person stranded. Not because of my male ego.'

'Don't worry, I wasn't thinking that,' I reassure him. 'Having met your mum, I get where your "rescuer" side comes from. She was in a caring profession, so it's either in your family blood or she's rubbed off on you. I can't believe I fell for Amber's nonsense again, though. She's a law unto herself, that girl.'

'I thought she did a stellar job. Would you rather we hadn't had our date?' He gives me a playful nudge.

'*No.*' I push him back, feeling like a fifteen-year-old girl with a massive crush.

James hands me my carry-on luggage, which he insisted on carrying for me. 'Have a brilliant time, Emma.'

'Thanks.' I suddenly feel shy. This is the moment where he'll either kiss me and send my hormones into a tailspin, or he'll leave without kissing me, and I'll spend my whole holiday wondering why. 'I hope you have a great time too – wherever you're going. We never got around to talking about that.'

'We had better things to chat about. Like how you spent the last few weeks pretending you didn't fancy me.'

'*Oh, you...*' I eyeball him as he deftly slips his arms round my waist, pulling me in towards him, and as our lips finally meet, it's like fireworks going off inside me. He tastes delicious, the scent of his aftershave heightening my senses.

We continue our embrace, lost in each other and barely aware of the passers-by making 'get a room' style jokey comments, until we eventually pull apart, laughing almost guiltily.

'See you soon?' he asks.

'Definitely.' I'm panting slightly from that mind-blowing kiss. 'You have my number now, so keep in touch.'

With one last lingering look between us, I turn and go through the security barriers, my body jangling with excitement that I might have finally met the real man of my dreams.

Chapter Forty

I reach the gate for our flight as boarding is about to begin. Cat and Amber are already in a short queue, so I join them.

'Get everything sorted?' Amber asks with a knowing look before I have a chance to say anything.

'Yes, much more than I expected.' I affectionately cuff her on the back of the head. 'I was going to give you hell, but as I just had the best kiss of my life, I'll let you off. This once.'

'And... *mission accomplished.*' She rubs her hands together with a self-satisfied smile.

'Tell me *everything.*' Cat grabs my hands excitedly.

'Seems I'll have to fill you in on board.' I gesture towards the airport staff member who's beckoning us forward.

He scans our boarding passes and we make our way along the skybridge onto the plane.

'Business class?' I gape at my two friends on locating our seats.

'Oh yeah,' says Amber. 'Did I forget to mention that? As well as the fee for the flight change, I used my rewards account to upgrade us – just on this short leg of the journey. There weren't enough seats left in economy.'

'But... that must have wiped out all your points.'

'So?' She shrugs. 'I had a boatload of them from my work travel. More than I knew what to do with. It's my way of treating us, and it's the least I can do, given you're paying for the whole trip.'

'Is that you starting to go soft, Amber?' Cat teases her.

'*Shut it, Cat.*'

A flight attendant passes, giving Amber a look.

'I'm not sure they would have let you in business class if they knew what you're like off the clock,' I say to her.

Once the initial excitement has worn off, I sit back and take a deep therapeutic breath, stretching out my legs in the space in front of me. After the events of the last two days, I still can't believe we're actually going. And all three of us as well. I still feel really sore about Sara, but Cat and Amber have been my friends for a lot longer. Plus, thanks to Lottie's insistence that I get out and have real experiences, instead of taking the easy route and doing things online, I now have new friends in my life (Cameron, Jana and Trudy) as well as a hot new bloke (fingers crossed!).

'Was that your phone buzzing there?' Cat says from the seat next to me.

'Oops, I still need to switch it to flight mode.' I reach down to retrieve it from my bag, expecting to see a message from my mum, who now knows I'm going away, and has been bombarding me with advice on staying safe abroad. But it's not from her.

Is it OK to say I thought that kiss was phenomenal? James x

I let out a restrained squeal of delight.

'What is it, honey?' asks Cat. 'Is that him?'

'It is.' I'm already grinning like a love-sick idiot. 'I can't believe how this has all turned out. I thought there was no way he'd be interested anymore after everything that went down last week. Amber, what did you say to him?' I look across the aisle at her and note that she's studying her folded up tray table a little too hard.

'*Amber...*'

'Mmm-hmm?' She tries to appear innocent, but fails miserably.

'Amber, what did you say?'

'Not much. Just that your self-esteem was on the floor, and that I'd slip him fifty quid if he'd make the first move.'

'*You didn't!*' Cat and I squawk in unison.

'OK, I made that up.'

I exhale with relief.

'The bribe part anyway.'

'You're joking, right?' I say. 'You didn't really tell him that. The truth please.'

She glances from me to Cat, and back again. 'I'm not joking. That's what I told him. Not word for word, but I said you'd been hurt, your confidence had taken a knock and if he messed you about, he'd have me to deal with. He was surprisingly receptive to the straight talk.'

I stare at her in disbelief. 'Amber, I don't know whether to hug you or wring your bloody neck.'

'You got a date and a snog out of it, didn't you? And I'm guessing he wants to see you again. Seriously, sometimes I wonder why I bother.'

Sadly, she has a point. 'All right. Thank you, Amber, for setting me up. I do appreciate it. But next time could you maybe share less about my... vulnerabilities?'

'Can't promise that.' She shakes her head decisively.

Cat and I roll our eyes in a resigned fashion. We both know I'm fighting a losing battle.

'So, Emma,' says Cat. 'That's been quite a change of heart with James?'

'Yeah, why did you think he wasn't interested anymore?' asks Amber.

'Well...' Now it's my turn to examine my tray table. 'I wasn't as grateful as I should have been when he came to my rescue on Friday night. I might have indirectly accused him of being a bit... stalkerish.'

'*You dipshit*,' Amber scolds me. 'That's why he left the bar after he told us what happened to you.'

'In my defence, I didn't know that you'd invited him along. It wasn't 'til the day after that I realised you guys were right about him – when Cat told me you'd done that, Amber. And by then, I was convinced that he hated me.'

'I suppose it was a reasonable enough assumption,' says Cat. 'It *was* the second time you'd told him where to go.'

'Exactly. And I wouldn't have blamed him for it.' I turn my attention back to my phone and tap out a reply to James, playing him at his own game.

It's absolutely fine to say that. It was certainly one of the best I've had... x

I hit the 'send' button and within moments he replies.

Just one of the best? Seems I need to get some more practice in. x

This sets off a flutter of flirtatious messages, which ends only when we're reminded over the PA system that all phones should now be in flight mode.

'Oh, you'll never guess what,' I say to Cat and Amber.

'James's parents are Lottie's neighbours – the ones who'll be looking after her when she gets out of hospital.'

'You're *joking*.' Cat's face is a picture. 'Tell us how that came about.'

I fill them in on my date with James and how I was terrified that his mum had told him everything I'd shared with her.

'That's *hilarious*,' Amber hoots. 'It could only happen to you, Emma. But at least you already have the parental approval.'

'I guess.' I cringe and settle back in my seat, where I indulge myself by delightedly reading James's messages over and over.

While doing this, my eyes keep being drawn to his mobile number. For some reason it looks familiar. Perhaps similar to the number of someone else I know? Then, a thought. *Surely not.* I open up an image in my photo library and flick between that and WhatsApp, doing a quick comparison.

'*Oh. My. God.*' I clamp a hand to my mouth, utterly astounded.

'What is it?' Cat calls across.

'Uh... give me a moment.'

I switch my phone out of flight mode, tap out a message to James and wait impatiently for his response. My phone sounds seconds later, leaving me gobsmacked.

'Just when I though this day couldn't get any weirder.'

'*Spit it out*,' Amber demands.

'OK...' I try to clear my muddled mind. 'So, you know how I used a scrap of paper I found on the shop floor to choose my lottery numbers?'

They both nod.

'Well, when I bumped into James at the bank on the day

my win was confirmed, he mentioned that he almost gave me his phone number on D-day night, because he was concerned about me.'

'So?' Amber prompts me to elaborate.

'So, I just asked if he wrote the number down. He said he scrawled it on a piece of paper he got from the shop keeper, but then ripped it up and put it in his pocket when he realised it wouldn't be well received. Anyway, he must have dropped part of it on the floor because it turns out I picked it up and used it to choose my ticket numbers. The first couple of digits were missing so I didn't recognise it as a mobile number.'

'What? So, you mean...'

'Yup. I've checked his number against a photo I took of my ticket when I was paranoid I was going to lose it somehow. There's no mistake. It's my winning numbers. In a different order, of course. The ticket shows them in numerical order. This is... *unbelievable.*'

'Wowsers.' Amber looks amazed. 'You found yourself one hell of a lucky number there.'

'Yeah, you did!' Cat is high pitched with excitement. 'James's mobile number hasn't just brought you a fortune, you found him too.'

'Easy,' I warn her. 'He's not quite my new man yet.'

'*Oh, come on!*' Cat and Amber yell at me in unison.

'OK, OK.' I assume a defensive pose with a coy smile. 'The signs are positive, so I guess I must have a lucky number after all.'

'That's better.' Cat reaches across and ruffles my hair. 'Honey, is James not wondering why you asked him that? It seems an odd question and I assume he doesn't know about your win yet.'

'Yeah, he is actually. I'd better message him back.'

Cat and Amber sit back in their seats, while I quickly sneak a response to James to say that I'll fill him in when the time is right (that's all I can commit to for now) before switching my phone back into flight mode. I then settle back in my own seat again as the plane pushes back from the gate, taxis to the runway and takes off.

Looking out of the window, watching Edinburgh and the surrounding area disappearing beneath us, I feel an overwhelming sense of relief at leaving behind the roller-coaster that has been the last few weeks. As well as a sense of expectation and hope for the future. With Lottie, Cat and Amber by my side, and my well-meaning but infuriating parents at slightly more of a distance – I know I'll be just fine.

To be continued in Another Lucky Number...

Another Lucky Number

A dream opportunity, but will it be lost in paradise?

Emma is off to the Bahamas with friends Cat and Amber. She plans to relax on the pristine white beaches before returning home to find a new career and continue her fledging romance with new love interest, James. That is until sexy Sebastien, who puts the 'hot' into 'hotelier', offers Emma the career opportunity of a lifetime at his chain of resorts. But there's a catch: the interview has to take place in three days, while she's there on holiday.

Emma needs some proper downtime, but an opportunity like this is too good to pass up. Afraid that she's punching above her weight, she enlists the help of her friends to get her interview ready, while still making the most of her tropical surroundings. But after a series of gaffs, a crisis of confidence, and with James unexpectedly turning up, her dream job looks like it's about to swim out of her reach.

Can Emma rise to the challenge and come out successful? And will her budding relationship with James survive the experience?

Coming in summer 2025!

Acknowledgements

This is my sixth book to be published, and in my eyes, it's my most important one yet – because of the circumstances in which I wrote it. Cryptic, huh? I'll explain...

Lucky Number started out with the title *As Luck Would Have It*. It was the first full-length novel I ever wrote, and I badged it 'my rehab book' because it helped me reclaim some quality of life after my body went into meltdown in 2014, and I was diagnosed with a disabling condition called Functional Neurological Disorder (FND). At that time, I had severe difficulty with many of my bodily functions: the physical stuff (like walking, talking, digesting my food and losing control of my body to agonizing and violent episodes of shaking and muscle spasms), the sensory elements (such as balance, hearing and vision problems) and the cognitive aspects (for example, issues with short term memory, word finding, reading and thinking, and my concentration was shot).

I wanted my life back and it felt like an impossible challenge. That was, until a conversation with an ex-boss of mine, Mel MacIntyre, during which she asked if I was using my time off sick from work to write the book I'd always wanted to write. At first, I was thrown by her question. I was far too unwell for that. But her words stayed with me and the seed that she planted grew into something special, helping me to identify what was missing from my recovery plan: 'physio' for my brain. So, I started writing – just ten to fifteen minutes at a time. It was gruelingly difficult and painful to even sit at a desk, but the thing about me is that I can be a determined little bugger. I kept at it, and as I wrote, it got easier and I could write for longer – until eventually I had written my first ever novel: this book, 'My rehab book' or if I'm allowed to be a little dramatic, perhaps even the book that saved me. Because it didn't just help me recover some of my cognitive capabilities, it gave me a renewed sense of self-belief when I badly needed one.

This is actually this book's second venture into the wild. Under the aforementioned previous title of *As Luck Would Have It*, it was published (in a much 'greener' version than now – a nod to my inexperience, not my climate-related values) for just six weeks before I was offered representation by The Kate Nash Literary Agency and I took it down from Amazon. This is – I guess – yet another reason why it's such an important book for me. Not only did it help me reclaim some quality of life and reignite my self-belief, it got me an agent. And while it was never picked up by a publisher because it doesn't sit in a defined genre, I received lots of very positive feedback that spurred me to keep writing.

So, with that in mind, my first thanks in these Acknowledgements go to this book. Bit of a weird one, I know. But without you, *Lucky Number*, who knows what path my life might have taken – and I suspect it wouldn't have been one that was so positive and brimming with a sense of purpose, achievement and fulfilment. It's hard having the 'disability' label attached to you in this world. I've been written off, demeaned, patronised... which means it's essential that I maintain my sense of identity and my self-esteem through my own actions and successes and the support and encouragement of those who believe in me.

Now, onto the humans, and front of the line is my

incredible husband, James, who may share the same name as the love interest in this book, but who is not the source of inspiration for him – well, not completely anyway. Thank you for your continued patience and support, which is nothing less than admirable. I know that having me incessantly interrupting your work to test out this, that and the other with you is challenging to put it mildly. I'm also pleased to credit you as the creative source of one of the scenes of my story (although I'll keep people guessing which), but I'm afraid I'm still resolute that that does not entitle you to ten per cent of the royalties. No matter which way you argue it.

Thank you to my amazing parents for your initial skepticism when I announced I wanted to write a novel (readers please note, this was pre my bodily meltdown – they're not heartless). Without the knowledge that you thought I was having some kind of early mid-life crisis, I might never have been fuelled by the need to prove you wrong. And on a more serious note, my heartfelt thanks go to my editor in chief from this book's first outing: my 'top Dad' who worked relentlessly to help me produce the best piece of work I could, and who acted as a second pair of 'editorial eyes' on my next couple of books before they went under the noses of my official editors. I've learned so much from you and I honestly don't know how to thank you for all the hours you put in, but rest assured it won't be with cash.

A huge thanks to my 'critical friends' from round one with this story: Mum, James, Angela, Geraldine, Rhona, Frankie, Amy, Alyson and Louise, for your extraordinarily helpful feedback, comments and suggestions. And for pointing out a few real clangers. I hope you'll enjoy this 'Rolls Royce version' just as much if you end up reading it. Thank you also to my first agent, Imogen Howson, and my current agent, Kate Nash, both of whom offered editorial advice and guidance when it was being prepared for submission to publishers. And to my highly professional 'editorial team' from this most recent editorial transformation: Fiona Leitch, Sandy Barker and Andie Newton, who between you have supported me through structural edits, copy edits and proof reading to get this book into tip-top shape. The time you have so selflessly given to me along with your feedback, advice, suggestions and corrections has been invaluable and appreciated more than you could ever know. Again, I don't know how to thank you for your support as well as your amazing friendship and brilliant banter, but I hope that one day I will be able to find a way (but again, it won't be in monetary form...).

A massive thank you also to Mel for planting the golden seed that helped me realise it was the right time to start writing again (I say 'again' because I had a couple of false starts with trying to write novels earlier in my life). That moment and what followed feels like a real 'Sliding Doors' point for me, in that, had things not fallen into place the way they did, I might not have gone on to publish the books I have or be sitting here penning these very acknowledgements right now.

To my entire family: Mum and Dad, my brothers, sisters-in-law, my niece and nephew (who are too young to be involved but who are a source of great joy in my life), and of course, James – thank you so much for believing in me, supporting me and being the best family I could ever ask for.

And finally, thank you to my readers (especially those of you who send me lovely messages), fellow authors who offer moral support, social media followers and avid supporters (you know who you are). Every tiny titbit you offer keeps me going and I thank you wholeheartedly for that kindness.

About the Author

Nina Kaye is a contemporary romance author who writes warm, witty and uplifting reads with a deeper edge. She lives in Edinburgh with her husband and much adored side-kick, James. In addition to writing, Nina enjoys swimming, gin and karaoke (preferably all together in a sunny, seaside destination). Nina has previously published *The Gin Lover's Guide to Dating, Take A Moment, One Night in Edinburgh, Just Like That* and *Stand Up Guy*. She has also been a contender for the RNA Joan Hessayon award.

Printed in Dunstable, United Kingdom